Outcomes and Perspective

The Complete Alexis Parker prequel series

Includes:

Assignment Zero

Agent Prerogative

The Final Chapter

G.K. Parks

Copyright © 2014 G.K. Parks

A Modus Operandi imprint

All rights reserved.

ISBN: 0989195821
ISBN-13: 978-0-9891958-2-9

For those who have made the ultimate sacrifice and have lost their lives in the line of duty, may they never be forgotten

Part I:

Assignment Zero

ONE

Introduction

The warehouse was only a mile from my location, but driving through city traffic was hell. I was on autopilot, and as I screeched around a corner, I briefly wondered how long I had been driving on the sidewalk. The flashing lights and sirens were on, and thankfully, pedestrians leapt out of my way as I flew to the location.

I made it to the warehouse within five minutes to find fire trucks and ambulances already on scene.

The fire department had a stationhouse only two blocks from here and responded immediately to my call.

Throwing the car into park and bolting from the door, I spotted Jablonsky sitting on the concrete as an EMT ran a flashlight in front of his eyes.

"What the hell happened?" I asked, relieved to see him alert and functioning. Only then did I notice the dark plumes billowing up from what was left of the building.

"Those sons of bitches rigged the building to explode." He tried to push the EMT away. "Where's Boyle and Carver?" he asked. "Oh for fuck's sake, I'm fine." He tried *to stand, but his balance was off. And the EMT pushed him back into a seated position.*

"I'll find out," I replied, already circling toward the back of the building as fear began to overtake my senses with every step.

"Ma'am," a fireman said as he tried to block my path, and I flashed my credentials at him, not slowing my pace. "Ma'am," he tried again as I sprinted toward the back. His job was to put the fire out; mine was to find my friends.

As the rear of the building came into view, I saw a fire truck and two ambulances. There was a bloody sheet on the ground. I raced toward it.

No, this can't be happening.

* * *

Four years earlier...

Pounding out the last half mile, I was relieved to cross the finish line and immediately put my hands on my knees as I sucked in some air. My heartbeat reverberated in my ears, and if I didn't thoroughly stretch, walking tomorrow would be a challenge.

"It's about time." Michael Carver tossed a water bottle in my direction. "As usual, you're still following my lead." I glared at him as I unscrewed the cap. "How did you ever pass the physical regs? You run like a girl."

"I am a girl, and just because I can't run a five minute mile doesn't mean shit. Frankly, my six and a half minutes are very respectable. You're just a freak of nature."

"Is that the argument you plan to use when you let a suspect get away?" Carver could be an ass. During the last five months of training at Quantico, he had been the bane of my existence, competitive, arrogant, a slight misogynistic streak, and always with the jibes.

"Thank god we get our field assignments tomorrow," I muttered. "If I had to spend another twenty weeks, let alone two years, with you, I don't know what I'd do."

"Who are you kidding, Alexis?" He grinned. "You know exactly what would happen." He cocked an eyebrow up. "Do you want to come over tonight? There's a chance we may never see one another again. We might as well go out with a bang."

"In your dreams." I finished stretching and found my keys. "Let me know who your supervisor is so I can send a sympathy card. Being forced to spend two years with you qualifies as a violation of the Constitution."

Not waiting for a response, I continued down the path to my apartment. It wasn't an apartment so much as a converted dorm room I had been assigned to share. The FBI and other law enforcement agencies used the Marine Corps base to conduct their own training programs, and I was relieved it was over. Although I had become close with Kate Hartley, my roommate, I preferred having a certain level of free will and privacy.

"Alexis Parker," she squealed and shoved an envelope in my direction as I walked in the door.

"What?"

"It's our posting. They issued our assignments early. I'm working white collar division."

"Big surprise," I teased. Kate had been a professional CPA for a few years before being recruited by someone at the Bureau. She wasn't up to snuff for fieldwork, barely managing to score high enough on the firearms proficiency test, but she could work magic with numbers and bank accounts. I put the unopened envelope on the table and found a change of clothes. "I'm going to take a shower. Do you feel like going out tonight?"

She looked astonished. "Of course. It's our last night. Everyone's meeting at the Blue Diamond later." I had meant dinner, not spending hours at a bar with a group of people who were tooting their own horns. "Aren't you going to open it?" She picked up the envelope and tried to hand it to me as I went past her on the way to the bathroom.

"Why? Do you think the courier is going to come back and rescind it if I don't open it immediately?"

"Smartass." She looked annoyed and went into her

room.

The time alone was a nice reprieve. Having a chance to think about things was typically a benefit, but I was nervous. Maybe I was going to be sent across the country to Alaska, Utah, or somewhere equally small. I liked the anonymity a large city provided. The FBI offices in the bigger cities had more divisions, plentiful resources, and opportunity for promotion and growth. I shut the water and tried not to let Carver's constant digs get to me. The actual agents had all been impressed by my physical and mental acuity. Carver was just intimidated and jealous, I hoped.

After dressing and giving myself a final word of encouragement, I went into the main room and tore open the envelope. I read and reread the words, looking for some clue as to whether or not this was a joke.

"Well?" Kate asked impatiently. She was standing in her doorway, dressed in a cute outfit.

"Office of International Operations." I didn't know whether I should be excited or scared shitless.

She stood behind me, reading over my shoulder. "At least we're going to be working out of the same city."

"Until they decide to send me overseas." Sometimes, I missed free will. She made a tsk sound and took the paper away.

"You have zero military experience. You're a law school graduate for god's sakes, and you don't speak Farsi, Arabic, or anything useful."

"Thanks." Sarcastic as always. It was nice some things never change.

"They do more than just fight the war on terrorism. Hell, we're all fighting the war on terrorism, but it doesn't mean you're going to the Middle East or anywhere overseas. They work a lot of the same cases Interpol does. Smuggling, forgeries, arms sales, et cetera."

"Wow, you just demoted me from operative to pencil pusher in two sentences."

She narrowed her eyes. "Do you even know what you want?"

"Dinner, preferably now."

Chuckling, she picked up her purse and met me at the door.

* * *

After we ate, Kate insisted we go to the bar. We were sitting on a few stools in the center, chatting easily. She had knocked back half a dozen tequila shots in the last two hours, and I was only on my second beer of the night. My life had taken many strange turns, and it was about to undergo another one. Everything in our government provided apartment was packed, and tomorrow, I'd load up my car and drive to a new city to begin a new life. This was what I wanted. The one thing I had been striving for since I turned twenty. I was twenty-four now, the minimum age required to become a Special Agent in Charge.

After working my ass off to complete my BA and pass the LSATs with flying colors, I received a scholarship to a decent law school with no intention of ever becoming a lawyer. It was just a stepping stone. Often, I was accused of being too serious. When I turned eighteen my entire life changed, and after spending the first two years of college completely lost, I witnessed firsthand how useful law enforcement agencies could be and found my focus. After law school, I sent my application to the Bureau, and by some miracle, they accepted me for training at Quantico.

"Parker," Carver called, sidling up to my barstool, "drinking your sorrows away?"

"What sorrows?"

"Your misery over missing me." He sat on the empty stool next to mine and swiveled in his seat.

"Clearly, that's the best thing about this entire situation," I deadpanned.

Kate turned to us. "Michael," she smiled, "where did you get assigned?"

"Los Angeles." He looked pleased.

"Alex is going to work for the OIO, and I'm assigned white collar out of the same office."

The smug look left his face. "Congratulations." He stood and picked up his glass. He leaned in and whispered in my ear, "I'm going to finish this and head home. Feel free to join me."

I snorted, and he walked away.

"You need to let loose sometimes," Kate commented, drawing my attention away from my to-do list for tomorrow. "Michael's interested in you, and he's going to be three thousand miles away. There's no reason you can't have some fun. The entire five months we've been here you haven't brought anyone home or stayed out all night."

"I'm not here to party."

"No," she swallowed the remainder of her shot, "you always have to be the best, practically perfect scores across the board on everything. All you do is workout, read, and study. You're avoiding living your life. It's almost like you're running away from something or someone."

"Drop it." I got up and put some cash on the bar. "If you bring someone home, try to make sure he's gone by the time I get up. I don't want my final morning in our apartment to be awkward while I'm rushing around trying to pack my car."

"Sure." She didn't look convinced, but she had learned it wasn't worth arguing. Stubborn was one of the things I did best.

*   *   *

The next morning, there were no strange men vying for bathroom time. Kate made a pot of coffee, and I filled my thermos and threw the few remaining unpacked items into a duffel bag.

"Alex," she just came up the steps from taking a box out to her car, "it's been fun."

"That's one way to put it." I shrugged, hefting the bag over my shoulder. "Give me a call whenever you get settled, and we'll go out for drinks to celebrate our new agent statuses."

"Sounds good."

Kate had a home elsewhere, and it would be a couple of weeks before her lease was up. This gave her some time to apartment hunt. I was a nomad, having moved from a dorm to a campus apartment to a studio apartment in law school. Setting down permanent roots was something I had yet to do in my adult life, and I would have to put it off a little longer.

Kate's position in white collar wasn't starting for another month. Unfortunately, Monday morning, I was expected to meet with my soon-to-be mentor, Mark Jablonsky, and hit the ground running. Not all of us had cushy desk jobs; although, the thought of only working behind a desk made me cringe. Sure, investigations were ninety percent pushing papers, but it was the ten percent that made the rest worth it. Until I had some time to catch my breath, I could live out of a hotel room. I made reservations last night and would stay in a weekly rental for the next few weeks while I apartment hunted and cut my teeth at the OIO.

After saying my goodbyes, I relished the five hour drive. It felt like freedom and the ability to make a choice. Admittedly, nothing from the time I turned eighteen until now felt much like a choice. It was all a string of theoretically good decisions in order to achieve a desired goal. Now that the goal was reached, things would be different.

TWO

Today wasn't going well. I sucked at interviews, and after spilling coffee on my blouse and having to find something else to wear, I was in a wrinkled, white button-up shirt with a black skirt, chunk heels, and my long, brown hair was tied back in a braid. My blazer must have been forgotten or lost somewhere between Quantico and my hotel room because I couldn't find it, so there was no way to hide the wrinkles on the white linen. An assistant provided a temporary security ID and escorted me to the OIO floor. It was daunting. The expansive room was full of desks, offices, and people who knew exactly what they were doing and why they were doing it.

I waited outside an office door, listening as annoyed words were exchanged inside. Obviously, bad days were contagious. Eavesdropping was neither polite nor a great way to make a first impression, but from the bits and pieces of the conversation I couldn't help but overhear, I felt certain I was the topic being discussed.

"Her scores were off the charts, expert marksmanship, superb physical ability, and near-perfect recall and deductive skills." The rest of the words were drowned out by a nearby ringing telephone.

Another voice replied, "No one performs at these levels and doesn't crash and burn. I don't want to waste my time."

"Do I have to make this an order?" the first voice threatened.

"No, sir."

A man, who strongly resembled Director Kendall, strode out of the office. He nodded in my general direction but didn't make eye contact.

"Parker," the same voice from inside the room barked, "get your ass in here."

"Sir?" I practically jumped out of the seat. It already felt like I had a lot to prove, especially since my training officer didn't want to train me. I stood up straight in front of his desk, waiting for something. The voice in my head mocked my militaristic posture and commented that being at Quantico surrounded by jarheads potentially ruined my devil-may-care attitude.

Mark Jablonsky glanced up from perusing my file. He had light brown hair and was in his mid-forties. Although he was dressed in a suit, it appeared he might have slept in it. At least my own disheveled appearance wouldn't be a point of contention for my new supervisor. "Sit down."

"Yes, sir." I sat primly as he rifled through his bottom desk drawer and pulled out a stack of stapled papers. He passed them across the desk, along with a pen.

"First, drop the *yes, sir, no, sir, three bags full, sir.* I can't stand that. In the office, it's Jablonsky. Second, fill these out."

"Okay." It was nice he wasn't quite so buttoned-up. He continued to skim through my records as I attempted to answer the basic questions on the page. The problem was, although basic, things like permanent address were beyond my current capabilities. It was obvious Jablonsky already regretted getting stuck with me, and not being able to do as he asked would just make the situation that much worse. I filled out what I could and turned the papers to face him.

We sat in silence as he read my file and picked up the forms, checking that everything was properly filled out. "Address?"

"I'm living out of a suitcase right now."

He nodded and continued scanning the pages. "You left off your emergency contact."

"I don't have one."

He let out what might have been a growl, or maybe he was just clearing his throat. "Most of the time it's a spouse, parent, sibling. Come on, Parker. Give me a name. Any name will do."

"I can't." He stared at me, not bothering to hide the annoyance or frustration. "I'm not married. I don't have any family to speak of since the people who adopted me washed their hands the moment I turned eighteen."

"Boyfriend? Girlfriend?" He softened slightly by my tale of woe which I found irritating. I wondered which of us would be more aggravated by the time five o'clock rolled around.

"Not that it matters, but I'm straight and single."

He let out a sigh and frowned. Snatching a pen from the cup on his desk, he scribbled something into the blank spaces. "Don't get yourself shot. I'll be your emergency contact, but under no circumstances are you to need an emergency contact. Do I make myself clear?"

"Crystal."

He leaned back in the chair and let out a chuckle. "Welcome to the OIO, Parker."

*   *   *

My first six months had flown by. I had found a one bedroom apartment on the sixth floor of a decent enough building. It was a bit old and slightly rundown, but it was in a safe neighborhood and within forty-five minutes of work. Jablonsky had warmed to my presence since our initial meeting, and although I had done little except shadow him and fulfill the other duties required of probationary agents, we were starting to find our rhythm.

"Parker," he barked, and I stood up from my desk and went into his office.

"Sir?" I knew it irritated him when I said it, which was often why I did.

"Cut the crap and tell me everything you know about Victor Spilano."

"Spilano owns and operates the winery and restaurant Specialty Vineyard. He's a wine collector and restaurateur. He's been suspected of importing and exporting black market weapons, namely military-grade assault rifles, small incendiary devices, and chemical components which could be used in the manufacturing of larger explosives. Customs has flagged his shipments, but they have not discovered any contraband during their numerous checks. Although Specialty Vineyard often pays for private charter flights, none of those have been stopped by U.S. Customs or TSA because he fails to file proper flight plans. We miss them every time."

Mark folded his hands over his stomach while he processed what I said. "Suggested course of action?"

"Continue surveillance, question employees, or perhaps place someone inside Specialty Vineyard to gain information on impending shipments." He nodded, encouraging me to continue. "Without solid evidence or witness corroboration, everything we have is hearsay and not enough to get a search warrant signed," I concluded.

"Very good." He glanced at his watch. "How would you like to go to dinner? I'm thinking someplace with a great wine menu. Go home, change into something not work appropriate, and I'll pick you up in an hour and a half."

"I've still got a dozen files to read and three to finalize."

"You'd rather sit behind a desk than get out there and do the job?" He raised a questioning eyebrow. "What happened to the agent who is constantly nagging me for more responsibility?"

"Fine, but you're picking up the tab."

"God, you sound like my wife." He smiled as I retreated from his office.

After going home, changing into one of the few things I owned that was elegant and not at all work-centric, I curled my straight brown hair and applied copious amounts of makeup. Twenty minutes later, my doorbell rang. Mark stood outside still dressed in his work attire.

"Did I interrupt your hot date?"

"No." I stowed my gun and badge in my purse and ushered him out of my apartment before he could get comfortable or start commenting about my belongings still being stuffed inside boxes that I had never unpacked. Unpacking was something that took time and effort, and it could be done as needed. For example, the silverware was in the kitchen as were the mugs. The actual plates and bowls were still packed because I subsisted off takeout and frozen entrees.

"When was the last time you went on a date?" he asked as we drove across town.

"Since when is that any of your business, Jablonsky?"

"Just some light conversation. I always did what I could to avoid having kids, like getting divorced twice, but you're practically the daughter I never had, especially since I'm old enough to be your father. I'd like to know you do something besides work all the damn time." He was fishing, but I didn't know why. "In the last two months, has there even been a single occasion when you've gone home earlier than I have?"

"Possibly." But the real answer was no. I spent most nights reading open case files, finalizing reports, and familiarizing myself with procedures and protocols.

"Yeah, right." He glanced at me from the corner of his eye. During the rest of the ride, he gave me instructions on the proper way of remaining unobtrusive. We were going out to eat. We weren't supposed to be federal agents attempting to get an inside view of a suspect's operation or monitoring his conduct. "Just remember to follow my lead," he said, handing the keys to the valet.

"Absolutely."

THREE

The service at Specialty Vineyard was excellent, and the food wasn't half bad either. My eyes roved the interior, gauging the layout, the patrons, and the staff. There was no sign of Spilano. He was probably apt at delegation. Why work when you could have someone else do it for you? Then again, there was the possibility he might be partaking in illegal activities and had to have unknowing third parties act as his proxy or cover for him.

"Tell me what you see," Jablonsky instructed in a hushed tone. I ran through everything I observed, watching as the smile brightened on his face. He was constantly in teacher mode which could be tedious and annoying. "So what do you make of the two guys sitting at the corner of the bar?"

Observation 101, you don't turn around to look. Peripheral vision, reflective surfaces, and some creativity were necessary for inconspicuous surveillance. I turned to look out the window, catching a glimpse of the men. Unable to get a better angle, I dropped my fork and cautioned a glance behind me as I returned to an upright position.

"What the hell is Carver doing here?" I whispered.

Jablonsky tried to look innocent, but amusement crinkled the corners of his eyes. "We'll discuss that later,

Alex. It's more of an outside matter."

He went back to eating, and I shook off the surprise. This was work. It wasn't an outing or event. But Carver's appearance meant Spilano was a much bigger fish than I imagined.

After eating, I went to the ladies' room. It was an excellent excuse to snoop around the less accessible areas of the restaurant; however, there were no suspicious crates shoved in any abandoned corners labeled guns and bombs. That would have made my job easier, but I liked a challenge. Having nothing additional to report, I met Jablonsky in the foyer, and we left the restaurant.

We barely spoke until he stopped the car in the garage underneath the OIO building. Work was only beginning for the evening, and I regretted not having a change of clothes with me.

"Practicality dictates always having a go-bag within reach," he chided. "Think of this as one of Mark's life lessons."

I filed the thought away for later consideration. Right now, I was focused on Spilano and the real reason we went to dinner. "Why was Agent Carver at Specialty Vineyard? The last I heard, he was working out of Los Angeles."

"Michael Carver," Mark tried to play dumb and failed miserably, "wasn't he at the academy with you?"

"Yes, sir."

He sighed in exasperation. "One of the few recruits who actually outperformed you from what I recall." I tried not to bristle at the dig. "We're working together to bring down Spilano. The LA office confiscated a shipment of detonator cord. The sender claimed it was Spilano's, but they've had trouble pinpointing the connection. Since Victor is a resident and business owner in our fine city, they sent over their crack team to assist us." He smiled, amused by some inside joke. "Do you think you can play nice?"

"I always play nice."

"We'll see. It's harder than it looks when someone doesn't think you can find your own ass with both hands. It's work politics. We're on the same side, but they think they can do better."

"Maybe that's because you're so damn old and out of touch," I teased. If we had been upstairs, I never would have said something so callous and insubordinate, but in the garage, I had some leeway.

"Watch it, Parker." He smiled. "If you start acting superior, I'll ship you out to LA with the rest of the arrogant lot." We stepped into the elevator and made our way upstairs.

"All right, people," Jablonsky announced, "let's get down to business." Two other agents remained in the office. He must have asked them to stay late. There was an analyst, another agent, and me. "As you all know, we've been trying to get something to stick to Victor Spilano. Our associates from Los Angeles are here to assist." I spotted Carver and the other man from the bar exiting the Director's office. "Agents Sam Boyle and Michael Carver will brief you on the situation."

Carver sauntered past, throwing a sly grin and a wink my way. So much for not having to see him ever again. Agent Boyle launched into an extensive briefing, complete with PowerPoint presentation and use of the Smart board.

Victor Spilano had been in California on winery business a month ago. Surveillance footage showed him in Napa and other parts of California's wine country. None of these areas were close to Los Angeles, and I wondered why the LA office was involved. As if reading my mind, the images shifted to LAX airport. Cargo containers and manifests listed the same vineyards Spilano toured as the source of the contraband det cords.

"After extensive questioning," Boyle continued, "the vineyard owners claimed these were not their shipments but shipments made by Victor Spilano while on their property. Right now, we have nothing solid to link Spilano to these crates except for the word of the men we caught red-handed."

"Convenient and controversial," Carver interjected. "We've been given some breathing room, but it's a short leash. The state department wants this sorted quickly and quietly. Your investigation into the business practices and black market ties of Mr. Spilano will expedite our investigation. By sharing information and resources, we'll be able to get this bastard off the streets and out of the arms business."

It sounded like a steaming pile of shit. Carver was feeding us the company line, and I understood Mark's position on playing nice. The LA office wanted us to hand over months of hard work to make them look good.

"Any questions?" Boyle asked, scanning the room.

"Just one." Jablonsky leaned against an empty desk. "Who's taking lead?"

Boyle played the question off good-naturedly. "Age before beauty, right? You have rank, Supervisory Special Agent. We'll assist your team. A bust is a bust, regardless of which coast makes it happen."

"Wise move," Jablonsky replied, immediately stepping away from the desk and taking point. "Tonight, I want all our records condensed, so we'll have one usable file for reference on our good buddy, Victor." He pointed to the analyst and the other agent. "The two of you, work with Agent Boyle." After a chorus of affirmatives, the three agents headed into the nearest conference room. "Rookies," he shifted his gaze from Carver to me, "or do you prefer the more appropriate term, probies?"

"I prefer when you're not being cute," I muttered under my breath. Luckily, Mark didn't hear me.

"Sir?" Carver questioned, waiting for whatever assignment we were about to be given as a child would wait to open a particularly large present on Christmas morning. The amusement on my supervisor's face was disconcerting. "What do you have for us?"

"You're both green. But you show exceptional promise. I've spoken to your supervisor, Boyle, and he assures me you can handle this."

Carver looked about ready to burst in anticipation, but something about the entire situation caused an uneasy feeling to settle in the pit of my stomach. Whatever was about to happen, I already didn't like it.

"The two of you are going undercover." Without waiting for a response, Mark went into his office, pulled out two files, and returned. "These are your cover identities and backgrounds. Make sure you have every bit of this memorized by tomorrow morning. Undercover work requires you to live and breathe being these people. Do what you have to in order to make me believe it."

"Yes, sir," we responded in unison.

Mark tossed a key ring to Carver. "Motor pool's lending you a vehicle for this op. Would you care to give Parker a ride home since I'm pulling an all-nighter with the boys?"

"It would be my pleasure," Carver said.

"No, it will not." I needed to work on holding my tongue. "Jablonsky, I'd be more than happy to stay and assist on the paperwork."

"If you want to be useful," he was back in teacher mode, "then you and your partner need to get used to working with one another. He's going to be the only one there if something goes sideways." He turned to Carver. "That goes double for you, kid." We both remained silent, and Mark sighed. "Get out of here and get to know your cover identities and each other. You need to be a believable couple by tomorrow, so Alex, stop cringing every time he gets within five feet of you. This isn't kindergarten. Boys don't have cooties."

I wasn't sure about that, but if we were partnered together, it was time to act like a professional.

"No cooties here." Carver smiled, his nose crinkling playfully.

"Carver," Jablonsky's tone had an edge, "unless absolutely necessary, don't get within five feet of Parker. She might shoot you."

I laughed, and the two of us headed for the elevator.

"Look who's turned into a teacher's pet," Carver teased as the doors closed.

"And look who's still an ass-kisser," I responded.

"I don't think Jablonsky needs to worry. We already act like a married couple."

I rolled my eyes, hoping once we were alone he would drop the macho attitude.

FOUR

An opened pizza box with two slices remaining sat on my coffee table. I leaned back against the couch and rubbed my eyes. It was two a.m. If I had to read my cover profile one more time, I would go insane.

"How long have you lived here?" Michael asked. We were both sitting on the floor. He was across the coffee table from me.

"Three years. I moved in the summer after graduating from Boston University with a degree in art history."

"No," he smiled, "not the fake you. The real you."

"Four months, give or take."

"I'm just amazed. It looks even less lived in than the apartment at Quantico. Why the hell haven't you unpacked or at least hung a picture on the wall or something? Maybe put up some wallpaper or paint."

"Is Michael Price a home decorator?" I asked, nudging his file with my index finger.

"No. He works at an art gallery, which is how we met."

"Then shut up."

"Classic Alex," he reached for one of the remaining slices, "if you don't want to deal with it, you bark at it until it goes away. Are you part Doberman? Because I'm okay with a little biting."

"Unbelievable." Being tired made me irritable. "All right, quiz me," I saw where his thoughts were going, "on this." I pointed to the folders.

"Name?"

"Alexandra Riley, but I go by Alex."

He nodded and gestured that I continue running through the phony background. We were supposed to be engaged. My art history background and Michael Price's position at the art gallery were how we met and supposedly fell in love. I was an up and coming artist, working at the gallery in the hopes of having my own show. While farfetched, the manufactured background provided ample opportunity to interact with Victor Spilano.

"How long have we been together?" I asked Michael, flipping the questions to him.

"Over a year. It was a year in," his eyes darted back and forth as he tried to remember, "September. The fourteenth, no, fifteenth." I gave him a warning look. "Come on, what's more believable than a guy not remembering the exact date of his anniversary?"

"I'll give you that one." We continued going over our backgrounds for another hour. By then, the pizza was gone. I had every inch of my cover and Carver's memorized. "I'm ready to call it a night." I tilted my neck to the side and rubbed the kink in my shoulder. "Any objections?"

"None." He looked tired too. "I'll see you in the morning, Alex." He got up, tossing the pizza box into my trashcan on his way to the door. "What do you call me?" he asked as I closed the folders and wiped the crumbs off the table.

"What?"

"I call you Alex, but what do I go by? Mike, Michael, Mikey, sweet-ums?"

Jackass, my mind responded, and I hid my amusement. There was a chance I might be a bit insane, more so when I was tired. "Whatever you want."

"Michael or sweet-ums." He winked. "The second is only acceptable postcoital."

I glared, and he let himself out of my apartment,

flipping the lock on the way.

*   *   *

The next morning, the four of us were uncomfortably situated in Jablonsky's tiny office. Boyle and Jablonsky looked exhausted; neither of them had gone home, based on the clothing they wore. They made copies of the pertinent information from the file and distributed it to everyone working this case. Our team was small, consisting of six people. The analyst and other agent from last night had already gone home. They would deal with the paperwork and coordinate the operation between this office and the LA field office. At least I was free from the paperwork for once.

"Do you two have your covers established?" Boyle asked, looking skeptical.

"Of course," Michael replied. I was mentally referring to him as Michael for the duration just to avoid any accidental slips when we were in the field. Calling him Carver in front of Spilano would not be good.

"You really believe these two recruits can handle an operation of this magnitude?" Boyle asked Jablonsky. It was intentional, so we'd know to act particularly careful since we were already on thin ice.

"I can't speak for yours, but mine's shown a great deal of promise. I don't expect to be disappointed." He looked pointedly at me as if to say *don't fuck up.*

"Then I'm gonna catch some z's." Boyle patted Michael on the back as he went out the door.

"Here's what's going to happen now." Jablonsky turned his computer monitor to the side so we could see as he began explaining how things were going to work.

There was a small art gallery near Specialty Vineyard. The owners were willing to cooperate with the Bureau, and they would corroborate Alexandra Riley and Michael Price's backgrounds. We were both going to be planted at the gallery and casually dine at Specialty Vineyard. At this point, the opportunities were endless.

"Question," Michael interjected. "What excuse are we

using to get close to Victor Spilano?"

"Whatever works. This isn't the time for handholding. You get in, try something. If it doesn't work, you try something else. You keep trying until you find an in and then you do whatever it takes not to lose it. Just remember, you cannot break cover."

"What if we encounter problems?" I asked. Although months of training and study had dealt extensively with the proper methods to handle situations like this, words on a page were nothing like the real thing.

"Be creative." Jablonsky pressed his lips together. "Try to develop a shorthand between yourselves. If things go south, at least you'll have immediate backup. In the event it turns into something life or death, don't sacrifice yourselves. Pull the badge and make the call. Just make sure it's not premature. If something looks uncertain, hold out as long as you can to make sure it is what it appears to be."

"Got it." Michael glanced at me. We were a team for the duration. At least he understood we had to agree before making a move. It was the only way to safeguard the mission and ourselves.

"Excellent." Jablonsky stood up. "Let's get the two of you situated at the art gallery so you can ease into your new identities. This ought to be fun."

After all the instructions, Michael drove to the gallery, Paintings and Pinnings, and found a metered spot a couple blocks away. The owners, Sara and Greg Sylvar, were accommodating. They closed shop at lunchtime to give us a complete tour and an insider's view of how the art world worked. Greg had an art history degree and recommended some light reading to help sell my cover. It was almost dinnertime when we left.

"I never realized the public was this amenable to law enforcement," Michael commented as we got back into the car.

"Maybe they were afraid we'd turn their information over to the IRS for a thorough audit if they didn't play ball." As he listened to my rambling, he checked the mirrors and backed out of the parking spot. "Jablonsky wants us to ease our way into becoming regulars at Specialty Vineyard, so I guess we should check in and then consider going to dinner."

"How old are we?" he asked, the demeaning quality I often heard when we were going through training was back.

"I'm twenty-four. You're twenty-seven?" I couldn't remember the date of his cover's birthday which probably meant spending so many late night hours memorizing things had let some minute details slip past. I'd need to refresh myself on it again tonight, just to make sure it was ingrained in my being.

"Yes, and so is Michael Price."

I wondered how deep cover agents kept things straight. It felt like we were suffering from dissociative identity disorders and had multiple personalities.

"That probably means we aren't in our seventies and hoping to cash in on the early bird specials," he said.

"Fine."

We went back to the OIO building. I reread our falsified backgrounds twice, cover to cover, before going home to change. Michael was picking me up for our date this evening. Undercover assignment here I come. I hoped no one would recognize us from last night. In the event they did, we'd need a decent cover story, and I had an idea.

FIVE

Having learned my lesson the last time I went out in a dress, I had a tote bag packed with a change of clothes. Spending the night in the office was more conducive when I was in either work attire or something more casual, like jeans and a t-shirt. In the event the maitre d' or one of the wait staff noticed our repeat presences, I had a cover story prepared. Mark could be my father, which fit perfectly since he often acted as a cross between a teacher and parent, and we had gone out for a nice meal. My fiancé was supposed to join us but had to woo a potential art dealer instead, explaining why he and Boyle spent the evening at the bar. It sounded good on paper, and when I ran it by Michael, he agreed it was plausible.

When we arrived at the restaurant, he turned on the charm, and I had no choice but to play along. The hostess seated us at a cozy table for two and lit the candle in the center for additional ambiance. A moment later, the server arrived, and Michael made some pretense of it being a special occasion. It was an excuse to order one of their finest bottles of wine. The man returned, presented the bottle, and poured a small sample into the glass. Michael swirled, sniffed, and did all the other pretentious things people do when pretending they know something about wine. After it met his approval, two glasses were poured, and we were left alone.

"Honey," he purred, "aren't you having a good time? You need to relax. We aren't at work."

Reading between the lines, I tried to appear more comfortable as I searched the room for Victor Spilano.

"You're just as tense," I retorted, glancing at him. "Maybe you need to drink some wine." I wasn't entirely sure drinking on the job was permitted, but there was no other way to blend in when your mark was in the wine business. Michael picked up the glass and held it out, waiting for me to clink mine with his. "Adorable."

"I must be the luckiest guy, getting to date you," he sounded snarky, "what with all these smart-alecky comments and everything."

"That's part of what made you fall head over heels in love with me. It's not my fault if I just swept you off your feet."

He laughed and picked up the menu, pretending to read as he studied something behind me. I hated not being able to see whatever had caught his attention. My back faced the front door. All I had was a great view of the bar, and if I tilted a little to the side, I could see a sliver inside the kitchen.

The server returned and took our orders. While we waited for him to return, Michael pulled out his cell phone. "Smile," he instructed. After he clicked a few photos, he passed the device to me.

Victor Spilano was standing off to the side of the foyer, speaking with someone in a business suit. I had no idea who the other man was, but as I skimmed the photos, I found a few close-up shots that might be viable for facial recognition.

Our meal arrived, and we ate while Michael continued to keep tabs on the mark. Eventually, his gaze shifted to the side, and I was ecstatic to have something more useful to do than try to see some indecipherable reflection in the glass surfaces of the bar. Victor stood against a back wall, speaking with a group at the table. It appeared he was schmoozing with the regulars.

After dinner, I ordered a dessert for us to share. Since Victor was in the building, we might as well hang around as long as possible. When the check was brought, Michael asked about catering and renting out the space for a private function. Within moments, Victor Spilano came to our table. He was unnaturally tanned with nearly black hair and a gauntness to him.

"How was your meal?" he inquired, resembling a shark by showing tons of teeth.

"Excellent." I smiled demurely, wondering which of us wore the pants in our pretend relationship. Since this was Michael's idea, I let him take lead.

"Michael Price," he extended his hand, "this is Alex. We work just down the street at Paintings and Pinnings. Normally, we have events at the gallery catered by a local bistro, but there's a very impressive artist planning a show, and since this place is fantastic, we were wondering if it would be possible to rent your restaurant for an evening or have you cater our function."

"Mr. Price, you obviously have exquisite taste. I'm the owner, Victor Spilano." He motioned to the bartender. "If you wait a moment, I'm sure I can scare up a price chart for our services. How many guests are you anticipating?"

Michael looked at me.

"It's invitation only." I tried to pretend I had some idea what was going on. "It should be in the ballpark of a hundred, maybe one fifty."

"We can easily accommodate you," Spilano insisted.

He went to the bar, and I looked at Michael. Flying by the seat of our pants on our first night conducting surveillance seemed like overkill. Were we pushing too hard? Would Victor become suspicious, or was I paranoid as usual? Michael gestured that I take it easy.

When Spilano returned with a printed sheet of services and features, Michael skimmed it and smiled. "Thank you so much. How much notice do you need?"

"Normally, a month, but if you're in a bind, I can probably scrape something together in as little as two weeks." If I didn't know Spilano was an arms dealer, I might have liked him.

We stood. Michael shook hands with Victor before putting his arm around my waist and escorting me to the door. As we stood outside, I could feel the unease of being watched. I cuddled up to Michael, unable to turn around to see who might be observing us, but it was best to sell ourselves as a couple. Michael kissed my temple and opened my car door, helping me inside as soon as the valet handed him the keys.

"That was fun," he said as we drove to the OIO building. "I believe our first day undercover was a complete success."

"You pushed too hard. We're trying to blend in, not draw more attention to ourselves. The only thing we were supposed to do was get a feel for the place, not start party planning."

"It'll get us inside. Doesn't Jablonsky ever let you call the shots? You never seemed particularly subservient at Quantico, so what the hell happened to you?"

"This is our first outing. I don't want to blow it. I'm under strict orders not to get shot."

"Paranoid much?"

"Screw you."

"That might help sell us as a couple."

"Do you ever take any of this shit seriously? You always talk a good game and throw out the jibes and the insults, but watching you tonight, I realize it's obvious you don't have any fucking idea what you're doing."

"I have a better understanding of this than you. Have you even been out of the office?"

"Oh and you have?" I asked.

Neither of us had any experience with this type of assignment. We were getting into hot water, and I wondered how Jablonsky and Boyle would react.

But I didn't have to wonder long. After we turned the photos over to the analyst, Jablonsky shut the four of us into his office.

"What the hell are you doing?" Boyle yelled. "You were given basic instructions. What you did was premature. Reckless. You shouldn't have made such an impact your first night out."

"Sir," Michael began, "an opportunity presented itself. There was no guarantee Spilano would be there any other night. For all any of us know, he might be going on vacation for the next three months."

Boyle looked annoyed. So did Jablonsky.

"It was a good call," I piped up. Although I didn't necessarily agree, I understood the basic tenet of this job;

never throw your partner under a bus. "Any suspicion could easily be mitigated. It isn't at all uncommon for the casual diner, looking to have an event catered, to ask for more information after enjoying a wonderful meal. We sold it from the beginning. From the wine to the dessert."

"Now you're drinking on the job too? You're federal agents. Why do you need to imbibe at work?" Jablonsky asked.

"To sell our cover. We aren't impaired. Would it make you feel better if we submit to a breathalyzer or a blood test?" I wouldn't back down. Maybe Michael made a dumb move, but we had to let it run its course.

"Tenacious. Goddamn tenacious." Jablonsky sighed. "Fine, fill out a report on everything you witnessed and get out of here. Tomorrow morning, we'll have an official briefing prepared for your next course of action, and whatever we tell you to do, you better pay attention this time."

"Operations like this aren't concluded in a day. Undercover work is slow. You aren't going to make a case in an hour. Some agents go undercover for months or longer. This is a marathon, not a sprint," Boyle cautioned.

"Yes, sir," Michael and I responded in unison. We needed to stop doing that.

"Parker," Jablonsky barked, "you wore that last night. Go buy some clothes to wear for working at the art gallery and going out on dates."

I nodded, and he jerked his head toward the door. We were dismissed.

I picked up my change of clothes and went in search of the locker room. After returning, I took a seat at my desk and began writing my report.

"You didn't have to back me up in there," Michael said. "I can take responsibility for my own actions."

"Stop being so impatient," I chided. "We're in this together, and I don't want my ass handed to me again because of the next dumb thing you do."

He finalized his report and picked it up to take it to Jablonsky's office. "See you tomorrow, Parker."

"Lucky me."

SIX

The next three weeks blurred into one monotonous day. Carver and I spent our fair share of time at Paintings and Pinnings, Specialty Vineyard, and work. It was beginning to wear on me. Undercover assignments were the pits. I hated paperwork, but constantly having to pretend to be someone else was just as tedious and soul-sucking. At least it was a learning experience. For future reference, if given the option, I wanted to work investigations, not gather intel.

It was Saturday morning; Jablonsky had given us the weekend off to help maintain our sanity. I slept until noon, and after getting dressed, I went for a run. It was one of the few things that cleared my mind. When I returned from my five miles, I found Michael standing outside my door.

"You're still running after something completely unobtainable?" he asked.

"Don't you have a life?"

"Yes, in Los Angeles. Until we get this sorted out, I'm stuck here." He followed me inside. "Plus, who are you to talk about a life? In the last three weeks, I don't believe you've unpacked a single box. Work is all you do. That's not much of a life." He went to my fridge and poured himself a glass of soda while I went into my room. "Running doesn't count as a life either. And you could have invited your fake fiancé along."

"Why are you here?" I stood in the hallway between my bedroom and bathroom, wanting to take a shower and go about my day without all this bullshit. We were off for the weekend. That meant I shouldn't have to deal with him.

"Boyle called. P&P is hosting an unplanned event tonight, and since we're supposed to be star employees, it would look suspicious if we weren't there. The surveillance van on Spilano has noticed some odd movements, so our bosses think it'd be a good idea if we were in the vicinity."

"But it's our day off," I protested.

"Honey, we don't get days off. It's part of the job."

"And you accuse me of not having a life." I shut the bathroom door.

The novelty of being a federal agent was wearing thin. I'd been assigned to Jablonsky for the last seven months, and although I still had a lot to learn, getting dragged into a long-term undercover assignment had never been on my radar. The few times Mark and I had a quiet moment, he would try to instill upon me vast amounts of facts and information he thought new agents should know. He hadn't wanted anything this large-scale to rest on two newbies either, but we were determined to make lemonade.

When I came out, Michael was on the phone. Rummaging through the fridge, I made a sandwich and sat at my kitchen table. He hung up and took a seat.

"Another shipment's been confiscated. Boyle wants to end this. He's sending an invitation to the gallery's gala to Spilano. Although it's short notice, it will give Victor a better understanding of the type of service we expect from his business, so he should show up."

"Why are we moving on him tonight? We already hired Spilano for the catering gig next week. While he's busy making sure the food prep and waiters are all prepared, we can snoop then."

"In case you forgot, we were told not to do anything," Michael rolled his eyes, "so Jablonsky's sending a few members of his team into the restaurant tonight. If Spilano's otherwise occupied, they might get a quick peek inside the back room of his restaurant. Whatever they find might be enough to tip his hand or catch him off guard."

"I didn't think we had enough for a search warrant."

"The rules have changed. A second source came forward and pointed the finger directly at Victor. The ink should be drying as we speak. Face it," Michael continued, "you don't even know what to do with a day off."

"I went for a run, and later, I planned to hit the range."

"That's not a day off. That's self-imposed training. Let me guess, after that you were going to curl up with a nice book or catch up on paperwork."

Dammit, I hated how he guessed my routine.

"Alex, we could have such fun together," he looked devilish, "but tonight, we're working. I'll meet you at the office, and we'll go to P&P together. Okay?"

"Fine."

*   *   *

After dressing for an art opening and ensuring my go-bag was in my trunk, I went to the OIO. There was no sign of Boyle or Carver, and I was relieved. I checked my e-mail, skimmed through the latest developments on a few other open cases, and went in search of Jablonsky. He was in his office.

"Knock, knock," I announced from the doorway.

He gestured me inside. "I'm glad the California boys aren't here right now." He looked exhausted. A crumpled blanket sat on the couch, but I filed that thought away for later. "Parker, this isn't normally the type of assignment I'd send you on. This was meant to be information gathering only, but things have changed. You're in too deep, or I'd pull you out."

"What's changed?" It wasn't that I didn't trust Michael, but he might not be aware of the current situation.

"We're sending in a team of agents. We have a search warrant, but I don't expect to find anything damning. Spilano isn't an idiot. He isn't going to keep anything incriminating at work or home, which are the only two places we know to search. Instead, we're hoping to panic him. If he's afraid his illegal activities will be discovered, he might do something stupid."

"So be on the lookout for stupid?"

"BOLOS," he joked. "The photograph of the man Carver took a few weeks ago pinged in Interpol's database. His name is Ivan Sarskov. He has peripheral ties to the Russian mafia. His family is known for dealing weapons to small groups in Chechnya, the Baltics, and parts of the Mediterranean. We're working under the assumption he's buying from Spilano, but things aren't always what they appear. Keep your eyes open and your ear to the ground." He blew out a breath. "Damn bureaucracy," he cursed quietly, "agents are raiding the restaurant tonight. We're hoping to get a look around without Spilano being there, but who knows how that will play out. Make sure you keep your cover intact. Don't do anything too ostentatious tonight, and keep Carver on a tight leash."

"I wasn't aware there was a hierarchy regarding our undercover work."

"Parker, it's my op which means I'm putting you in charge of making sure Carver doesn't act recklessly."

"Can I have a taser instead?"

"Get out of here."

I left the office and was in the midst of speaking to the analyst concerning Sarskov and Spilano when Michael appeared behind me in a snazzy suit. The analyst started over, and once the briefing concluded, we went downstairs to the garage and headed for the gallery. During the drive, I warned Michael to keep a lid on things and do his best to blend in.

"How can I blend in when I'm dressed like this and with you on my arm?" He attempted suave, but given the current pre-op jitters I couldn't shake, the compliment fell on deaf ears.

We pretended to be in the know on all things art related as we worked the party, doing our best to remain in one another's company most of the night. A guest had some questions on purchasing a particular photograph, and since I *worked* at P&P, I led him to one of the owners. By the time I returned, Michael was deep in conversation with Spilano. I hurried over, hoping it was nothing but casual conversation.

"Alex, you look stunning." Victor smiled and hugged me. "Your beau was just telling me you have yet to decide where to have your rehearsal dinner."

I smiled brightly, wanting nothing more than to knock some sense into Michael.

"Honey," Michael wrapped his arm tightly around my waist, "what do you think of having it at Specialty Vineyard? You absolutely raved about the food, and the restaurant is lovely."

"So lovely." I smiled at Victor. "Can you excuse us for just a moment?" He nodded and turned back to gaze at the art. I dragged Michael into the next room and angrily whispered to him, "What the hell are you doing?"

"He started it. Just follow my lead. It'll be fine." Without waiting for a response, Michael went back into the other room, leaving me no choice but to follow.

"Well?" Spilano looked at us expectantly.

"It's decided." Michael put his arm around me again and crushed me against his side. "It will be the third Thursday in April. We still have a million other plans to make. Cake and flowers and linens. You know how women are." He gave me a squeeze as if this was my idea. "But we can't live without them, can we?"

"I'd like to see you try." It was said in a kidding tone, but Michael got the point and backed off a little. "Since it's still three months away, can we wait to decide menu choices? My mom's a vegetarian and his sister is currently trying out Veganism. We're hoping to get everyone to agree to chicken or beef by the time the wedding rolls around, but who knows how that's going to work."

"No rush." Spilano gave us a questioning look, and without permission, Michael leaned in and kissed me passionately. I was fighting the urge to shove him away, when I heard Spilano quietly excuse himself. Making sure the coast was clear, I bit Michael's lip, and he stepped back.

"Hey," he exclaimed.

I gave him my most lethal, drop dead look. "Don't."

This entire evening was going horribly wrong. Carver couldn't follow orders, and there was a chance Spilano might be getting suspicious. There was the even more frightening possibility that if we were still undercover in three months, we'd have to fake a rehearsal dinner. God, if I had to spend three more months with Michael Carver, one of us was going to resign. Hopefully, his personal constitution was pliable or his pain threshold was low because I worked too hard to get here.

The next hour was fine. Spilano worked the party, talking to the other guests and the owners. He discussed business, asking about the number of caterers, the liquor and wine choices, and whether they wanted to do a floating event next week that could begin at the restaurant and wind up at the gallery or vice versa. Just as I began to think Carver didn't sabotage the op and it would be okay, Spilano took a call. He turned crimson and then blanched. Hanging up, he turned to the group he was speaking to and quickly extricated himself.

"Is everything okay?" Michael asked him as he rushed past.

"No. The FBI is raiding my restaurant."

SEVEN

After Spilano left, I dialed Jablonsky and told him Victor was on his way. I was sure there would be the threat of lawsuits for harassment and the usual rigmarole of protests that went along with search warrants. Sighing, I wasn't sure if we had to stay the rest of the night at P&P or if we were free to go.

"I can't believe you bit me," Michael muttered.

I took to leaning in a secluded corner of the gallery. What I wanted was to go back to the office and get started cataloging whatever evidence they might be collecting. But since I was stuck here, I wanted time alone to think. The warrant had been for weapons and shipping manifests. At the very least, we would be able to go through the restaurant's order forms for something sinister.

"You're lucky that's all I did. You try something again, and you'll have a new career as a soprano."

"Feisty," he remarked, positioning himself next to me. "I did say I was okay with a little biting, but I never expected you to take it so literally."

We stood silently as the party died down, and the remaining guests trickled out. When there was no reason left to stay, we went back to the office and didn't exchange a single word the rest of the night.

As Jablonsky predicted, the search was inconclusive. The records had been run and rerun, and although we cross-referenced them with alleged weapons trafficking, it seemed more hit or miss. There was something here. There had to be. Surveillance still had eyes on Spilano and his restaurant, but now that he'd been tipped off, he would be more cautious. At least he would if he had half a brain. Boyle was adamant that criminals always trip themselves up, and we'd catch him red-handed. This seemed to be an unrealistic pipe dream, but he had years of experience dictating otherwise.

"Parker?" I looked up. The sun had risen without my noticing. "You're in early," Kate commented on her way to the coffeepot, "especially for a weekend."

"I guess." I wasn't about to tell her I didn't go home last night. "What are you doing here? I thought desk jockeys only work weekdays." It was part of the back and forth we exchanged whenever we ran into each other in the halls or elevator.

"Tell that to my supervisor." She continued on her way but brilliance struck, and I called her back.

"Can you do me a favor?" I held up the stack of shipping manifests. A few had account numbers listed. "If you get a chance, run down these accounts." I explained the situation and how we obtained the information because I didn't want to risk tainting the investigation with any illegal actions.

"Fine, but that means you owe me. And I'm cashing in the first night we both have off. Pub crawl and you're buying," she smiled evilly, "until I find an attractive gentleman to foot the bill." Maybe the research was true. Kate was in her thirties and clearly at her sexual peak. I just wished she would grow out of this juvenile and semi-reckless behavior.

"A restaurant with a bar and we'll split a bottle of wine."

"Deal." She copied the relevant account numbers and promised to call as soon as she had something solid.

Getting up, I stretched. The office was a ghost town. It

should be easy to sneak out and go home without anyone making a fuss. As I made my way toward the elevator, I spotted Mark's office door cracked open. What was he doing here on a Sunday?

I went to the door, but stopped myself from knocking. Inside, he was asleep on the tiny couch in the corner. Tomorrow, I would give him hell for busting my chops for working such crazy hours when he was clearly doing the same.

Once home, I changed and crawled into bed. Everything I read blurred into a constant running thought wisp in my brain, and there was no off switch. My brain was gnawing on something. It was nonstop and frustrating as hell. Eventually, I dragged myself out of bed and found a blank notepad. Starting at the beginning, I listed all the facts I knew to be true about Victor Spilano, Specialty Vineyard, and the confiscated weapons. The one piece that didn't fit was Sarskov. Why would one arms dealer have any interaction with another? It made no sense. Arms dealers weren't card carrying members of an exclusive club, just like drug dealers didn't go to a weekly gathering to exchange sales advice. The only reason competitors would meet would be to make threats.

The databases said Ivan Sarskov was a businessman. He owned half a dozen strip joints. His suspected ties to the Russian mafia were unsubstantiated, at least from a legal standpoint. The guy didn't have a jacket. He was clean, just like Spilano. The only difference was Sarskov's two brothers had been arrested for drugs, gambling, solicitation, and assault. Maybe being the black sheep in the family wasn't a bad thing. Either that or Ivan had gotten all the brains and kept his illegal habits under wraps. My guess, he was running drugs and girls out of his clubs, maybe weapons too.

I stopped writing and paced my apartment. Strip joints were Petri dishes for crime, but Specialty Vineyard was an upscale restaurant. The facts didn't fit the accusations. "What am I missing?" I asked the empty room. No one answered which was probably a good thing because if I got an answer that would mean I was certifiable. Why was an investigation ever opened on Victor Spilano anyway?

Even before Boyle and Carver showed up, Jablonsky sent Spilano's file across my desk. The investigation was in the works and had been for months, but no one told me what the impetus was. It never seemed important to ask until now.

"Carver," Michael answered on the second ring.

"What made Victor Spilano a person of interest?"

"He's selling and smuggling weapons. That violates dozens of federal and international laws."

Before he could continue with the history lesson, I interjected, "Originally."

"Huh," he sounded puzzled. "Hang on." I heard some papers being shuffled around. "Traces of plastic explosive were identified by TSA on one of his wine shipments four months ago."

"Who was the seller?" Could we have been wrong all along?

"I don't know. It's in the official report. You mean to tell me you haven't memorized the entire thing by now?"

"Ha. Ha." My mind raced. Everything I needed was at the office. The problem was I also needed some help to access it. It was Sunday, and after the long hours the team had been putting in, I didn't think calling in an analyst was a good idea. I was still the newest agent and somewhat of a joke since I had yet to complete a case.

"You can't go through four months of research by yourself," Michael said.

"Sure I can." I hung up, changed, and went back to the office.

When I got there, Michael was sitting at my desk. Two boxes full of files, surveillance photos, and documents were on the floor. He had the computer running a search as he leafed through the condensed file Boyle and Jablonsky compiled at the beginning of the op.

"Okay, so from what I've read, Spilano was questioned at the time his property was confiscated by TSA. As predicted, he claimed to possess no knowledge of explosives, C4 or otherwise. And since there were no actual weapons within the shipment, the items were returned to him, minus the packaging," Michael said. I pulled up a chair and sat next to him. "We probably would have let it go, but less than a week later, Spilano traveled to Pakistan. He was gone for two weeks. According to his passport records, he went from Pakistan to India, then Dubai, Turkey, stopped at Greece, hit England, and then home."

"Vacation?"

"He cited business for his reason to travel."

We lived in tumultuous times, and many of the places in the Middle East and even Eastern Europe were considered hotbeds for terrorism or other illegal activities. Even innocent travelers could come under scrutiny. The traces of explosive on his packing crates the week before had done nothing to alleviate his questionable travel itinerary. One plus one equals two, right?

"What did Boyle say about all of this?" I asked.

"We were keeping tabs on Spilano for obvious reasons, and when we uncovered actual weapons, it was the first solid lead we had. That's when he found the files your division compiled, and we hopped a plane."

I rubbed my face. It just didn't feel right.

"You seriously can't believe this guy is being set-up," Michael said.

"Something doesn't jibe." I pointed out the flaws in our reasoning, particularly concerning Sarskov, but Carver wasn't dissuaded.

"Why did he rush out of P&P last night if he isn't doing anything wrong?"

"I don't know."

"What about the two separate parties who pointed us to Spilano? He was on their property. He used their resources to make shipments, and lo and behold, the shipments are nothing but contraband. But he's innocent, I forgot," Michael huffed. "You've lost your damn mind." He got up and slammed the chair against the desk.

"Did I ask for your help?" His comments pissed me off. "This is my gut instinct talking, so I'll react the way I see fit. You can get the hell out of here." I slid his chair out of my way and rolled in front of the computer, typing a search on Ivan Sarskov.

Having reconsidered his options and blown off enough steam with his minor temper tantrum, Michael came back to the desk. "If you're right about this, I'm taking half the credit." He scooted the chair back and opened the second box of files. "But if you're wrong, I'm not taking half the heat."

"Son of a bitch," I caught his eye and winked, "all of the benefits and none of the consequences. I wish I had a partner like yours."

EIGHT

"Don't tell me Parker's work ethic has rubbed off on the rest of the team." Jablonsky sighed as he walked up to my desk and stared at the scattered files and notes.

"She can be persuasive." Carver didn't bother to glance up from the computer.

"I didn't ask you to help." I dropped my pen on the paper and blinked a few times. My eyes were dry from spending so many hours reading. "What are you doing here, Jablonsky?"

He ignored my question and read over my shoulder. "Are you moonlighting for a defense attorney?"

"No." My answer was succinct, but he wanted some elaboration so he nudged the back of my chair. "Something doesn't feel right."

Michael mumbled something derogatory about women and their intuition.

"My office, now." Mark led the way and shut the door. "What do you mean it doesn't feel right?"

"Sarskov and Spilano, they don't fit. Not together. What if everything has been circumstantial and Spilano's just been in the wrong place at the wrong time?"

"Jesus, Parker." He rubbed the stubble on his chin. "We've had corroboration. Evidence. Hell, we even had enough to get a search warrant. How can you start doubting the entire operation now? Why?" His volume increased with every syllable. "Are you spiraling into some kind of nervous breakdown? I thought you showed promise as an agent, but agents don't do this. You're wasting your time, Carver's time, and now my time. Get out."

"But sir," it felt like I had just been punched in the gut, "why would one arms dealer be colluding with another?"

"Maybe they're debating territory. Maybe they want to join forces and open Guns 'R Us. Maybe they're best friends from college. Who cares? Your job is to investigate Victor Spilano." He paused, his face red from yelling. "Actually, your job isn't even to investigate; it's to gather intel while undercover. How's that going? So far, I'm not sure you've brought anything worthwhile to my attention. It seems Carver has to make all the moves, doesn't he?"

"This is bullshit." I turned and walked out of Jablonsky's office, not waiting to be dismissed. Michael glanced up but remained speechless. "Go home." I shook my head, trying to shake off the verbal barrage I just dealt with. "Spilano's dirty. Our job is to nail scum to the wall, and he's scum."

To his credit, Michael didn't waver. He remained at the computer, searching for additional information and connections between Sarskov and Spilano. Jablonsky stayed in his office, likely fuming over my insubordination. I wasn't sure what to do. I was told to stop, but the little voice in my head said we were close to something. After my nerves regrouped, I continued at a faster pace than before, convinced any moment Mark would ask for my badge and resignation.

"Oh my god, Alex." Kate interrupted my thoughts as she ran down the hallway toward us. "Do you have any idea what you've stumbled upon?"

"What?"

Michael turned in his chair, and Jablonsky came out of his office at the sound of Kate's commotion.

"Agent Hartley," Jablonsky gave her a skeptical look, "has Agent Parker dragged you into this cockamamie research project also?"

"Sir," Kate looked frightened to be spoken to in such a way by a superior, "it's not, I mean, yes." She took a deep breath and started over. "The spending in these accounts doesn't coincide with the purchases listed."

"Which means?" Michael asked, giving her his full attention.

"The records are falsified," Jablonsky said, shooting an *I told you so* look my way. "It speaks to Spilano's guilt."

"No," she interjected, correcting herself quickly by adding, "sir."

"Sit down and take it from the top." I kicked a chair toward her, and she sat.

"The list of transactions and authorized purchases don't line up." Although she was starting over, it still made no sense. "These accounts belong to Victor Spilano, and from this purchase order, we can conclude Spilano made these purchases. But it's not physically possible that all the account activity was conducted by Spilano."

"I'm sure he has assistants at the restaurant who can place orders." Jablonsky wasn't willing to give even an inch.

Carver picked up the paper Kate dropped on the desk and read it, passing it to me as she continued to explain the situation.

"He's the victim of identity theft," I said aloud, dumbfounded. Kate put a finger on her nose and pointed at me, something that started as a joke back in our shared apartment.

"You've got to be shitting me." Jablonsky grabbed the paper out of my hand and stormed to the elevator. The three of us exchanged looks. I wasn't about to follow someone who castigated me for conducting a proper investigation.

"Does this change everything?" Carver asked.

I looked to Hartley, hoping she could give us an answer. Numbers were a foreign language, and she was our translator.

"It's possible." She didn't sound convinced. "Were those purchases a principal component of the case?"

"No." Although Spilano might be the victim of identity theft, it didn't exonerate him from the weapons charges. Two people pointed the finger at him for being responsible, and no amount of questionable purchase orders affected that fact.

"Our criminal is also the victim of a crime. How ironic," Michael chimed in, adding nothing useful. "Nice to see you again, Kate."

"Likewise. I never expected to see the day when Carver and Parker would be working together."

I glanced at Michael, waiting for him to say something inappropriate or childish. Instead, he showed a level of restraint I didn't believe him capable of.

"We got partnered together on this Spilano thing. It hasn't been so bad. She's just turned the whole case upside down which means either she's a genius or she's going to tank both our careers. Either way, it'll be one hell of a ride." He nodded to me. "I'm gonna phone Boyle and ask what he thinks. Your boss doesn't agree with our supposition but maybe mine will."

"Thanks."

He walked into a conference room and shut the door. I closed my eyes and tried to calm the panic away. Jablonsky was furious. Kate's findings didn't reinforce my theory; all they did was throw a monkey wrench into the mix.

"Are you okay, Alex?" Her voice interrupted my pity party.

"I've never done this before. Those five months at Quantico did nothing to prepare us for this. I've been here for seven months, working under Jablonsky, and just when I think I might be turning into an investigator," I bit my lip and took a breath, "I might have sabotaged all of it."

"You're being too hard on yourself."

"Disobeying my supervisor's orders, trying to find some reason why a dirtbag isn't dirty, dragging you into it," I let out a sigh, "I'd say I'm coming unhinged."

"Cease and desist."

"That's the problem. I can't."

"Why not?" She stared at me as if there was something seriously wrong, like I might have sprouted a third arm.

"Do you ever feel like something is off, and it just keeps nagging at the corners of your mind until you figure it out?"

She nodded, but she looked confused.

"That's this case," I said.

Michael came back into the room. From his expression, it was hard to determine if we just got support or a secondary chewing out. "He hung up. Jablonsky just phoned." The three of us sat in the office, studying the mountain of paperwork in the interim.

The elevator dinged, and Jablonsky came toward us. He looked more controlled. "Well, if Nancy Drew and the Hardy Boys are done screwing around, we have to rework the entire case from the bottom up. Let's get to it."

NINE

By Monday evening, the powers that be still believed Victor Spilano was an arms dealer. This wasn't a court of law, so the general approach was guilty unless proven innocent. The forensic accountants, Kate included, were going over all purchases and charges with a fine tooth comb. Since we didn't know exactly what we were dealing with, we were told to hold back on the assumption it might be identity theft. It was possible the out-of-state orders were being made by an unidentified accomplice or associate. We had no right to be privy to the inner business workings unless we had proof of their illegal nature. Nothing Kate discovered was illegal. Honestly, with the way Boyle reacted to the situation, I suspected he thought Kate was overzealous, just like me.

"C'mon," Carver stood in front of my desk, "let's get out here."

Jablonsky had shunned me since yesterday afternoon, and the whispers and looks I got from the other agents made my pariah status obvious.

"Don't stand too close. You might catch leprosy," I warned.

"Alexis, turn off the computer. We have a dinner date."

"Specialty Vineyard has been shut down since Saturday night."

"But Michael Price and Alexandra Riley don't know that." He grabbed the back of my chair and rolled me away from my desk. "You think people are talking about you now, just see what happens when I throw you over my shoulder and carry you from the building."

"You wouldn't dare." But instead of risking it, I stood and collected my belongings. "Shall we meet there?"

"I'll pick you up at your place. In the event he spots us, two cars will look suspicious as hell."

*   *   *

The investigation was stalled. My hunch didn't pan out, and unless the accountants discovered something damning, the raid was a complete waste of time and resources. If anything, we were moving in reverse. Specialty Vineyard closed after the raid to avoid bad publicity or so Spilano could put his affairs in order and get out of Dodge. I was kicking myself for failing to follow orders and for turning the investigation into a witch hunt. Perhaps I wasn't cut out for this job.

After arriving at my apartment, I stared at my open closet. The clothes I was forced to buy for this operation hung inside, many with tags still attached, taunting my stupidity. There was a knock on the door, and I answered.

"You're going to need a jacket to hide the shoulder holster and badge," Michael remarked, entering my apartment. He was dressed in street clothes, a pair of jeans and a button-up shirt, not the more sophisticated business attire I had grown accustomed to.

"Too bad we're all not lucky enough to conceal our credentials underneath an untucked shirt."

"Don't knock the shirt." He was being playful. Nice, even.

"Am I getting fired?" I asked, trying to figure out why he had the sudden change of heart.

"No. Am I?" He smirked and sat on one of the stools at my counter.

Retreating to my room, I changed into a dark pair of jeans and a black sweater. If he could do casual, so could I. Returning to the kitchen, I put my gun and badge in my purse.

"Did you get any additional instructions, or are we just putting in an appearance and calling it a night?" I asked.

"The latter." He followed me to the door, locking it on the way out. "Y'know, it's a lot more fun to best you when you're coming at me with your A-game. Right now, everyone thinks I'm brilliant just for being stuck with you. Granted, that is a burden, but not to the extent people believe."

No response seemed pertinent, so I got in the car. Carver cast a glance my way every few minutes but didn't speak.

After he parked the car, he reached for my arm. "None of us know what the fuck we're doing. So get over it. Do your job. And if you believe in something, don't back down."

"Fine."

"I mean it. I want to kick your ass fair and square to prove once and for all your scores on the exams were a fluke and not actually two points higher than mine."

"Cocky bastard," I retorted, offering a grin.

"Ah, there's my fiancée. I was beginning to wonder what happened to her." He opened the car door. "Come on, honey. It's time for dinner."

We strolled toward the restaurant, but as predicted, there was a notice on the front door. Specialty Vineyard was closed until Wednesday. On the bright side, it was Michael's gas and quarters that paid for this little venture. I turned back toward the car, and something caught my eye.

"What is it?" he asked once he noticed I was no longer next to him.

"I don't know."

Veering off the sidewalk, I turned into the alley that ran along the side of the restaurant. The alley contained two dumpsters and not much else. It was narrow and culminated in a dead end. Something had caught the light and reflected it. Kneeling down next to a few wine crates beside the dumpster, I still couldn't determine what I saw.

"Alex," Michael flipped the lid on the dumpster and peered inside, "what do you make of this?"

I stood up and looked inside. It was brimming with packing materials covered in Russian mailing labels and writing. My heart sank. Obviously, my insistence that two arms dealers couldn't be in cahoots was dead wrong. I turned away, and the same shiny glimmer caught my eye again. This time, I spotted the source – a single diamond on the concrete beside the crates. Now what did we stumble into?

"Do we call it in?" I asked.

After taking a photo of the diamond with my phone, I dug out a tissue and picked it up. I doubted it was large enough to provide a usable print, but since I was in hot water, every move I made had to be by the book.

"And say what? There are some suspicious looking airmail stickers in the garbage outside the restaurant. For all we know, it's from the caviar," Michael said. I held up the diamond for him to examine. "And someone lost the stone on her engagement ring." He looked skeptical. "Let's get out of here before we blow our cover. I'll swing by the OIO, and we'll give them the heads up." Calling in a team to swarm the place wouldn't help my credibility, and it would compromise our fake identities.

Slipping out of the alley as inconspicuously as possible, we went back to the car. There had to be more to the story. Russian shipping crates, diamonds on the ground, and weird purchases on Spilano's business account, maybe it all added up to weapons dealing. We drove past the alley, and Michael turned down the next street. The restaurant was on the corner, and through the windows, we saw a few men inside.

"Is that Sarskov?" he asked.

"Maybe. It's hard to tell."

Michael turned at the next corner and whipped the car around.

"What are you doing?" I asked.

"Recon," he turned and grinned, "you in?"

"I'm already on thin ice, might as well light a fire while

I'm at it."

"You're mixing metaphors," he chastised. Finding a shadowed place on a side road with a decent view of Specialty Vineyard, he parked the car. "I say we stick around and see if anything happens. Anything solid might just be your redemption."

Glancing at him, I saw an unfamiliar determination. Maybe Carver was more than just an arrogant asshole.

"When the director's ripping into both of us, I promise not to throw you under the bus." It was the only consolation I could offer.

"Noted." He reached into the back seat and pulled out a camera case. "How illegal is it to photograph someone already under surveillance?" It was a debate from our academy days. He zoomed in, and we had a front row seat to the activities inside Specialty Vineyard.

TEN

Three men were inside. From the way the other two bustled about, it was obvious Ivan Sarskov was in charge. However, there was no sign of Victor Spilano. Maybe he was in the back or out of view. Our angle only allowed us to view what was happening diagonally from the large middle windows.

"What do you think they're looking for?" Michael asked, but I didn't have an answer.

"Maybe they're hungry. Who knows?" I sighed. "Where do you think Spilano is?"

"Out back, counting diamonds or packing up a box of AKs," he kidded, but it made me take pause. There was something to that statement; the gnawing in the recesses of my brain insisted.

"TSA recovered a box of detonator cord. There had been traces of explosive materials on the initial wine shipping box but not a single firearm." I squinted into the darkness, trying to see something that wasn't there. "We never found the actual explosives."

"Shit," he looked at me, "you think that's what the Three Stooges are searching for?" We both looked toward the restaurant, but the men had moved out of our line of sight.

"Assuming the diamond in the alley is part of the

payment, I'd say whatever they are looking for is long gone."

We continued to watch as figures crossed in front of the window, but whatever they were doing, it didn't appear they were making any headway. The same could be said for us.

A car pulled up and parked illegally in front of a hydrant. Spilano got out and rushed inside. Even though I couldn't read lips, it was obvious heated words were exchanged. Spilano screamed at someone just out of view. Carver decided to try to get a better angle and got out of the car and headed across the street.

Things were going from bad to worse. I kept my eyes on the restaurant as I unzipped my bag and removed my credentials and nine millimeter. I tucked my badge into my front pocket and my gun into the waistband at the small of my back, pulling my sweater down over both. It wouldn't be prudent to waste time looking for either if the situation required immediate action. Jablonsky's words about not breaking cover echoed through my mind, and I hoped the jitteriness was a result of my probationary status and never having been in a situation like this before. Innately, I knew better.

Getting out of the car, I looped around to a position on the opposite side of the street from Carver. He cast a glance my way and motioned me over. Since we were still undercover, we needed to act like it, especially out in the open. Although dusk had settled and only the street lights provided illumination, plenty of people and vehicles remained in the vicinity. It was imperative we act with finesse. No one else paid any heed to the closed restaurant. Clearly, our interest was already out of the ordinary.

"Alex," Michael tried to downplay his nerves, appearing macho and in control, but I noticed the tremor in his hands, "any ideas?"

"We've got nothing concrete. Jablonsky warned us not to blow it prematurely."

"I've never had that problem. I don't want to start now."

"Then we wait it out." It was the right call, but it wasn't an easy one.

The nearby bus stop provided a perfect angle to Specialty Vineyard and a feasible cover. We sat down, and Michael turned to face the restaurant, once again forcing me to lack a decent angle to watch what was happening. Thankfully, he still had the camera on, and he flipped the viewfinder around so I could watch on the screen as he scooted closer and caressed a strand of hair that framed my face.

He whispered in my ear, "Maybe you were right all along."

I kept my eyes on the camera's screen as Sarskov stepped into view. Spilano cowered but refused to meet Sarskov's demands. The restauranteur gestured emphatically to the door.

"Looks like a standoff," I muttered as Michael pulled me into an embrace. His breath hitched, and I felt his sudden exhale against my neck, causing a chill to travel down my spine.

"Someone's called in reinforcements." As he continued to watch, three car doors slammed in a chorus of impending doom.

"How many?" I asked. They parked across the street from Specialty Vineyard and out of sight of the small screen I was monitoring.

"Three. I can't be positive, but I'd say one of them is Sarskov's brother, Sergei."

Do we wait? It was the only question on my mind.

"The other two might be his enforcers." Michael swallowed.

"Call for backup." I pulled away and looked him in the eye. Without further instructions, I was in charge, according to Jablonsky. I just wondered if that still held true. "I'm going to gather more information."

"Are you out of your fucking mind?"

"Absolutely." Taking a deep breath, I stood up. "Call it in. Ask for advice and wait for instructions."

Striding across the street, I wanted to look like I belonged. Alexandra Riley was an employee of P&P and a constant frequenter at Specialty Vineyard. There was nothing abnormal about going to the restaurant and knocking on the door. I repeated this over and over as I approached the restaurant. Despite my attempt to remain in character, the pessimistic voice in my head explained the precise reason why two new agents were never partnered alone together. We had our training and muscle memory to rely on, but we lacked experience.

Even though the front door was locked, there were enough people inside Specialty Vineyard for the casual observer to believe the restaurant might be open. First, I tried to push open the door. Then I knocked and pressed my face against the glass. No one had any visible contraband, not even the two enforcers sitting in the back corner. Sarskov was standing in the middle of the room, talking to his brother, Sergei, while the other man whispered to Spilano in the opposite corner of the room. The original third man was nowhere to be seen.

At the sound of my knocking, all eyes turned to me. I spotted Spilano and smiled, offering a slight wave. He came to the door, cracking it open but not letting me inside.

"Alex, we're closed," he apologized, trying to force me away.

"Oh, I'm sorry. I didn't realize. I just finished for the day and thought we could work on the menu for my rehearsal dinner. I hoped to get started and surprise Michael. He should be along in a few minutes."

"Another time." Spilano stared into my eyes, and I saw fear and panic on his pasty and sweaty visage. He tried to pull the door closed.

"Are you okay?"

He tossed a nervous glance toward the men at the table. The other man, someone I recognized as an employee of Specialty Vineyard, came up behind Spilano.

"He's fine. Why don't you stop by tomorrow afternoon, Ms. Riley, and we'll take care of you then."

"Okay," I offered him a friendly smile, "I'll see you tomorrow."

Heading down the street the way I came, I hoped Carver had been instructed on proper procedure in this situation. Leaving Spilano inside left a bad taste in my mouth.

Regardless of who he was or what he had done, he was terrified. The lack of imminent danger would make a tactical breach premature and sacrifice our entire operation, but not reacting might lead to sacrificing our prime suspect. Surely, I wasn't supposed to worry about an arms dealer who could be plotting to kill potentially hundreds of people or selling to groups or individuals intent on mayhem, death, and destruction. My moral compass was so skewed I had no idea which way was up.

I rendezvoused with Carver, and he wrapped his arms around me and whispered in my ear, "Boyle's putting a tactical unit on standby. The surveillance team assigned to Spilano isn't here because they've been covering his house. Somehow, he eluded them because, until I called, they thought he was home. Jablonsky's on his way to determine the veracity of our claims and take point."

I told Carver everything I witnessed. He went rigid and swallowed.

"We're on our own until then." I slipped out of his grip. "Let's split up and try to maintain eyes inside."

ELEVEN

Carver was positioned near the alleyway. There was an alcove for a storefront close by, and he leaned against the far wall. I was at the bus stop, monitoring the movement inside the restaurant. Since we weren't prepared for this sort of operation, our only method for communicating was via cell phone.

"Do you want to talk dirty?" Carver asked, letting out a nervous laugh.

"Sorry, but this isn't a nine hundred number, and you wouldn't be able to afford it if it was." Maintaining radio silence was SOP, but we didn't have radios. Also, despite his bravado, he was nervous. Hell, I was nervous. Rhetoric was one way to pretend we weren't unraveling at the seams. Even if I'd never admit it, I was happy to have the light banter cutting through the tension. "How long do you think it'll take Jablonsky to get here?"

"It's only been a few minutes. I'd say, depending on traffic, at least twenty."

"Traffic's a bitch."

Carver chuckled at my comment, and we went silent as the men moved around. After my brief interruption, Spilano was forced to take a seat at the bar, and he hadn't moved since. The two enforcers sat at the table, keeping tabs as the Sarskov brothers did something out of my field of vision. The other man, the one who worked at Specialty Vineyard, was seated a few stools away from Spilano, and although his back was to me, it looked like he was in the midst of a conversation with Victor.

"You got eyes on Tweedledee and Tweedledum?" My affectionate names for the enforcers.

"Negative."

The waiting was torture. Carver's harsh exhales would cut the silence every now and again, but other than that, we were focused on the objective. Ivan emerged and barked something to the two goons at the table. One of them got up, grabbed Spilano by the collar, and shoved him toward the back. The other goon grabbed Spilano's co-worker and dragged him out of view.

"Carver, they're heading your way. The muscle has Spilano and his co-worker."

"They just exited into the alley," he said. Casting a quick glance at Carver, I saw him edge closer. "What's happening inside?"

The original man, who had been assisting Ivan Sarskov, opened the front door and went down the street. Without manpower or resources, I had no choice but to let him go. Hopefully, we'd be able to identify him later from the photographs taken. Only Ivan and Sergei remained inside Specialty Vineyard. "I don't know. Someone just left, but the Russians are still inside."

The streets were emptying. With the restaurant closed and the nearby shops having locked their doors a half hour ago, there was a severe lack of pedestrians. The dim light and the angle made it impossible for me to see into the alley, but I heard the scuffle. It occurred almost simultaneously with Sergei exiting the front door. He got into an SUV and drove away, leaving the two meatheads behind. Ivan strode through the restaurant and out the other side door and away from the impending fracas. The party was now completely in the alley.

"Michael?" I asked. He hadn't said a word since I heard the noise in the alley. A cry of pain carried across the street, and fearing the worst, I reached for my gun and dashed into oncoming traffic. "Michael?"

"We need to move in before someone gets killed." He dropped the call, leaving me hanging.

I sprinted across the street and glanced both ways to make sure no one was coming back. Michael was several feet from the alley and entered without waiting. I was half a block away when I heard the authoritarian announcement, "Federal agent, don't move."

Rushing to get to him, I slowed before hitting the opening. Leaning my back against the wall and wishing we had worn vests on this outing, I looked around the corner. One of the enforcers had Spilano pinned against a wall, clearly in the middle of knocking the shit out of him. The other brandished a gun and was in a standoff with Carver. The Specialty Vineyard employee was curled into the fetal position on the ground.

"I said drop it," Carver commanded. He held his badge in his left, and he placed his right on top, trying to steady his aim.

The assailant with the gun snorted and smiled. "Do you believe this?" he asked his pal, who had yet to release Spilano.

"Sir, drop the weapon," Carver insisted.

I took a step into the alley, using the brick wall as partial cover. The two thugs looked at us.

"Put the gun on the ground and put your hands in the air," I ordered.

The man with the gun smiled, tilting his head down and lowering his arm ever so slightly. Carver took half a step forward, and the goon brought his gun up to fire. It all happened in an instant, but Carver flinched, and I pulled the trigger. The gunshot reverberated in the enclosed space, and the man dropped the gun, clutching his chest as he sunk to the ground. His partner released Spilano and took off running.

"You got him?" I shouted to Carver, who was finally moving again. The temporary paralysis had worn off, and he kicked the gun out of the wounded man's reach, pulling a pair of cuffs from his back pocket.

"Go," he yelled, but I was already in pursuit.

Running as fast as my legs could carry me, I was gaining on the fleeing unsub. The adrenaline created a numbing haze, and I functioned solely on instinct. Turning a corner, I continued chasing after the man who was slowing down. In another block, after shoving my way through a crowd of pedestrians and shouting "federal agent" on the way, I had him cornered.

"I surrender." He turned with his hands in the air. He had no choice. He had trapped himself on a dead end street.

"On the ground, hands behind your head. Lace your fingers together." Having to approach and physically cuff a man who only minutes earlier had assaulted Spilano was disconcerting, but thankfully, he didn't try anything.

"You killed Boris," he said, resigned to his own fate. His words hit hard, and I swallowed the bile that rose in my throat. "Don't shoot." His accent was thick, but I understood why he surrendered.

"Don't give me a reason." I hauled him to his feet. We made it half a block when the government-issued vehicles, complete with sirens and flashing lights, pulled up.

"Agent Parker," Jablonsky said, taking custody of my suspect, "where's Carver? He called for backup."

Another agent shoved the handcuffed man into the back of the car as Mark ran after me. More sirens were on the way, and I spotted an ambulance. Mark radioed our location as we continued to the alley next to Specialty Vineyard.

"Michael," I gasped down some air, winded from anxiety and the run, "are you okay?"

He nodded, and Jablonsky shoved him away from the bleeding man. A second later, EMTs were on the scene, along with enough federal agents to make it look like they were casting extras for a new *Men in Black* movie.

"Who fired?" Jablonsky asked as the EMTs put the guy on a stretcher and loaded him into the back of the ambulance.

"I did."

Mark confiscated my gun, sniffing it for the telltale scent

of cordite. Carver was staring at me, and only when he grasped my arm did I realize I was trembling.

"Are you both okay?" Jablonsky asked.

"Yes, sir," Michael replied, but Mark looked at me uncertainly.

"Are you all right to drive back to the OIO building?" he asked, and Michael nodded. "Take Parker with you. We're going to have a shit ton of paperwork to fill out, incident reports, an internal investigation, psychological evaluations, lots of fun stuff." I wasn't sure if his tone was berating or simply matter-of-fact. "Get going. I'll see you at the office." Michael led me out of the alley, but before we made it across the street, Mark called to us, "Make sure you're prepared to tell us exactly what happened tonight."

Under normal conditions, they would have separated me from Michael immediately. Apparently Jablonsky believed in bending the rules sometimes.

We got into the car. The only thing I could concentrate on was the man bleeding on the ground. Boris. Did I kill a man named Boris tonight? Did he have a family? A real job besides beating people up? How did he end up in that alley, believing he could shoot his way out of the situation?

"Alex," Michael interrupted my thoughts, "thanks for having my back."

"You hesitated." My words came out a whisper. "You can't hesitate." I shut my eyes and curled up on the seat, facing the window. "It isn't fair." I wanted to throw a dozen accusations at him. I wanted to blame him, but I held back. "What's going to happen now?"

"It'll be okay. You didn't do anything wrong." The unspoken implication hung in the air, but it didn't need to be said. As far as I was concerned, it never had to be said. Assigning blame wasn't going to change anything.

TWELVE

Michael touched my back, and I jumped, scrambling to get as far away as possible. It made no sense how it happened, but somewhere between Specialty Vineyard and the OIO building, I had fallen asleep. Passed out might have been a more accurate term. Fighting to get the seatbelt off while pretending I didn't just react like a wounded animal was nearly impossible. Before I even realized it, Mark was on the other side, opening my car door.

"Adrenaline crash, it happens to all of us," he said matter-of-factly. "It's a shock to your system to go from one extreme to another. Get a cup of coffee. It'll help level you out. We have a long night ahead of us."

"Yes, sir."

A couple agents escorted Carver away as Jablonsky watched me pull myself together. "Most agents never have to pull their piece," he began, "and an even smaller percentage actually have to fire on another human being. You have some shit ass luck, Parker." He led me toward the elevator. "I'm sorry I have to welcome you to the club."

"Hate to be here," I mumbled. Swallowing carefully, I felt nauseous. The possibility of stomaching coffee seemed almost impossible. "Did I kill him?"

Jablonsky hit the elevator stop button and turned to me.

"First, you never ask a question like that. We are not in the business of murder, so words like kill are negatively charged. Second," I wondered if I was turning green because he softened, "he's at the hospital. When they brought him in, he was still alive. No reason to assume otherwise." He hit the button for the elevator to resume. "And your file indicates you're an expert marksman. Obviously, you need more practice." He winked and offered a genuine smile for the first time in days.

Exiting onto the main level, I turned the diamond over as evidence, along with my phone. Everything else would rely heavily on my statement and Carver's. Mark insisted I get cleaned up and changed. After flushing my stomach contents, changing into regulation attire, and rinsing my mouth in the sink, I pinned my hair into a tight bun and went to be debriefed by my fellow agents and write my report.

*　　*　　*

Another all-nighter spent in the OIO building. This time, I actually was exhausted. The only thing I wanted to do was climb into bed, curl up under the covers, and vanish into thin air. After signing my report, I brought it into Mark's office. He was sitting on the couch, staring bleary-eyed at the mountain of paperwork before him.

"You're out for the next seventy-two hours while the shooting is put into perspective. I'll call with a verdict, but from what I've read so far, you have nothing to worry about."

"Okay."

"Spilano's in custody. His employee, Henry Rubin, is being held for questioning. Tech's running the diamond you found in the alley, and we issued BOLOs for Ivan and Sergei Sarskov. Whenever we determine who the other man is, we'll add him to the list. Dmitri Porchankov, the man you arrested, is being interrogated as we speak."

"Sounds good."

"Are you gonna be okay?"

Melting down in front of my supervisor was not

professional and never a good idea. "Sure, why not?"

"Carver said you saved his life tonight. Around here, that counts for a hell of a lot. Sometimes, it's everything." Remaining silent, I waited to be dismissed. It was about time I played by the rules. "You're a good agent, Parker. I'm sorry I doubted you," Mark said.

I went into the hallway. The morning shift had just arrived and was getting read in on what happened over the course of the night.

"Alex," Kate bounded up and hugged me, "I heard what happened. Are you okay?"

"Fine." I pulled out of her grasp. "I just want to go home." She looked at her watch. Her purse was still on her shoulder.

"Come on, I'll take you."

*   *   *

The next seventy-two hours was utter agony. The first twenty-four I spent in bed, barely moving unless absolutely necessary. But by Wednesday morning, the total stillness was replaced with the dire need to do something. Anything. I spent the remaining forty-eight hours of exile unpacking my boxes, organizing my apartment into a livable domicile, and running over a dozen miles on the treadmill. Regardless of what I did, I couldn't escape the sound of the gunshot, the blood spreading across Boris' chest, or his friend telling me I killed him. For all I knew, he was alive, and if he wasn't, I didn't want to know.

Granted, in a situation where it was him or me, there was only one obvious conclusion. Similarly, the situation was him or Carver, and still, there was just one clear-cut choice. It wasn't even a choice; it was a fact. The one thing I didn't understand was how Michael could hesitate. How could he not pull the trigger to save his own life? Some people signed up for this job with the misguided belief they were going to save people. I had never been one of those idealists, but ironically enough, it could be argued I saved Michael Carver. If only I believed it, maybe the shooting would have been that much easier to stomach.

"Knock, knock," Jablonsky called from outside my apartment door. It was noon on Friday, and even though I was conflicted, I still wanted to get back to work. Obviously, there must be some loose wiring in my brain. Opening the door, he smiled. "Looks like you weathered the storm rather well."

"It's all about survival, right?"

"That's my girl. Now get dressed. This isn't a vacation."

"You could have called," I remarked as I quickly got ready. "Why does everyone keep insisting on picking me up?"

"The way you drive is frightening," he deadpanned, "but more importantly, after work, you have an appointment you'd try to shirk if it weren't for your fearless leader showing you the way."

"What?"

"It's a surprise. Mandatory, but still a surprise."

Not bothering to ask anything else, I let him drive to the OIO building. The fun was just beginning.

Upon arrival, I was sent directly to Director Kendall's office. Boyle and Carver were already inside, and Mark grabbed an extra chair from the hallway before shutting the door. The four of us sat in a semi-circle around Kendall's desk. He had yet to speak, and I knew we were moments away from an all-out barrage.

It began with Jablonsky and Boyle being dressed down for assigning two junior agents to monitor a volatile situation without backup or a senior agent to provide guidance. From the way the argument went, I was surprised neither of them was forced to relinquish their badges; although, there was the threat of a demotion. No matter what kind of explanation Mark or Sam provided, Kendall wasn't buying it. Since things were already going this poorly, I was positive Michael and I would be reading the classified section of the newspaper by the end of the day, searching for a new career.

When the director turned his tirade on us, I sat as still as a statue, steeling my nerves and determined to show no sign of emotion. Sometime during the yelling and screaming, his outburst stopped. Maybe I was experiencing a break from reality because it sounded like he was complimenting our quick thinking and dogged investigation tactics. What did everyone else write in their reports? My recollection of Monday evening didn't involve heroics and superior deductive reasoning skills but rather a balls to the wall, fly by the seat of your pants, bend over and kiss your ass goodbye, holy shit, we're so screwed retelling of the events.

"Agent Parker?" Kendall asked, and I looked up from the spot on his desk I had been staring at since the yelling started. "Are you listening?"

"Yes, sir." I sat up straighter and made eye contact. "We overstepped our position."

"No." He cast an angry glare at Boyle and Jablonsky. "You and Carver showed initiative. You discovered a key piece of evidence, and by interceding, you might have prevented Mr. Spilano from suffering a tragedy. You are both junior agents," he settled his gaze on the space between Carver and me, "and you shouldn't have been expected to make that call. But you both exhibited a great deal of promise. You're dismissed." Carver stood, and I followed suit. "It's nothing personal, but you're riding a desk for the next two weeks, Parker. You won't have your firearm returned until after you pass the psych eval and re-qualify."

"Yes, sir."

We left the office, leaving Jablonsky and Boyle to deal with the rest of the fallout alone.

THIRTEEN

In the last three days, the investigation had come a long way. The pile of paperwork on my desk promised another long night, but it was a welcome relief. This was what I spent years trying to achieve, and if it were over in just a matter of months, that would have been devastating. Starting at the top, I only cracked open the evidence file concerning the diamond and other items found in the alley before being summoned downstairs.

"Agent Parker," Dr. Weiler stood and extended his hand, "it's a pleasure to meet you." When the director said I had to undergo a psychological evaluation, I didn't realize it was happening today.

"Sure." I shook his hand and sat in the offered seat. The incident report and my personnel file sat on top of his desk. "I assume this is in regards to Monday evening."

"Yes." He didn't say anything else. I had been through enough interrogation courses at Quantico to know what to expect. Silence was often enough pressure to force a suspect to open up. Needless to say, I remained tight-lipped. After a few minutes of listening to the whir of the white noise machine, he began again. "Why did you want to become an agent?"

"Why not?" I shrugged. At this rate, we'd be here all day. Maybe I could get him to fast track this whole thing. After all, I had a lot of paperwork to do. "Government job provides great benefits, a certain level of job security, and preferential experience in the event I ever make the leap to the private sector." At least that was the argument Kate had made many nights in our apartment.

"Good." He picked up my personnel file. "Is there a reason your emergency contact is Agent Jablonsky?"

"He's a federal agent. Seems like a decent choice for an emergency contact, don't you think?"

"You're being evasive."

"I don't see what any of this has to do with getting my gun back and going back to work."

"So you just want me to sign this form and send you on your way?" It was a trick question. I knew it, but I couldn't help myself.

"That would be great."

He picked up the pen and held it over the paper. "You ever shoot anyone before?"

"No."

"Now you have. How's that? Any nightmares, trouble sleeping, images of the event, reconsidering the things you did and hoping it would change the outcome?"

"I'm dealing with it."

"How? Alcohol? Drugs? Talking to someone about it?" That explained the sudden interest in my emergency contact.

"Unpacking. I moved into an apartment, and I unpacked. This is where I am. This is my life and where I belong."

"Okay," he signed the form and held it out, "but you're going to stop by a few times in the next couple of weeks and let me know how you're handling things. If it becomes too overbearing, we'll talk about it." He forced his card into my palm as I reached for the form.

"Fine." I snatched the paper and headed for the door.

"Parker," he called, "whatever it is you have outside the job, you need to use it as your fallback. It's the only way anyone remains sane when they're forced to do what you did."

Mumbling some type of agreement, I was just happy to be free from the Jungian, Freudian, or other obscure psychological babble he might want to instill upon me.

My desk upstairs was comforting. The paperwork was something I knew how to handle. A few hours later, I had familiarized myself with the evidence and who the current players were. I just picked up the transcript for Victor Spilano's interrogation when Mark came out of his office.

"It's five o'clock," he announced. "You're done for the rest of the weekend. Monday, you can catch up."

"But," I gestured to the stack of files, "I'm just getting started."

"Monday," he insisted. "Carver," he yelled across the room, "finish up and meet us."

I gave Michael a confused look, and he smiled like a Cheshire cat. "Are you planning to take me somewhere to kill me?" I asked.

"No, now let's go."

* * *

"I don't drink tequila." I pushed the shot away. "You know how they make that, don't you?"

Michael picked up the glass and downed it. Clearly, fermentation inside a worm didn't bother him.

"Fine, anything you want." Jablonsky motioned the bartender over. "Fair warning, if you order something girly, you will be teased mercilessly."

"Belfast car bomb," I said.

The bartender smiled and poured. Dropping the shot into the pint, I took a sip. "Now would you like to explain how this is a mandatory part of the job?"

"You've been working your ass off. You went through hell Monday, and we've still got a lot of shit left to deal with concerning this investigation. Blow off some steam, get your head on straight, and Monday, we'll start over. Plus, I'm buying."

"Well, when you put it that way."

An hour later, there was the very strong possibility I was

drunk. Not so drunk to do anything stupid, like take Carver home, but drunk enough that talking about the shooting seemed like a decent conversation topic. Carver was at a table, talking to a couple of agents who were regular frequenters at the bar. Only Mark and I sat alone at a corner booth. When my babbling on the shooting ebbed, he laughed.

"You got some brass balls, Alex." He looked toward Carver's table to make sure he was out of earshot. "I screwed up letting the two of you run things. It was stupid. Carver's green, much greener than you. He got lucky."

"Did Boris get lucky?"

"He's still in the ICU. The docs think he'll pull through."

I blinked back tears. Drinking made me emotional. Damn Irish whiskey. Knowing a would-be killer was going to live shouldn't make me this happy, but the fact that I didn't kill someone made me overjoyed. I could go another day knowing I hadn't taken a life, justified or not.

"Another thing," Mark motioned for another round, but I shook my head, "you were right."

"About?" I spotted Kate in the corner, chatting up some attractive guy. I blinked, trying to remember what we were talking about.

"Spilano's not an arms dealer. I know you didn't get far enough into the transcripts, but apparently his business associate, Henry Rubin, cut a deal with Sarskov. We have one hell of a mess to sort through."

"So that's why people aren't treating me like a complete moron anymore," I slurred. It was time to go home. "Good to know." Locating my phone, I dialed a cab. It would arrive in a few minutes, and I wanted nothing but to sleep off this entire week.

"I'll wait with you," Mark said.

As I walked past Carver and his pals, he smiled. "To Alex." Michael held up a shot glass, and they drank. My guess was half of them didn't even know who I was. Then again, it probably didn't make a damn bit of difference.

"Y'know, you shouldn't ride me so hard about working late when you're camping out in your office day in and day out," I said to Jablonsky. The cool breeze had a sobering effect, and since we were off duty, this might be the only opportunity I had to chastise my superior.

"You noticed?"

"Hard to miss."

Mark was quiet for a time as I waited for an explanation. "My wife served me with divorce papers a week ago. Maybe it's had more of an impact on my job performance and professional relationships than I wanted to admit. Might be why I came down so hard on you when you brought up the possibility of Spilano's innocence. It's just so frustrating being wrong all the time."

"I'm sorry." There wasn't much else to say. Smirking, I dug through my purse until I found Dr. Weiler's card. "Maybe you should talk to a professional."

"Goddamn." Mark burst into a contagious fit of laughter, and by the time the cab rolled up, we both had tears streaming down our faces. Stress and alcohol could cause some crazy side effects. As the cab drove away, I caught sight of him, wiping his eyes and snickering. We'd be just fine.

FOURTEEN

By Monday afternoon, my gun was returned. I no longer felt like an incompetent joke. Although I was still chained to a desk, the investigation was taking off and there was plenty to do. Victor Spilano requested protective custody until the lunatics who ransacked his restaurant were identified and captured. The last I heard, he was in an undisclosed location and guarded by a team of agents. Boris Romanski was still in the hospital under lock and key, and since it had been a week since the shooting, there was some teasing concerning my failure to use the proper double tap or three to center mass firing methods. The guy was lucky I wasn't a stickler for rules, or he'd be six feet under.

The second enforcer, Dmitri Porchankov, sang like a canary. This was particularly easy to do when you didn't know a damn thing. The only thing we had him on was assault and destruction of property. He hadn't been armed and surrendered. It would be hard to get any serious charges to stick to him, and he'd been through the system enough times to realize it was best to give up whatever he had, cut a deal for a reduced sentence, and get the hell out as soon as possible.

This left the still unidentified third man and the Sarskov brothers. The local PD was assisting in the search, but the Sarskovs weren't at any of the strip joints or in any of their usual hangouts. They had gone underground. A couple of agents from organized crime were meeting with their father to see if some type of arrangement could be reached, but blood was thicker than water. The only one left to break was Henry Rubin.

"Mr. Rubin," Jablonsky began. We were inside one of the interrogation rooms, and Mark was taking point while I learned the finer skills of conducting a successful interview. "Things aren't looking so good for you." Rubin's representation sat next to him, but neither said a word. "Selling explosives is a serious offense. It's even worse when you're involved in international trafficking." Mark made a sound as if he were trying to suck something loose from between his teeth. "The way I see it, you're stuck holding the bag."

No one said anything as I leaned against the back wall, watching for micro-expressions or a shift in Rubin's eyes. He swallowed but didn't move. Maybe his hearing was impaired.

"What proof do you have of my client's involvement?" the lawyer asked.

Smiling, Jablonsky lifted the case file off the table. "His fingerprint is on the diamond recovered from the alleyway. Did I mention it's the same alley where some hired guns almost killed two of my agents? By the way, those men are in custody now." He let this fact sink in as he leaned his hip against the side of the table. "They're looking for a break and are willing to deal."

"What can you promise me?" Rubin asked. This was the first time he looked up from the table.

"Nothing until I know what you have to offer." Mark was playing hardball, and the lawyer cast a stern look at Jablonsky.

"I would like to confer with my client alone."

"That won't make him any less guilty," Mark muttered, heading for the door.

I opened it, and he walked through.

"Are you paying attention, Parker?" he asked as we went down the hallway in search of coffee.

"Yes, sir."

"Then drop the sir." He filled a mug and handed it to me as he reached for another one for himself. "His attorney is worried. Right now, he's probably asking what happened at the restaurant, who was there, and what exactly Rubin is involved with. At some point, a decision will be made based on his degree of involvement and how much damning evidence we might have."

"Does this happen often?"

"Not as much as I'd like. Mostly, we get threats and suggestions to go screw ourselves."

"Well, there's that."

"Yep." Jablonsky glanced at his watch. Was Rubin more afraid of Ivan and Sergei than us? By the time I was down half a mug, the door to interrogation opened, and the agent posted outside gestured to Mark. "Now we see what's going to happen."

Back inside, Rubin tried to work out a deal. After some negotiation, he explained in vast detail how purchases made from the California vineyards had been altered on scene by a team of locals the Sarskovs hired. The team would intercept the crates in transit, switch casks of fermenting wine for a stockpile of weapons, detonator cords, and incendiary materials, and then replace the shipment before anyone was the wiser. Victor Spilano was a puppet. He had no idea what was going on, but when these disguised business ventures and profit margins were made so appealing by his business manager, Spilano had no choice but to sign the orders. He never knew what happened to the shipments because Rubin claimed they were shipping mishaps.

The weapons shipped from California arrived by boat and were trucked to the locations, loaded up, and sent across country. Or at least that had been the plan before TSA confiscated the suspicious crates. Rubin insisted he didn't know who the source was overseas. The Sarskovs had come to him with this proposition. For his trouble, he was given a percentage of the profits and told to keep his mouth shut. The latest payment had been in diamonds.

"We need the rest of them." Jablonsky cast a look at Rubin. "Any idea where the Sarskovs might be?" Rubin shook his head emphatically; even if he knew, he wouldn't say. "Want to tell me who the third guy is?" Again, the headshake. "How 'bout we try what the hell the three of you were looking for inside the restaurant?"

That question caught Rubin unprepared. I saw the flash of fear in his eyes and the reflexive tightening of his jaw. "I don't know," he lied.

Mark let out a breath and came over to me. He whispered some orders and went back to the table. I left the room to tell Boyle to send a team to tear the place apart. Whatever they were looking for might still be there.

By the time I returned, Rubin's lawyer was halfway down the hall, and Rubin was escorted back to a temporary holding cell. The OIO wasn't equipped for holding prisoners the same way a police station was, but we found some extra space just for him.

"What happened?" I asked as I fell into step beside Jablonsky.

"He said all he's going to. We need to find whatever they wanted, or we need to find them. My guess is there's one remaining shipment to uncover. Either it's somewhere in the vicinity of Specialty Vineyard, or it's still out there. Either way, we need to get it off the streets."

As the crime scene investigators tore Specialty Vineyard apart, I remained at the OIO building, researching every known fact about Rubin and the Russians. It sounded like a name for a rock band from the sixties. The discrepancies in the restaurant's financial records had been explained, and like I thought, Spilano was clean. Sure, he had been duped by his business manager, but being gullible wasn't a crime. Phoning his protection detail, I asked if they could question him again about the third man inside the restaurant. Upon our initial interview, he claimed he didn't know the man, but he had been flustered. Maybe having a couple of days to calm down jogged his memory.

Boyle grabbed a chair and pulled it up to my desk. "Agent Parker, any progress?"

"None to report. The team's still at the restaurant, and I asked the guys to go over the facts with Spilano once more." I was out of ideas. "Did you need me to do something, sir?"

"Would you mind going through the seizure information and see if there's something we missed?" Although posed as a question, it was not.

"Right away."

Boxes of paperwork filled the conference room. Ivan and Sergei each had a box of their own that organized crime had sent over, and it took some time to find the proper documentation. Opening the jacket from the initial suspicious bust, I settled into the chair and rubbed my eyes. It was going to be another long night.

FIFTEEN

There was nothing to find. Boyle didn't need a federal agent to go over the records. He needed a magician to make evidence and leads appear out of thin air. Frustrated, I shoved the materials back into the box and stomped to the coffeemaker. It was empty. Muttering about how others should follow proper etiquette, I poured the water in the top just as Carver came down the hallway.

"Facial recognition got a hit on our third man from the footage we took Monday night," he announced.

Forgetting the coffee, I trailed him to Jablonsky's office. Inside, Mark and Sam were reviewing the photos and information the crime scene unit found.

Without standing on ceremony, Michael barged in to spread the good news. The third man was Vlad Yenisof. The name didn't ring any bells, so Jablonsky picked up the phone to have the analysts run a full profile on the guy. Everything felt like it was falling into place.

While we waited for Yenisof's file, the rest of the diamonds Ivan paid Rubin were delivered. Carver signed off on chain of custody and took them downstairs to get cataloged and run for additional trace elements that could be pertinent to furthering our investigation. It was getting late, and Jablonsky had just ordered me to go home for the night.

As I stood at my workstation, shutting down my computer, Vlad Yenisof exited the elevator in a dark suit. Standing next to him was Director Kendall, and the two were having a serious discussion. Stunned and unsure what to do, I gaped as Yenisof was shown to Jablonsky's office.

"Alex," Michael said, and I jumped. "What are you staring at?"

"The third man," I jerked my chin to the closed door, "he's in there."

"We've brought him in already?"

"No." Something was off.

Ten minutes later, Kendall emerged and barked at us to get back to work. Technically, I should have left, but it was like watching a train wreck. We sat down, still staring at the door until Yenisof exited and vanished behind the elevator doors. It was a scramble to beat Michael to Jablonsky's office.

"What just happened?" I asked, standing in the doorway.

"The third man works for Homeland Security," Boyle informed us while Mark muttered expletives under his breath. "Our search pinged in their database."

"He was a plant?" Carver asked.

"Yes." Jablonsky slammed the drawer closed so hard the entire desk trembled. "This operation is officially over."

Again, it felt as if I'd been punched in the gut. Everything that happened was for nothing. Carver was almost killed, and I almost lost my job because of this. This steaming pile of bullshit.

"How? We've got missing explosives, missing Russian gangsters, and a bag full of diamonds," Michael babbled, but it was what we were all thinking. It was what I was thinking.

"We're done," Jablonsky said. "Part of this job is knowing when to walk away, and we're fucking walking. Now go home. Both of you." There was no room for argument, and Carver and I backed out of the office.

Inside the parking garage, Michael looked at me. We weren't satisfied with our orders. "Now what?" he asked. He held his car keys uncertainly. The right move would be to follow orders and let it go.

"Come over," I said, getting into my car and starting the engine without giving him time to ask a question or protest.

* * *

Chinese food containers were strewn around my living room as we reconstructed all the facts we knew. Ivan and Sergei were responsible for smuggling weaponry into the United States. Ivan used Henry Rubin as his patsy and paid him handsomely in diamonds. I was sure the payment was just as illegal as the rest of the business, but the techs could worry about that detail.

Rubin was perfect. As the business manager for Specialty Vineyard, he had access to the business' finances. Since Victor Spilano was a wine collector and traveled often in pursuit of his personal and professional love, Rubin figured he'd put all the blame on his partner. No one would have been the wiser if TSA hadn't gotten a hit on the explosive residue. Compounding this was Spilano's questionable travel itinerary, which raised yet another red flag. The only reason any part of the investigation ever came to fruition had been out of sheer luck.

"Homeland oversees all law enforcement agencies and the infrastructure. It's part of the new world we've been living in for over a decade," Michael surmised. "You know this must be rough on Jablonsky and Boyle. They were probably used to the old way of doing things and were forced to change. At least you and I don't know any better."

"Clearly, we don't know any better, or we wouldn't be connecting the final dots to something that's over."

"They never received the explosives," Michael continued. "I'd wager that's what they were searching for in the restaurant. Maybe they figured the shipment had come in and was down in the wine cellar, or Spilano located it and wanted a cut of the illegal gains."

"Yenisof was there to make it believable. My guess is Homeland already confiscated the missing shipment. Maybe they even put a stop to the international source. We could dig around in Interpol's files to look," I suggested but thought better of it and shook my head the instant the words left my lips.

He stared off into the distance, not focusing on anything. "We'll never know. Will we?"

"Probably not, but we did explain almost all of it." I let out a sigh. "Michael, it doesn't matter if it's this assignment or our hundredth assignment, we'll never really know what happens. We collect evidence, statements, maybe even surveillance tapes, but it's all supposition."

"My god, you're cynical and jaded already." But he didn't argue. Instead, he looked at his watch. "Six hours until we're back at work. Want to pull an all-nighter like we used to at Quantico?"

"No," I got up and stretched, listening to my bones pop, "but you can crash on the couch if you want."

"Thanks."

"Just remember, I sleep with a loaded gun so don't try anything."

He laughed. "That's not surprising." Pulling the extra pillow off my bed and a blanket from the linen closet, I brought them out to the couch. He had thrown the empty takeout containers into the garbage and put the leftovers in the fridge. He was amused by something, and I looked at him confused. "Y'know, it's not like your roommate is going to come home and stop us this time."

"Nothing happened."

"It almost did."

"No. It really didn't. But if you want to keep up this crap, I will rescind the offer to let you sleep on the couch."

He pantomimed zipping his lip, and I went into my room, making a show of shutting the door.

I was asleep the moment my head touched the pillow. These long hours were taking their toll. Thankfully, when I woke up, Michael had already left. The blanket was folded neatly, and the coffee was brewed.

Arriving at work an hour later, Jablonsky had left the

file on my desk. We had to go over the final report. From what I read and what Michael and I pieced together the night before, our deductions seemed accurate. The only loose thread was the whereabouts of Ivan and Sergei Sarskov.

I finished the paperwork and debrief and did my best to wash my hands of everything. During my first major assignment, I had shot a man and almost lost my job, and what did I have to show for it but a case that Homeland Security had taken possession of. On the bright side, Victor Spilano was cleared and I no longer had to be Alexandra Riley, fiancée of Michael Price.

Carver and Boyle were leaving tomorrow on an eight a.m. flight for Los Angeles, and Jablonsky would continue to mentor me in the fine art of being a federal agent. Hopefully, there would be no more major pitfalls or screw-ups.

SIXTEEN

A few days later, I stopped by Mark's office on my way out. It was one of the first nights I was leaving at a reasonable hour. There were no major cases that required additional man-hours, and I was trying to take the shrink's advice and forge some type of life outside the office. Kate and I were going out on the town tonight.

"Hey," I knocked on the doorjamb, "I'm heading home if there's nothing else."

"Come in and close the door." Obeying his request, I sat down. Hopefully, I could catch Kate before she left since it looked like our plans were getting cancelled. "A guy over at Homeland told me the Sarskovs are in custody. The international arms dealing ring they were part of has been disbanded, and all the key players we know about are no longer a threat to national security." The way he said it sounded like he was mimicking someone. "I didn't tell you this though."

"Tell me what?" I asked, smiling.

"Good." He reached into his filing cabinet and pulled out a bottle of scotch and a glass. "Shall we drink to a job well done?"

I spun the bottle; it was fifty-year-old Macallan. "How can you afford this on a government salary?"

"A friend of mine sent it over as a coping mechanism for the divorce." He looked glum. "Instead, I think we should use it to celebrate." He poured some into the glass and slid it across the desk to me. He then poured a few fingers into his coffee cup and put the bottle back into the filing cabinet. We clinked our cups and took a sip. "Parker, you have something rare. You've got this natural instinct about things. It's something most agents learn, but you haven't been here long enough for that. We're lucky to have you."

"Thank you," I paused, "sir."

Mark snorted. "When we're drinking expensive scotch, it's Mark."

"Hell of a first assignment. Do most people end up with their first major case being taken away by another agency after they have to shoot a suspect in a dark alley?" I stopped. "Jesus, I sound like a cheesy action flick."

Mark laughed. "Let's call this assignment zero. With any luck, your next one will be better, and that will count as the first."

"I knew girls in high school that took a similar approach to losing their virginity. I'm not sure it works that way."

"We'll keep it quiet," he insisted. "Now get out of here."

*　　*　　*

A couple of weeks later, another case presented itself. We were doing things by the book this time, so hopefully, it would all pan out without any more undercover work or another department taking over our investigation. As required, I saw Dr. Weiler a couple of times for the perfunctory and semi-hostile appointments. The verdict seemed unanimous. I was about as mentally stable as anyone else who wanted this type of career.

There was a joint task force being formed between Interpol and the OIO, and I hoped Jablonsky wasn't going to get us roped into it. It had something to do with illegal art sales. Worst case, I might score a free trip to Europe, but for now, I was happy to be in the city.

"Have you heard?" Mark asked as I went into his office to have a requisition form signed.

"Please tell me we aren't traveling across the globe."

"No. Well, I don't know. But the director was exceptionally pleased by the work you and Agent Carver did. Despite the reprimands he cast upon Boyle and me, he thinks the four of us make a good team. He's extended them a permanent position at the OIO. Although, I don't think Sam has any desire to leave Los Angeles."

"And suddenly, I'm much more open to the possibility of travel."

He signed the form, and I went back to my desk. This was one hell of a life.

Part II:

Agent Prerogative

SEVENTEEN

Several months later...

Stepping off the plane, I resisted the urge to kiss the tarmac like the Pope. Instead, I squinted against the too bright sun, thankful to be on solid ground. The flight from Paris back to the United States had been long and crowded. There must have been at least four infants on the plane who screamed in chorus for the last three hours. My head pounded, my stomach was unsettled, and I just wanted to go home.

"Parker," a voice called from behind as I moved with the rest of the deplaning herd. "Parker." I sighed and stopped walking. "Alexis," my supervisor, Mark Jablonsky, tried again. I waited for him to catch up; he met me in his wrinkled suit, looking about as haggard as I felt. "This is a joke, right?" He held up his cell phone.

"Of course not. What were you doing for the last eight hours?" I asked as we continued through customs, flashing our passports and federal agent credentials. It would make picking up our firearms seem less suspicious to the overzealous TSA agents.

"Sleeping." Mark looked incredulous. "I can't believe you spent the flight writing your report on our joint task force. Just because we've spent the last few months in Paris working with Interpol to bring down an art forgery ring doesn't mean you have to hit the ground running as soon as we land. Wouldn't you like a break?"

"I'd love one, Jablonsky." We made it to the luggage carousel, and I grabbed my suitcase and overstuffed duffel. "That's precisely why I spent the last few hours getting my paperwork in order." I had sat in my cramped seat with my laptop resting on my thighs as I rehashed everything the director would need for our debrief. All the while, Mark snored in his seat two rows behind me.

My role as special agent with the Office of International Operations required an extended overseas investigation as we assisted Interpol in identifying art forgers in Paris, worked in concert with their undercover operative, Jean-Pierre Dubois, and arrested seven different smugglers, all of which were being prosecuted in the EU before any charges would be brought against them in the US. Proof of my dedication could be found in the first degree burns on my thighs from my overheated laptop. Now that I was home, I wanted to go home and not back to the office.

"You know we still have to go through the unofficial debrief before we can call it a day," Jablonsky warned as he led me from the airport and into the parking structure.

When we left for Paris, he had driven the two of us in his government-provided SUV. Therefore, I had no choice in the matter since my car was still at the office, and I was under orders, given that Mark was my supervisor.

"Yes, but after that, I can go home." I smiled. "I don't have to spend the next few hours writing my report. It's finished." I tried to hide the smug look but failed miserably. "That's why you got the e-mail notification on your phone."

"Damn overachiever." He shook his head.

"Face it, I'm a genius." He snorted and unlocked the doors so I could throw my belongings into the trunk and get inside the vehicle. "And the answer is no. I'm not helping you catch up on paperwork," I declared.

"Stop being so insubordinate, rookie," he teased as we headed for the freeway. "Your two years aren't up yet. I still own your ass."

Mark and I had a good relationship. It started out a little rocky, but he was a great mentor and an even better friend. I was twenty-six, and Mark had at least two decades on me. Sometimes, I was convinced he thought of me as a daughter. In the twenty-two months that I had gotten to know him, he finalized his third divorce and seemed as disconnected from the rest of the human race as I was. He had some friends but no spouse or children of his own. I had always been a loner with no family, few friends, and my career being my sole focus in life. Needless to say, we clicked.

All new recruits at the Office of International Operations, which was part of the FBI, had to undergo twenty weeks of training at Quantico followed by two years of supervision by an actual agent. Jablonsky must have hit the jackpot when he was assigned me. In the last two years, I had filed more paperwork than I thought possible, gone undercover to find an arms dealer, and most recently, I had spent the last few months in Paris stopping art forgers. It was a hell of a life.

We drove back to the OIO in silence, and I appreciated it. The pounding in my head had subsided to a dull ache, and the queasiness had abated. The only trick would be to get my internal clock back on east coast time. When the SUV came to a full stop in the underground garage, I took my bags out of the trunk and found my car keys. Unlocking my car, I put everything in the back seat, hoping to make an even faster escape as soon as possible.

"I'll meet you upstairs in the conference room," Mark called as he went to the elevator.

Taking a deep breath, I wanted to hug my car. I was home. Sure, Europe was great, but there was something to be said about being home. My car. My apartment. My furniture. And my bed. I let out a relieved sigh. My pillow. Grinning like an idiot, I went to the elevator and rode up to the OIO floor.

"Excuse me," I said to a man's back, "but that's my desk."

"I know." Michael Carver, my rival from Quantico and my support on the arms dealer case, spun around in my chair. "Welcome home, Alex."

"You're supposed to be in Los Angeles. You work out of the LA field office." The jetlag must be causing hallucinations.

"I got transferred six weeks ago. Agent Sam Boyle and I are the newest additions to the OIO family." He winked. "It's because the director was so impressed by the awesome job the two of us did last time."

If I remembered correctly, Carver had almost gotten himself killed and Boyle and Jablonsky had been chewed out for letting two probationary agents call the shots, but I didn't quibble over details. The goal was to be debriefed and go home.

"Whatever." I opened my desk drawer and grabbed a notepad and pen. "But this is my desk."

"C'mon, Alex, don't you know how to share?"

"Nope." I tried to hide my smile. "It is nice to see you again, Michael." I walked away before he could come up with a cheeky response.

After going over the information regarding the arrests, our time in Paris, and anything else the powers that be deemed pertinent, I found my way back to the parking garage. Jablonsky was upstairs, typing his report, and we were both scheduled tomorrow afternoon for the much more official debrief and meeting with the Interpol liaison. Right now, I just wanted to go home and crash. Even though it was around five, my body was on Paris time, and I was convinced it was getting close to bedtime.

Letting myself into my apartment, I found the place covered in a layer of dust. The air smelled stale, and the room was stuffy. I cracked open the fire escape, changed the thermostat, and ordered a pizza. While I waited for dinner to arrive, hoping it would be twenty minutes or less as promised, I changed the sheets on my bed, pulled out some clean towels, and unpacked my luggage. After eating,

I took a shower and went to bed before eight. I woke up at four a.m. and cursed my screwed up sleep schedule. Having nothing better to do, I spent the rest of the night cleaning my apartment, writing out a grocery list, and running on the treadmill. By eight a.m., I was ready to go back to work.

When I arrived at the OIO building, Jablonsky wasn't in yet, and I got reacquainted with my co-workers and friends. A dozen open cases needed attention. As I perused the folders, it felt like I was starting over. Being gone for an extended amount of time must have that effect. It's not like time stood still while I was away. Once again, I was behind.

"Playing catch up?" Michael asked from his desk, diagonally across the room from mine.

"Sucks," I retorted. "Did you leave all of this for me yesterday? Or were you trying to figure out where I keep the good pens?"

"The good pens are in the top right drawer," he teased, "and I thought you'd want everything waiting when you got back. You're like a damn robot. Predictable as hell." Letting the comment go, I glowered at the files as I began making personal notes on the current open cases. "If you want, we can get together this weekend, and I'll catch you up to speed." Judging by his expression, I wondered if he was being sincere. "Dobbs did the same for me. I'm just paying it forward."

"Thanks."

"Don't mention it."

EIGHTEEN

After our meetings and conferences, the file on Paris was closed and no longer our concern. It was nice to be back in familiar territory where English was the only language spoken. Settling behind my desk with a soup cup filled with coffee, I read my e-mails, office memoranda, statements that had been passed along by Homeland Security, and began again on the stack of files. It was Thursday, and although I was trying to adjust, the trip had left me exhausted and overwhelmed.

"Y'know, you could call in sick tomorrow," Carver suggested, jerking his chin at my blank notepad.

"I'm not sick."

Jablonsky came down the hall and went into his office. He nodded to Michael. If my boss could do it, so could I.

"It's just one more day, and then I'm off this weekend." Or so I hoped.

"Maybe you need to change your batteries or plug into the wall or whatever it is robots do," he quipped.

I gave him a death stare, and he went about his business.

The rest of the day and the next moved at a snail's pace, or at least I did. Friday at four, I called it quits and went home. Curling up on the couch, I didn't move unless it became absolutely necessary.

Saturday afternoon, there was annoying knocking at my door, and without looking, I knew it was Michael. He had a messenger bag slung across his chest, a six pack of beer in one hand, and a plastic bag with the logo from the deli down the street.

"I've come prepared for everything," he announced, entering my apartment. "And I do mean everything." The innuendo was not lost on me, but I chose to ignore it. Michael was a bit of a flirt, and sometimes, it was hard to tell when the teasing stopped and the serious began. My general approach was to take everything non-work related as a joke. "Was I wrong to assume your fridge is empty?"

"Not at all." I grabbed the bag from his hand and poked my head inside as I carried it to the coffee table. "But I would have ordered in."

He shrugged and put the beer in the fridge before coming back into the living room with all the necessary work documentation still inside his bag. "It was on my way." He took a seat on the floor and began pulling out stacks of paper as I evaluated the sandwiches and got up to get some plates and flatware. "This feels like déjà vu," he surmised.

"Are you here for good?" I put a paper plate and napkin in front of him. Grabbing a turkey and cheddar sandwich, I struggled with the incorrigible plastic wrap as Michael watched.

"It looks that way. Afraid I'm moving in on your territory and going to outperform you, again?"

"Ha." I met his eyes. "But I thought you liked it in LA."

"The OIO might be a better fit. Now, do you want to catch up with me or with the paperwork because frankly I'm good with either?"

"Maybe a bit of both."

Carver spent hours going over leads and the current circumstances surrounding a dozen cases that made their way to our office. He didn't complain once, despite the constant questions I posed. It had grown dark outside, and my notes were plentiful. Everything that I could glean from the files was instilled within my being. Anything else I should know could be picked up from investigating or observing.

"You think you have it all down?" he asked, packing everything back into his bag.

"Yes. Thank you."

"Well, the way I remember it, I owe you. This probably doesn't quite make up for that, but it's a start."

I shook my head. "You don't owe me. Let's not talk about that. I didn't get fired. You didn't get killed. It's all good." He looked a little grim. "What's it like working in my neck of the woods?" I rerouted the conversation to something more pleasant.

"Pretty good. If you and Jablonsky weren't shipped off to Paris, I might still be in LA. So if things go south, it's your fault." He looked mischievous. "Want to grab dinner and tell me about your trip?"

"Okay."

I changed out of my tank top and sweats and into something more appropriate and treated Carver to dinner. It was the least I could do. We ate and talked while we sat at a back booth in the neighborhood sports bar. It was Saturday, so with the exception of some college sports fans, the bar was rather subdued. Afterward, he walked me home and collected his belongings. Although I'd never admit this to him, I was glad to have another familiar face at the office. It was also nice not being the only probationary agent. Someone else could be picked on and forced to do the menial tasks and the shitty assignments.

*　　*　　*

Several weeks later, I was no longer a probationary agent. After the official paperwork was forwarded to the pertinent parties and I had some options concerning transferring to a different office, Jablonsky took me out to dinner. Apparently, the rest of the team had been invited. Seeing as how Carver and I graduated Quantico together and were both active agents now, everyone wanted an excuse to celebrate on the government's dime.

"Welcome to being full-fledged members of the team," Sam Boyle, Carver's supervisor, toasted. If Mark told me this was a social outing, I would have declined. Crowds and parties weren't my scene, and the dozen members of the OIO present counted as a party in my mind. "Any idea where you might want to go from here?"

I glanced up, wondering what Michael would say. He shrugged and picked up his bourbon. Maybe I could learn a few tricks on keeping my mouth shut from him.

"Parker," Mark commanded my attention, "are you planning to stick around?"

"That depends on how many more overseas assignments you want to drop in my lap," I retorted, and he chuckled. "Are you counting the days until you're rid of me?"

There was the briefest flicker of emotion across Mark's face before he said, "I'm counting the days until you stop being a huge pain in my ass."

"In that case, I'm not going anywhere. Someone's gotta keep you in line."

"Watch it. I'm still your boss."

The conversation found a focus which was no longer me, and I stared into nothingness as I considered what I wanted to do with the rest of my life. This was the first time I felt like I belonged. The first place I had an apartment and a real home with people I cared about, even if they were just curmudgeonly federal agents. Leaving it to start over somewhere else seemed counterproductive. Maybe I just hated change. Tomorrow, I'd ask Mark if there was a permanent position for me at the OIO or if a transfer was necessary, but tonight, I was determined to celebrate.

An hour later, the chorus of cell phones began with Jablonsky and ended with Carver. There had been a development on a major case, so we were all summoned back to work. Boyle glanced at Carver, who by all accounts had one too many to go back to work. The problem with being in law enforcement, you were always on call. That meant being drunk was never allowed, but something that happened all too frequently.

"Parker," Boyle directed his comment to me, "why don't

you and Carver take the rest of the night off. You've earned it." He didn't want to point out Carver's condition to the rest of the table. "Just make sure to show up first thing in the morning, and we'll get you up to speed."

"Aye, sir."

Mark paid the check as the rest of the group left. "Congratulations, again," he whispered, putting his jacket on. "I'll see you first thing in the morning."

"Absolutely," I paused, "sir." He hated it when I called him that. Narrowing his eyes, he headed out the door as Michael and I stared at the empty table and the remainder of the bottle of champagne. "What the hell?" I picked up the bottle and refilled my glass and then poured the last few drops into his.

"Agent Parker." He held up his glass, smiling like a kid in a candy store.

"Agent Carver." I grinned. Tomorrow would be business as usual, but tonight, I didn't see any reason to let perfectly good champagne go to waste.

Outcomes and Perspective

NINETEEN

The next morning, I was happy to report I wasn't hungover. Carver didn't appear to be either, but maybe he found an EMT to hook him up to a banana bag between then and now. He was pretty wasted last night when I shoved him into a cab and gave the driver his address. Luckily, he pulled it together and showed up looking professional and ready to work.

Last night, a tip came in on an impending robbery. One of our cases, which we had made little headway on, involved a string of robberies. Most of them involved liquor and grocery stores, but each time, the ATM was the focus of the theft. Since ATM's were considered bank property which fell under the jurisdiction of the federal government, we were assisting the FBI in tracking the robbers. While dozens of anonymous tips flooded the hotline over the last two weeks, none had shown any promise. An individual caller last week had given a location, and believing it to be a hoax, we didn't do anything to safeguard against the robbery. Last night, confirmation came in on the tip.

The thieves were escalating, and our tipster had provided additional details, naming future locations including a bank. We pulled phone records, but the call originated from one of the city's few remaining payphones. Nearby CCTV footage was being compiled to see if we could identify the tipster based on timestamp. Once that was accomplished, facial recognition would run nonstop until we put a name to a face. Honestly, I was glad I wasn't here last night, examining the call logs. Every once in a while, the job was more tedious than fulfilling.

"In my office," Jablonsky barked the moment I left the conference room. I followed him down the hall and shut the door as instructed. "Are you ready for your first assignment?"

"I'm pretty sure we've been there done that."

"True, but you're not wet behind the ears anymore. Until we identify our tipster and find out how he knows what's about to happen, the director wants to place an agent inside the bank. The bank manager has agreed, and given the demographic of employees, you fit the bill."

"Why? Because I can count without using my fingers?"

"Wow, you're just full of positive attributes." He outmatched my sarcasm. "Most of the bank tellers are women, early twenties, either starting a career or working while continuing their education. If we send you inside, no one will be suspicious."

"Because I don't look like a federal agent?" This was a sexist world we lived in.

"That and because you got carded last night at dinner. The waiter wasn't even sure you were twenty-fucking-one."

"He needed glasses, and he's five years too late for that." Sighing, I didn't want to be insubordinate. "Fine, point me in the right direction, and I'll assist on all your banking needs."

"Excellent." Mark led me down the hallway and into another conference room where a few seasoned agents counseled me on the proper methods for blending in and keeping an eye out for suspicious behavior.

Around lunchtime, I met with Mr. Brandon Sharpe, the bank manager of Mutual One. He ushered me into his office and told his assistant not to bother us while he conducted the interview. After we finished, he gave me a tour and announced he'd call in the next few days to let me know if I got the job. I was positive I was a shoo-in.

When I arrived back at the OIO building, the techs were still trying to pinpoint the source of the tip. They had yet to find a usable angle from the city's surveillance cameras. The two other locations our tipster mentioned were being scouted. One was an ATM on the street that was going to be monitored by a twenty-four hour surveillance van, and a tactical team would remain on standby. The second location was a convenience store with an in-store ATM. Agent Boyle was being sent inside to work the counter and keep an eye out. At least I wasn't the only one getting an undercover assignment. Who knows, maybe before I started my bank job, the thieves would be arrested.

"How come you get to play dress-up?" Carver asked. He approached my desk and looked over my shoulder as I reread the robbery reports, the FBI's memos, and what the OIO compiled on its own.

"It's because my legs look great in a skirt."

"Okay." He didn't know if I was kidding or serious. That made two of us. "Boyle wanted to know when you're starting at the bank."

"Two days from now. I start training Thursday morning." I shut the file. There was nothing else to learn. At least working as a bank teller didn't require an elaborate, planted background. "I'll finish learning the ropes by end of business Friday, and by Monday, I'll be stationed at the front counter."

"Where's the bank's ATM?"

"Front foyer as soon as you walk inside." I bit my lip, recalling the single bank security guard who had been chatting up one of the loan officers. The guy was probably sixty, not necessarily the best theft deterrent. "There's going to be a team nearby. If the thieves make a run at the ATM, I'll radio it in, and by the time they think they're getting away scot-free, tactical will be pointing assault rifles in their faces. Should be simple."

"Assuming you notice them jacking the machine," Carver retorted. "You might be bogged down counting some old lady's pennies."

"I can multitask."

"Great," Jablonsky said from behind, "then you can go over the bank security systems while you brief your backup unit."

"Right away, sir," I said to annoy Mark as I grabbed the relevant folder. Glaring at Carver for getting me in trouble, I brushed past him and into one of the conference rooms.

*   *   *

By Monday morning, the techs had given up trying to identify the tipster. There weren't any good angles to locate him, and even when they tried to follow him from the phone booth, he looked and dressed in such a nondescript fashion that they lost him in a throng of people. Boyle was positioned at the convenience store, but aside from some punks who were more interested in stealing beer than cash, there hadn't been a blip from any of the three locations. The tipster hadn't called since, so without even a peep, we had no new developments or leads.

My heels clacked against the tile floor as I entered the bank in a mid-length skirt, a cute blouse, and my long brown hair flowing behind me. I didn't look like a federal agent. One of my co-workers offered a smile as I reached across and lifted the latch to get behind the front counter. Mr. Sharpe came out of his office to welcome his newest employee.

"Alex, welcome to the Mutual One family," he gushed. I hoped he acted like this with everyone and not just me or else he'd blow my cover within my first ten minutes on the job.

"Thank you, sir." I logged into the computer with my bank-provided access code. "I'm ready to get to work."

He nodded, understanding the double meaning and went back to his office.

As customers filtered in, I scoped out the layout in between entering deposits and handing out cash for withdrawals. The entrance and exit were separate doors directly in front of me. The ATM was positioned between the two doors, against the wall. The left side of the room was comprised of loan offices, three separate cubicles, and a small waiting area with a couple of couches, a few tables, and a television. The right side contained a file room and Mr. Sharpe's office with a door to the vault and safe deposit boxes that were nestled on the main floor but walled in so as not to be seen by your average customer. Upstairs contained more offices for other people with titles, two bathrooms, a break room, and a corridor that led down a back staircase to the vault and safe deposit boxes.

Around lunchtime, the pace picked up as more customers entered the bank. I tried to pay attention to the employees to see if anyone seemed off, but there was too much of a rush to focus on anything other than work. It was two o'clock by the time the clientele trickled to a stop. With the obvious lull, I was told to go on break. I went upstairs, did a thorough assessment of the restroom and break room, and returned to my post at the front counter. As I sat on the stool behind the counter, I spotted Jablonsky waiting for a loan officer. He stretched and caught my eye but did nothing obvious to compromise my position. Either he was checking up on me, or there had been a new development.

Outcomes and Perspective

TWENTY

At five o'clock, the security guard locked the front doors. The tellers performed a final count of the money in the drawers, put the cash into zippered envelopes, and brought them to the smaller bank safe to wait for the morning. Wishing everyone a good night, I went outside and walked the two blocks to my car. Shutting my door, I put the key in the ignition and started the engine before dialing Mark's number.

"It's about damn time," he said. "The ATM got hit early this morning."

"What do you mean it got hit?"

"Our robbers waited for rush hour traffic, attached a chain to the contraption, and drove off before our agents could intervene."

"Shit." My mind tried to process an appropriate plan of action while I exited the garage and turned down the next street. It looked like another late night would be spent in the OIO building. "What about a description of the vehicle? Did they get tag numbers?"

"We got the car. It's a rental, wiped clean. Forensics is going over it. They haven't found any prints. We checked everything, even the lever to adjust the seat. We're pretty sure it's at least a three-man team. From eyewitness accounts, two men got out and hooked some chains to the ATM, and another drove the getaway vehicle."

"ATM's have cameras."

"They wore masks. Our IT team is trying to come up with a possible solution. But as I was saying, we have the vehicle. Hell, we even have the ATM. The only thing we don't have is the money. Treasury Department's putting us in contact with an expert on ATM thefts to give us a usable timetable and evaluate the evidence. He should be calling in a few minutes. Are you on your way?"

"Of course." It sounded like our robbers had seen one too many movies. This was real life. You couldn't just haul off an ATM and believe you would get away with it. *That was highway robbery*, my internal voice made the pun, and even I cringed at the pathetic attempt at humor. "What about Boyle's location?"

"Nothing yet. We've doubled up surveillance. If these assholes show up, we'll nab them." The sound of metal on metal filled the airspace. Mark needed to oil that filing cabinet. "When you get here, come to my office. We need to devise a better plan for protecting the bank."

*   *   *

I knocked on Jablonsky's open office door, and he glanced up. Clearly, someone wasn't having a good day. He blew out a breath and rubbed his forehead. He motioned that I remain silent. He was on speaker with someone important from the Treasury Department. After a couple *yes, sirs* and *we'll do our best, sirs*, he hung up.

"Are we having fun yet?" I asked, trying to hide the smirk. His glare quickly squelched my playful attitude.

"We're a group of incompetent imbeciles. Or so say the higher-ups." He looked ready to explode as he tried to tamp down his rage. "Assuming our tipster is on the level, we're going to do all we can to grab the guys at the convenience store. Until then, we have nothing. It's bad business, hoping for another crime to be committed."

"What did the expert say?"

"Twenty minutes to get into the ATM. They dragged it off, took it to a secluded location, emptied it, and left the car and the machine behind." He slammed his palm on top of the desk. "Fuck."

"What do you want me to do?"

He looked up as if he forgot we were having a conversation. Maybe the stress was leading to premature senility. "Don't let anything happen at the bank. We're keeping the team outside, and hopefully, we'll stop them before they do any more damage."

I nodded.

"Does anyone you work with seem suspicious?"

"No. But I've barely spent any time with these people."

"You have amazing instincts, Parker." He frowned, considering something. "I trust your judgment. Off the record, has anyone set your radar buzzing?"

I shook my head.

"Let me know if they do."

"Absolutely."

"All right. Go home. There's nothing for you to do here. I've turned another group of IT guys onto the tipster's phone message, and forensics is still evaluating the car. When something surfaces, I'll let you know."

*   *   *

The rest of the week, I evaluated each of the Mutual One employees. No one seemed involved. Frankly, unless one of them was the tipster, they all had alibis for the latest ATM theft. This was a small branch of a neighborhood bank. This wasn't some giant national savings and loan. Most of the customers had been coming here for years or were new additions to the community. The tellers knew them by name, and no one seemed out of place. At the same time, no one seemed too comfortable or familiar with the layout either. Jablonsky was barking up the wrong tree.

After spending the day undercover as a bank teller, I went to work at the OIO. Our floor looked like a ghost town, and a sick feeling settled in the pit of my stomach.

Yes, it was Friday, but something was off. I dialed Carver's cell phone. Hopefully, he would insist I had gone insane.

"Parker, I can't talk right now. The convenience store just got knocked over."

"Is Boyle okay? Did we get the guys? What about an ID?"

"Sam's fine. If you're at the office, you might as well stay there. We'll bring the party to you." He hung up without another word.

Dammit. Things were not going the way they were supposed to. Maybe we were all incompetent imbeciles. I reviewed the alleged progress we made on the vehicle and the recovered ATM, but realistically, there was no progress. No prints, no leads, nothing helpful. We were chasing ghosts, and it didn't look like they could be caught.

Two hours later, Carver, Jablonsky, and a team of agents came in. Mark shut himself inside his office, slamming the door for effect. Carver said something to the rest of the suits with him, and they scattered. He grabbed a chair and pulled it up to my desk. I raised an eyebrow and waited for him to say something.

"It's a four-man team. Three men, one woman. She was a decoy. She goes in, starts asking a dozen questions about lottery tickets, and while she's there, two guys go to the ATM, dark jackets with the collars turned up and baseball caps low on their faces. Boyle notices them, goes around the counter, and the chick clocks him with a glass bottle. By the time he recovers, the guys are gone."

"Shit."

"The car they were driving had no plates. It was a black sedan, older, maybe from the nineties. Our surveillance team was in hot pursuit for almost two miles and then they vanished."

"How the fuck did they vanish?" I wished I had a door to slam in frustration.

"Don't know." He rubbed his eyes. "The good news is they didn't get anything from the ATM, and Sam's working with a sketch artist to get a composite of the woman out over the wire."

"Where is he?" I glanced around the office.

"Emergency room. They wanted to make sure he didn't have a concussion. We have the security camera footage from inside and outside the convenience store," he continued. "Frankly, it's just a matter of time."

"Great. What are we doing until then?"

"Jablonsky's on the line with the director and someone from the FBI. We need a foolproof plan to stop these assholes. They didn't get anything today, but we didn't get them either."

"Let me rephrase. What are *we* doing in the meantime?"

Carver wasn't assigned to the surveillance vans, and since I was only working the bank, we were free to do whatever needed to be done on the investigation.

"Dial up the security cam footage, and I'll go make some popcorn."

TWENTY-ONE

Carver and I spent the evening watching and rewatching the footage. He noted a few details about the car they drove and the fundamental stats for the men involved, height, weight, and race. I noticed a reflection in the glass on the counter, and after sending it down to the IT department, we had a reasonable representation of the woman's profile. When Agent Sam Boyle returned to the OIO with his clean bill of health and a couple of stitches, he verified that's what she looked like. Between the profile reflection and the rendition the sketch artist made, we issued a BOLO on her and ran it through the news channels. Maybe we'd get lucky.

It was after midnight when Jablonsky left his office. He didn't say a word, and given the fact he was lugging a stack of files around, I suspected he had an early morning meeting with someone at a different agency concerning our current failure. This was, by all accounts, the FBI's operation, but since we were part of their organization, we were helping. Or trying not to impede the investigation. At this point, our usefulness was somewhat questionable.

"They're lucky," I said, breaking the silence. Carver and Boyle both turned to look at me. "It's not that we're screwing up. And it's certainly not because they're better than us. They've been lucky up until this point, but it won't last." Something scratched at the corners of my subconscious. "The tipster has to be on the team or someone close to one of the thieves. It's the only way he'd know what's going on, and it would explain why he's gone to such extremes to conceal his identity from us."

"But why would someone involved in the thefts report himself?" Carver asked.

"Maybe to taunt us. Maybe as a game to prove he's better," Boyle said. "Or because he doesn't want to be doing this, but he isn't sure how to get out of the mess he's in."

"We need to find the girl." I picked up the sketch and looked at her picture. "She's the best lead we have right now."

Boyle was kicking himself for letting her get the drop on him. He had been duped by a pretty face. It was a stupid mistake. Unfortunately, we were all human. Mistakes did happen, even if they weren't supposed to.

"Go home, Sam," Carver said. "Alex and I will run through this a few more times. You've had a rough day."

Boyle nodded and collected his things.

"Sir," I called after him, "you prevented them from getting the money."

"Yeah. Too bad I didn't stop them from leaving."

"We'll get them. It's just a matter of time." After the elevator doors closed around Boyle, Carver whispered to me, "Do you think we will get them?"

"It depends. If they're smart, they'll stop now and go into hiding. But if they were smart, they wouldn't be robbing ATMs and one of their own wouldn't have called in a tip."

"So it's just a matter of time?"

I shrugged. "Probably."

The two of us spent the next couple of hours reviewing the reports from the forensics lab, our tech support, and the agents in the surveillance van. The only thing we needed was a lead on the robbers' identities or whereabouts. Carver remained at his desk, searching the vehicle database in the hopes the make, model, and dents and dings on the car would lend themselves to tracking the owner. I stayed at my desk, trying to correlate the tipster footage to the two thieves inside the convenience store. The tipster could be one of the thieves, but then again, the tipster could also be any Joe Schmo off the street. I despised endless possibilities.

At three a.m. my computer let out a resounding ding. Facial recognition had gotten a hit on the woman who assaulted Boyle. Not only did we have a name and her previous arrest record, but we also had a current address.

"Do you want to knock on some doors?" I called to Carver.

He answered my question with a bright smile.

After the proper paperwork was signed, an entire assault team accompanied us to Roxie Henderson's apartment. No wonder the woman had a record. With a name like that she was just a stone's throw away from stripper or prostitute. The team flanked the front and rear exits. We didn't know who might be inside.

Carver knocked on the door as I stood to the side of the frame with a group of well-armed men behind me. "Ms. Henderson, open up." We listened for noise coming from inside. "Federal agents. Ms. Henderson, open up."

After a minute passed without any sound or movement, Carver stepped back and reached for his gun as one of the tactical team approached the door with a battering ram. After one good swing, the door popped open. The frame splintered where the deadbolt had been. The tactical team went in with guns poised, and Michael and I brought up the rear.

A chorus of clears echoed through the living room, kitchen, and bathroom. Michael and I found Roxie passed out in bed with a needle in her arm.

"That's one way to spend the stolen cash." Carver radioed for EMTs and checked her vitals. "She's breathing. No sign of an overdose." He lifted her eyelid and checked her pupil. She mumbled something but didn't move.

I glanced at the paraphernalia littering her dresser. "Heroin?"

"That would be my guess." He stepped out of the room,

and I followed.

"On the bright side, she didn't make a run for it."

"I doubt she even realizes anyone is inside her apartment, including herself." He sighed.

"Can someone take a look at this," one of the tactical guys called from the kitchen.

Michael and I exchanged a look. It would have been childish to play a game of Rochambeau to decide who was going into the kitchen and who had to babysit the drug-addled thief, so instead, I strode to the kitchen without giving Michael a chance to protest.

The refrigerator was open, and for all intents and purposes, I was willing to accept that our team found it that way. Inside were stacks of cash, schematics on four different models of ATM machines, maps listing the locations of the hits, and a set of blueprints. No one touched anything, but I crouched down to get a better look. This was a lot more than we bargained for, but there was no reason to look a gift horse in the mouth. Something did seem strange though.

"Any sign of anyone else living here?" I asked. I got a couple of headshakes. "How 'bout signs of recent visitors?" This time, I got a shrug. "All right, we need an evidence team down here." One of the men radioed it in, and another went downstairs to wait for the EMTs to arrive. "Carver," I headed into the hallway, "does anything about this situation seem strange to you?"

He kept one eye on our unconscious prisoner. "Like what?" The house was neat and tidy.

"I'm not sure."

"Did you find any evidence of substance abuse anywhere else?" Carver asked as I wandered through the living room.

"None." Nothing about her apartment, the building, or the neighborhood screamed addict. The walls were covered with photographs of her friends and family. She didn't look the type. Even stoned out of her mind, she still didn't resemble an addict. There was no liquor, wine, or even beer in her fridge. No empty bottles in the trash. Not even a cigarette lighter to be found anywhere else in her apartment.

"You think someone did this to her?" Michael reached the conclusion I did.

"Maybe. Or maybe she's got a Type A personality and likes to keep the dirty little secrets hidden away, so no one will suspect her world is anything other than perfect."

"Damn, you're cold and cynical."

Eventually, the EMTs showed up and checked her vitals. She roused slightly as they put her on top of a stretcher and carried her down the stairs. She was going to the hospital and getting handcuffed to the bed. At least we found one of the thieves. Three more to go. Maybe we could get her to talk. The doctors could evaluate her for other drugs, check for track marks, and since she was a captive audience, we'd have the opportunity to get some real answers.

TWENTY-TWO

"Welcome back, Ms. Henderson," Carver said. "I believe your luck might have run out."

She looked utterly bewildered. Her eyes searched the room, trying to determine where she was and what was going on. She jerked her arm and realized she was restrained.

"You're in the hospital," I said. "Do you remember what happened?"

She shifted her gaze to me, surprised anyone else was nearby. Frankly, I didn't want to be here anymore than she did, but after the evidence team set to work in the apartment, there wasn't any other place for me to go. Plus, Carver needed support from a female team member, or so he claimed.

"Hospital?" She jerked her arm again, rattling the bed's railing. "Why am I in handcuffs?"

"See, I guess you must have missed the part where we placed you under arrest on account of you being higher than a kite," I said.

"Federal agents, ma'am." Carver showed his credentials. He probably practiced that in the mirror when no one was around. He reminded her of her rights and got back to business. "You assaulted an agent. You were positively identified as an accomplice in a robbery, and we found you in possession of narcotics."

"And also under the influence," I chimed in. "Not to mention the tons of evidence in your apartment. At this point, it's in your best interest to cooperate."

Roxie looked flummoxed. She tugged one final time against the restraints, apparently believing if she could get her wrist free, she could escape the hospital after giving Michael and me the slip. But the handcuffs didn't budge. "You don't know anything. You don't have anything on me. It's all lies. You're fucking liars."

"Okay." It was morning, and I had been up all night and had no patience for games. Michael, on the other hand, wasn't ready to throw in the towel.

"Ms. Henderson," he paused, "Roxie, may I call you Roxie?"

"Whatever."

"Roxie, you need to be aware of what's going on right now. There was a search warrant issued for your house, your car, and your office. The police and the FBI are tearing through your life to figure out what other ATMs your friends are planning to rob, who your friends are, and what you've done with all of your ill-gotten gains. You were caught red-handed with enough evidence to put you away for the next couple of decades. How do you think your life is going to end up when you're spending the next twenty years in a federal penitentiary?"

She shuddered, her defiance weakening. "Liars," she hissed.

"We aren't," I said. "You know we aren't. You know exactly what was inside your apartment. The man you clocked with that bottle yesterday afternoon, he's our boss. Things aren't looking good for you. Do you have a family? A mother? Father? Anyone? Because the harder you make us work to find the rest of your team, the worse it's going to be for everyone you know. There will be questions, searches, tons of embarrassment. Maybe they're involved. Maybe they're helping you or covering for you. Who knows? Maybe we'll bring them up on accessory charges or interfering in an investigation."

"Don't." She looked miserable, largely due to the low following her high, but maybe a little bit because of the threats.

"Tell us something," Michael insisted. "Anything you say can only help you."

"How?"

"We can speak to the prosecutor, the judge, testify about your helpfulness," I said. "Maybe you were keeping everything at your apartment for someone else. Maybe we can mitigate your involvement."

"The drugs aren't a common thing. Not anymore. I cleaned myself up. I have a job now, a life, but," she faltered as tears threatened to spill, "it was supposed to be something small and simple. It wasn't supposed to be this." She took an unsteady breath, and Carver cautioned a glance at me. She would break since she was already broken.

I went to the door and dragged the police officer, who was standing watch, inside. We wanted someone else to corroborate her statement. The officer stood in the corner, flipped on a tape recorder, and relayed the pertinent information. Carver informed her we were taping the interview, and she continued her story.

She worked as a receptionist at an auto body shop. Every day, she answered phones, made appointments, and filled out work orders and bills. After working there for almost two years, she got involved with David Slidle. He was a charismatic, adventure-seeking mechanic. One day, he introduced her to some of his friends, none of which had a name she was willing to share. They talked fast cars and daredevil stunts. She never expected all this talk to turn into anything illegal.

"What did you think was going to happen?" Carver asked. "You're telling me the conversation went from skydiving and bungee jumping to bank robbery?"

"Not bank robbery, knocking over vending machines."

"So they were knocking over vending machines first?" I asked.

"I don't know. I guess." She covered her face with a

hand. "I never saw it happen. I thought they were just fooling around. Shooting the shit. You know how guys are." She peeked at me with one eye, hoping for some support. "Then last week, David calls. He's in a bind, and he needs me to meet him near the pier." Carver looked about to interrupt, and I put my hand on his forearm, wanting to see what she was going to say first. Derailing her now didn't seem ideal. "I find him and his two asshole friends with a fucking ATM, ripped open, under a bridge. They get in the car, laughing and congratulating one another. I had no idea." She moved her hand away and stared wide-eyed at the ceiling. "No freaking idea."

"Why didn't you report it?" Carver and I asked simultaneously.

"How could I? I drove the fucking getaway car. I was an accomplice." There was no point in arguing about should have, could have, would have, so I waited for her to continue. "Then they said they had another couple of scores mapped out. They knew how to do it now. They could break into the ATMs with no problem. Just get in and out, but they needed a distraction."

"Why did you agree?" I asked.

She looked ashamed. "Because it was more money than I would make in a year." I didn't see how that was true. ATMs didn't hold that much cash. Either they had a bigger score in mind, or they misrepresented what could be gained from their dumbass thievery. "No one was supposed to get hurt. It was supposed to be simple. The government and the banks have been screwing us over for years. It didn't seem that wrong."

It always annoyed me how people could justify illegal behavior. It was like speeders who were infuriated for getting pulled over for going ten above the limit as if that was acceptable, even though it violated the stated law.

"Tell us what happened," I said.

"You know what happened. I go inside the convenience store and talk to the clerk. David's two friends go inside to break into the ATM while he waits in the car, but the clerk sees what's going on and comes around the counter. I didn't know he was a cop. You gotta believe me. I didn't know what to do, so I picked up one of the glass soda bottles and hit him over the head. We ran out of there, and that was it." She looked pensive. "Is that guy okay?"

"He'll live," Carver said. "What happened afterward?"

"David dropped me off at home. I was scared shitless. This wasn't supposed to happen. I had my life back on track. I'm a good person." Yet another of the things people say that I found irksome. "But I didn't want this life. I don't want to hurt anybody. I don't want to steal. I just wanted things to go back to normal." She sniffled and tugged at her wrist again. "But normal's over."

"What'd you do?" I asked, knowing where the story was going.

"I had my cut and David's. All of his notes were in my car. I wanted to burn them, but I was afraid he'd get mad and his friends would do something to me. So I found the only out I ever remembered." She glanced at her arm. "Three years clean and sober down the drain because of some guy and his friends. That was who I was. Not who I wanted to be. Not anymore. It was all for nothing, wasn't it?" She searched my eyes for an answer, but I didn't have one. She turned to Carver, but he backed away.

"Thanks for your help, ma'am. If we have any other questions, we'll be back." He stepped toward the door.

"Wait. What's going to happen to me now?" she asked.

"We'll do what we can to have your charges reduced," I promised. "Until then, you'll remain in police custody, pending a hearing."

TWENTY-THREE

"Buy you breakfast?" Carver asked.

We just finished the paperwork on Roxie Henderson. The evidence from her apartment was being bagged, cataloged, and evaluated as we spoke. Jablonsky called to check on our progress. He was on his way to the office and suggested Carver and I take a couple of hours to get some rest before continuing with our day. Boyle had gotten word on the current situation and took a team to David Slidle's apartment. There wasn't any news on that front, so if we wanted to step out, now might be our only opportunity.

"C'mon, you've been going nonstop for the last twenty-four hours. Jablonsky will ream you a new one if you don't take a break."

"It's not that." I rubbed the grit out of the corner of my eye. "I can't determine if I'd rather sleep or eat."

"Fair enough." Carver led me to the elevator. "Go home and get some sleep. You can always grab a sandwich at your desk."

I yawned, perhaps due to his suggestion.

"Are you going to stay awake long enough to drive home, Parker?"

I thought about it, knowing once I was home my brain

would start churning around Roxie and David. "Actually, I changed my mind. Breakfast sounds great, especially if you're buying."

"Are you sure?"

"Absolutely. Added bonus, you can drive."

We went to a nearby diner and took a seat at an empty booth. I ordered an espresso and scrambled eggs with toast. Carver went with steak and eggs and black coffee. We stared into nothingness, zombified by the long hours. After our meals arrived and the caffeine kicked in, conversation didn't seem quite as challenging as it previously had.

"Do you believe her?" he asked, skewering the last piece of steak with his fork. "Henderson," he elaborated as he chewed.

"I don't know." I motioned to the waitress for a refill. "Her place didn't match the heroin, but she has priors for possession and B&E. It would make sense why she'd be afraid to call the cops. Who believes a former addict with a rap sheet?"

"You do." He finished his coffee and wiped his mouth.

"Maybe. Maybe not. Some things still don't fit. Everything incriminating was at her apartment. Maps, blueprints, schematics," I sighed, "cash. She could be running the show." I glanced out the window into the bright morning light. "There wasn't a single item in that apartment that indicated a man had been there. If it's all her boyfriend's fault, like she insists, why aren't there any pictures of the two of them? There's no razor, extra toothbrush, t-shirt, jacket, whatever. There should be something."

"Do you think he removed everything from her apartment in case she got caught? Frankly, she cold-cocked Sam, so of course, she was going to get caught."

"I guess we wait and see what turns up at Slidle's place and take it from there." I took a final sip of my espresso. "Do you think they'll scatter now that we have Roxie and David?"

"They might not know. Or the three men might be together." Carver dropped some cash on the table and stood up. "Where do you think Jablonsky went last night?"

"Maybe he had a meeting with someone from another agency. He'll tell us if we need to know."

Michael gave me a strange look as if to say *when did you become so patient*, but the question never formed into actual words because our phones rang. That was never a good sign.

"Parker," I answered as we went outside to Michael's car. The team was at Slidle's apartment, but there was no sign of our suspect. Either he happened to be out when we came knocking, or he got wind of what happened at Roxie's and took off.

"All right, we're on our way," Carver said, disconnecting his call. We exchanged glances. "No rest for the wicked."

After entering the address into the GPS, we arrived at Slidle's in less than twenty minutes. The tactical team had done a decent job hiding the van, so hopefully, if David returned, we wouldn't spook him.

We went upstairs and located apartment 419. The door was ajar, and Carver announced himself as he went in. I followed and glanced around. The place was a mess. Empty bottles were scattered around the room. Papers and maps covered the rumpled, unmade bed in the center of the studio apartment.

"Any cash or signs of his involvement in the thefts?" I asked.

"Nothing conclusive yet, but we just started," one of the other agents said. "Don't you have eyes? Have you seen this place?"

"Any evidence of Roxie Henderson?" Carver asked, opening the fridge and checking the contents inside. As he shut the door, he spotted a photo of the two of them in a magnetic frame. "Never mind." He tapped the photo with his pointer finger. "At least we know they're dating."

I wanted nothing more than to start in one corner and search every inch of the apartment, but it wasn't my job. We had a search team to do that. What Michael and I needed to figure out was where David Slidle might be hiding.

Pulling on a pair of gloves and trying not to disturb anything more than necessary, I began at one end of the apartment, and Michael began on the other. We worked around the techs as we searched for a receipt, appointment book, or calendar, anything that would lead to our suspect.

I heard footsteps in the hallway outside the apartment, and I cocked my head up. Everyone else heard it too. Michael took point, and resting his hand on the butt of his gun, he approached the door. I came around on the other side to provide cover if necessary.

"What are you doing in my apartment?" a voice asked from the hallway.

"Mr. Slidle?" Carver kept his gun and badge out of view.

"Who are you?"

"Why don't you come inside? We can discuss this in person." Carver hoped to get Slidle closer before announcing he was a federal agent in case the man decided to run. They tended to run far more often than they should. Slidle didn't budge, so Carver took his credentials from his jacket pocket. "Federal agent, Mr. Slidle. Don't move." Of course, he moved. In fact, he went running in the opposite direction, back to the staircase. "Shit."

Carver raced out the door with me at his heels. I didn't know if anyone else from the team would assist in the pursuit or if they'd simply go back to cataloging all the crap in Slidle's apartment. Since Carver and I were the two newest agents, we always had the fun job of chasing down the runners.

We were coming up on the second floor landing when Slidle put a hand on the banister and leapt over, landing in a crouch on the ground floor and taking off out the front door. Carver continued pursuit, jumping over the last four steps and repeating this process on the final flight of stairs. I ran down the steps as fast as my legs could carry me. Slidle burst out the door and out of sight, followed half a minute later by Carver.

When I broke through the front door, I came to a dead stop, searching in all directions for the two men. Catching a glimpse of Michael to my right, I took off in that direction. Slidle zigzagged across traffic in the hopes of losing Michael. I crossed the street, hoping not to be splattered against someone's windshield like a bug.

The screech of tires and the blare of a horn made my already pounding heart leap into my throat. The sound wasn't for me, and since Slidle was on the other side of the street, I hoped Michael was okay. After crossing, I glanced down the street to the last location I had seen him. He was still up and running.

My attention returned to Slidle, who was clearly a total moron. Not that I was complaining since he was still running from Michael but had reversed course and was heading back in my general direction.

"Slidle, freeze," I ordered, but the man kept running.

Apparently, he had been a bulldozer in a past life and hurtled toward me. I grabbed the back of his shirt, landing on top of him and bringing him down hard on the pavement with a resounding oomph. He tried to roll me off of him as we struggled on the ground. He wasn't willing to give up without a fight, and I was in no mood to let our suspect get away. As I kneed him hard in the ribs and flipped him onto his stomach, Michael came up behind me.

"You got him?" he asked.

"Just about." I clicked the handcuffs in place and hit Slidle in the kidney on my way up for good measure. The two espressos before sprinting through the streets threatened to cause cardiac arrest. "Do you mind dragging his sorry ass back to the apartment building?"

"It'd be my pleasure." Carver hauled Slidle to his feet. "If you try anything else, one of us will shoot you." He cautioned a glance at me.

I took a few deep breaths and tried to walk off the pounding in my chest. I nodded that I was okay, and we went back to the apartment to turn over another piece of crap.

TWENTY-FOUR

"If you're innocent, why did you run?" Jablonsky asked David Slidle. We brought Slidle in for questioning, and despite his protests that he was brutally assaulted, his scrapes and bruises weren't life-threatening.

"Some guys were ransacking my apartment. I didn't want to mess with any psychopaths."

I chuckled, glad to be in the observation room and not in interrogation.

"I never realized the federal government employed psychos. I want my lawyer," Slidle said.

Carver came in and handed me my handcuffs. "I disinfected them for you."

"Thanks."

We watched as Boyle entered the interrogation room to assist Jablonsky. "How the hell did you catch up to him? From what I remember, you run like a girl," Carver teased.

"I would have caught him sooner if you weren't in my way," I quipped. "But he did backtrack, so it wasn't too hard to get him on the ground. Although, it might have been easier had we not just finished breakfast."

"Do you want to watch the interrogation, or do you want to see what was uncovered at his apartment?"

I considered the question and decided to see what we

found instead of listening to Slidle whine and bitch about how his rights were violated. Plus, it would be an hour before his lawyer got here which meant the questioning was over until then.

Trailing Michael back to his desk, I saw the files and photographs spread out for our perusal. It looked like a much weaker version of the evidence we found in Roxie's apartment. There was maybe a grand in twenties that had been recovered from under the mattress and a layout of Mutual One. At least she had been on the level about something.

"Any idea who the other two chuckleheads are?" I skimmed the official report and evidence list.

"No idea. But we're getting a subpoena for Slidle and Henderson's phone records. Maybe we'll figure it out. They must have been in contact, right?"

"Sure." I went to my desk and found the aspirin in my top drawer. Popping two and swallowing, I shut my eyes and tried to think. I had a headache and was running on fumes. Sleep would have been the better choice instead of breakfast. Too late now. "Has anyone pulled employee records for the auto body shop? If Roxie and David work there, maybe the other two goons do too. Or maybe someone there will remember seeing them."

"Here," Carver pulled out a sheet of paper and read the names on the page, "I'm not sure if we've run backgrounds on any of them yet." He scanned the rest of the forms on his desk, looking for a note but came up empty. "Do you think they have previous records?"

"What do you think?" I asked.

"Mr. Upstanding Citizen doesn't just decide to steal a fucking ATM on a whim."

"Probably not. Split the list with me."

He wrote down half the names on a separate sheet of paper, and we got to work. While we were running the names through the law enforcement databases, looking for previous records, particularly ones involving burglary or larceny, Jablonsky appeared near my desk.

"Parker, would you like to explain how Mr. Slidle ended up with bruised ribs and complaints about pissing blood?"

"He resisted arrest," I said, not bothering to look up. I didn't use excessive force. He had at least eighty pounds and six inches on me. Sometimes, my lack of height and weight required creativity to subdue a fleeing suspect, and he pissed me off. "The guy barreled right into me. I had to take him down. You always taught us not to let a suspect get away."

"Where were you?" Mark asked, turning to Carver.

"Trying to get across the street." We explained the dynamics of the chase to Jablonsky.

"Good work. It's nice to know the two of you can get things done while I'm gone. No more handholding," he quietly added. "Nicely done."

I suspected he was congratulating himself on his training techniques, so I kept silent, pretending I didn't hear a word he said. We were all suffering from sleep deprivation, so if he needed to self-congratulate himself, it was fine by me.

When Carver and I finished our background checks on the list of employees, we didn't get any hits. It was possible the other two thieves lacked a record or used fake names and identities when applying for the job. After all, it was difficult enough finding work without a criminal record. Jablonsky had been in and out, revisiting interrogation a few times. Maybe Slidle had given us another lead.

"I'll check with Boyle and see if we uncovered anything new," Carver said. "Can you see if Ms. Henderson has decided to be more forthcoming after getting some sleep?"

"On it." I picked up the phone and dialed the local police precinct.

She was still at the hospital under police supervision. After being passed around from department to department, my call was forwarded to the officer who recorded the conversation that morning. Unfortunately, the more Henderson recovered, the less talkative she became. It was timing that had gotten her to speak as freely as she did. With nothing else to do, I put my head on top of my desk and waited for someone to come back with an update.

*   *   *

"Parker, go home," Mark said softly. I opened my eyes and sat up. My neck was stiff, and I wondered how long I had been asleep at my desk. This gave new meaning to the term sleeping on the job. "You helped bring in two suspects in the last twenty-four hours. It's time to go home and get some rest. That's an order."

"Sir," I mumbled in protest, rubbing my eyes.

"You know I hate being called sir. Just for that, you're going home. Stop by in the morning before you go to the bank. Understood?"

"Yes," I narrowed my eyes at him, "sir."

He waited for me to collect my belongings and go to the elevator before he continued down the hallway. Being asleep and called out on it by my superior was not how I envisioned this day ending, but I was too tired to beat myself up over it.

Arriving at home, I locked my door, considered eating or showering, decided against both, and set my alarm for five a.m. When the buzzer went off, I considered throwing it against the wall. Nixing that idea, I crawled out of bed, showered, dressed for the bank, and packed a separate bag with regulation attire in the hopes we could simply go and nail the remaining two suspects instead.

I made it to the OIO building at six and spotted Boyle in his office. I knocked on the door, and he gestured for me to enter. Jablonsky, Carver, and the other agents from yesterday had gone home. We all deserved a break.

"Agent Parker," he poured a second cup of coffee from his personal machine and placed it in front of me, "Jablonsky asked that I brief you on our findings from yesterday."

"I just wanted to apologize for," I stared at the floor and added timidly, "falling asleep at my desk."

He laughed. "You're salaried, not paid by the hour. It's perfectly fine. But you probably don't want to make a habit out of it. Vicious rumors of narcolepsy may spread throughout the office." He took a sip from his mug. "Point out a single seasoned agent who hasn't fallen asleep at his desk, and I'll show you someone who isn't doing the job properly. Now, let's get down to business. I'd hate to make you late for your backup career."

Outcomes and Perspective

TWENTY-FIVE

Sam Boyle spent an hour and a half detailing the evidence found in our suspects' apartments. The court order had been issued for Roxie Henderson and David Slidle's phone records, but no identifications had been made on the other two team members. After sobering up and recovering from her low, Henderson wasn't willing to give an ounce. She hadn't spoken, except to the medical professionals attending to her. After getting a clean bill of health, she was moved to lockup at the precinct. If we needed her, someone could put in an order for her transfer, but right now, she served no purpose. The local cops would take a crack at her, but I was certain she said all she was going to say.

David Slidle had lawyered up. He wasn't talking unless it was to complain about the treatment he received during his arrest. Boyle rolled his eyes at this. No one believed Slidle was brutalized. Frankly, if I slammed his skull into the pavement a few times, I might have even gotten away with that. However, I wasn't in the business of getting my rocks off by knocking around shitheads. So he had some bruises and scrapes, so did I. All part of the job.

"What am I doing in the meantime?" I asked after Boyle concluding the briefing.

"Same thing you've been doing. Keep an eye on the ATM in the bank. I don't know if the ATM bandits are going to ground or if they'll try to make the final score, so keep your eyes open. And don't get bogged down in the details or descriptions," he indicated the stitches on the side of his face, "because it smarts when you do."

"Dignity mostly?"

"Unfortunately, yes." He scratched an eyebrow. "We're keeping two tactical units on standby in the event anything occurs. But half their team is in custody, so it'd be insane for them to try to distract, break in, and get away by themselves, especially after everything."

"Are we any closer to identifying them? What about the tipster?" It seemed we had stopped focusing on this mysterious informant. From the limited footage we had, it wasn't Roxie. Maybe it was David, but for an informant, he was highly uncooperative. That left one of the two remaining team members or a possible third party.

"Hell if I know," he replied, and I looked at my watch. "Get to work, Parker. If you need anything, we'll be on standby, awaiting your call."

"Let's hope I don't need anything." I went to the door. "Agent Boyle, if you happen to capture the rest of the thieves before close of business today, feel free to spring me early."

"Clearly, you love working at a bank," he teased. "Hell, Parker, maybe in the future you should consider a full time position with corporate America."

"I'd put a bullet through my brain before that would ever happen."

"Hey, y'never know."

* * *

Another three days were spent at the bank. It was Wednesday, hump day, and even though it was the middle of the week, the proverbial hump, it was annoying the way Annette, the teller, so cheerfully announced this. Maybe she just left the employee lounge after humping Ted, the loan officer, because I couldn't figure out why anyone would be this cheery working in a bank. Frankly, it was depressing. We handled other people's money and financial problems, not even our own. Pull it together, Parker. You're not a teller. You're a federal agent. I shook off the boredom and handed the elderly woman the roll of quarters she requested.

"Are these old quarters?" she asked.

"Excuse me?"

"With the eagles on the back. The way quarters were meant to be."

I stared at her, wanting to reach into my purse, pull out my nine millimeter, and ask her nicely to step away from the counter.

"Miss," she shook the roll of quarters in front of my face, "are they old quarters?"

"It's a mixture." I gave her my best attempt at a smile, hoping I didn't look like a deranged, homicidal clown. "It'll be a surprise, just like the toy in a cereal box." She accepted that answer as if it were perfectly logical and walked away. "I need a break." I put my face in my hands and tried to shut out the world.

We hadn't made any progress identifying the ATM bandits. Jablonsky had been trying to negotiate a deal with Slidle to get names in exchange for a reduced sentence, but the problem was we didn't have much on him. The only thing we had was some cash and a layout of the bank. Most of our evidence was against Roxie. She assaulted Boyle and all the evidence had been lined up and waiting for us in her apartment. Slidle's representation must have realized how weak our case against his client was because he had been stalling as much as possible. We needed to catch the other two or gather more evidence, which was why I was stuck behind the counter at the bank from hell.

"Excuse me, but I don't think you can accurately do your job with your face buried in your hands," Carver said.

"What are you doing here, Michael?" I brushed my hair back and gazed across the empty lobby. "Have you come to free me from this torture?"

"No." He grinned, enjoying himself.

Annette glanced at us. "Alex, is this your boyfriend?"

"Honey," Michael cooed, further irritating me, "you haven't told your co-workers about me yet? Tsk, tsk." He gave Annette his high wattage smile. "I'm Michael."

"Why don't you take a break?" she suggested. "It's dead in here anyway. I can cover for you for ten minutes."

"Great, thanks." I grabbed my purse and went around to the opening to get away from the counter. "What are you doing here? Did we get them?" I whispered to Michael, hoping I was free to leave.

"No. We're taking another run at Roxie and David, but it doesn't look promising."

"This is ridiculous. Are we even positive there were four to begin with? Could it have just been two? Maybe Sam got hit in the head harder than he realized and was seeing double."

"Doubtful." He did a quick visual sweep of the bank, eyeing the ATM which no one even visited today. "They want to pull the vans off the bank. We might have spooked them. By now, they must know we have half their friends in custody."

"Great," I muttered sarcastically.

"Look, Boyle and I are positioned across the street, and the vans will be nearby. Just don't panic if you don't see your support parked a block away." He kissed my cheek, remaining in character. "I'll let you get back to work."

Maybe I should suggest we move the ATM outside, disconnect the cameras, open the cash door, and leave a note saying 'free for the taking, will assist with haul-away'. It might be the only way to get the rest of the thieves to make their move.

*   *   *

After work, I stopped by the OIO and knocked on Jablonsky's door. He looked the way I felt. This wasn't working. We were wasting resources and manpower on bringing in two suspects for which we had no leads, no description, and no feasible plan. We had to get Slidle or Henderson to give them up or else we'd never catch them.

"We got another tip an hour ago," Mark said after I

finished my tirade. Briefly, I considered he might be lying, but he wasn't into games. "The voice sounded the same. We have teams running traces, looking through footage, doing everything we can." He shook some thoughts loose in his brain. "Who knows? Anyway, if we're to believe our tipster, the team's been rebuilt, and they're planning something big. He didn't say what it was, but it will be their last job before they disappear for good."

"Sounds like our tipster's a nutcase."

"He was right the last time. It's all we have to go on, Parker. Boyle and Carver are running this new information by our friends in custody, but until we have something solid, stay where you are."

"Are you putting the vans back on the bank?"

"No." He frowned, and his forehead creased. I knew Mark well enough to know he thought this was a bad idea. "They'll be close. One is covering the road from the east and the other on the west. If they do a snatch and grab on the ATM, we'll get them. Did Carver tell you he and Boyle are staking out the bank from across the street?"

"Yep."

"Okay. If we get verification they're hitting the bank, I'll put every spare agent on it. They won't get away again, and if not, then we'll be here, trying to figure out a better plan to get these bastards off the street. They've been making us laughingstocks, and I am no one's laughingstock." They'd pissed off Boyle and now Jablonsky. Whoever they were, they were going down.

TWENTY-SIX

It was getting close to five o'clock on Friday afternoon. I stifled my yawn and reached for the deposit slip. The man I was helping smiled brightly and asked for my phone number as I printed his receipt and slid it to him.

"Thanks, but I'm already spoken for."

The security guard had just locked the entrance, hoping to deter any last minute customers from coming inside the bank. A few people went to the exit as the man stood before me, not willing to take no for an answer.

"Here," he looked behind his shoulder, and something caused the hair on the back of my neck to stand at attention, "let me give you mine instead." He turned his receipt over and scribbled something on the back. Looking down, I knew what it was going to say. "Don't make a scene," he warned.

"Of course not, sir." I remained calm and detached as I hoped everyone else would leave the bank before things went from bad to worse.

The instructions were simple. He wanted an escort to the vault, and if I failed to comply, he'd shoot up the place. My phone was on the counter, and I needed it to get word to the team outside.

"All right," he jerked his head to the side, "get moving, and if you push the panic button, I'll kill you."

I'd like to see you try, I thought as I moved deliberately slow, giving as many customers enough time to get out of the bank as possible. The fewer possible casualties, the better. I scanned the room, trying to identify the rest of the bank robbers or determine if there were any other bank robbers. Placing one hand on top of my phone which was just out of his line of sight, I slipped it into my blazer pocket. As soon as I got the chance, I'd speed dial Carver. Hopefully, it wouldn't be enough to tip off the thief.

"Okay, there's no reason anyone needs to get hurt here, but you must know, I don't have access. I'm just a teller," I said quietly. Two men stood near the back wall, and from the way their jackets hung on their bodies and their faces were obscured by sunglasses and caps, I knew they were here for the robbery. "You don't want to draw attention to yourself. Let's not alert anyone else, okay?" If he thought it was strange I was offering helpful hints on conducting a heist, he didn't let on.

"Hurry up."

Opening the latch, I went around the counter, my eyes never leaving him. He wasn't disguised or trying to conceal his identity, which either meant he was cocky enough to believe he'd get away without incident or he was willing to kill anyone who got in the way. By my calculations, those weren't good odds.

"Alex, what are you doing?" Annette asked, causing him to turn toward her. I saw the gun on his hip, just underneath his shirt and knew things could get bloody any second.

"Nothing. It's almost closing time. I just need a moment alone with my friend. Finish with your customer and call it a night. I'll close up," I said as nonchalantly as possible. She continued to look at us questioningly, but I continued toward the staircase, urging the bank robber along.

As we began our ascent, I noticed him signal to the other two, who had remained off to the side near the empty couches and closed loan offices. Thankfully, the loan department had gone home for the night, and there were only three tellers, the security guard, and the bank manager still in the building, in addition to a few straggling customers. Containing the situation was the best I could hope for. If the three or four customers in line would just finish their business and leave, it would make this entire situation easier for everyone involved.

"You've done this before?" the man asked as we made it to the top of the steps. "No one remains this calm."

"You're just like a fucking mugger. If I cooperate, you'll take what you want and go." I tried to sound frightened and angry, but I was weighing my options concerning the chances of attempting to subdue him. The only problem was the two goons downstairs. I needed backup in the form of tactical support.

"Smart girl." He stared with dead eyes and removed the gun from his hip. "Now take me to the safe deposit boxes." Apparently, he was smart enough to realize breaking into the vault would be too time-consuming and obvious. At least with safe deposit boxes, there was no way of knowing what went missing. There were no surveillance cameras in the room, and the locks were simpler to break, even if there were two per box. Someone had done their homework. "Move." He raised the gun and maintained a steady aim as I led him to the other staircase and descended the steps.

"It's right here." I opened the door and swallowed, leaning against the opposite wall and trying to make myself small and less intimidating, not that he was intimidated by my barely five foot six physique.

"No. You'll make a run for it. Get inside."

I obeyed, and he shut the door.

"Don't try anything." He jerked the gun, indicating I should take a seat.

I slid to the floor, and as he began searching for a specific box or set of boxes, I felt the number pad on my phone. Pressing the two and the call button, I hoped Carver would answer.

"Why are you doing this?" I asked, hoping Michael could hear me. "Robbing a bank is a great way to ensure you'll spend the next twenty years in prison. What about your two friends in the lobby? They have automatic weapons, don't they? Are you planning to mow us all down after you get what you want?"

"Shut up, bitch," he growled, prying open one of the boxes.

"Or do you think because you're just hitting the safe deposit boxes no one will ever know?"

"I said shut it." He kicked the table in the middle of the room toward me as a threatening gesture.

"It's an excellent plan, except for the fact I can identify you. At least your friends have caps and sunglasses on." That was everything I knew about the situation, and all the information I could relay to Carver. It was up to him now.

"I swear to god, if you make one more sound, I will blow your fucking brains out." He dropped what he was doing and towered over me, pressing the muzzle of his gun against my forehead. "Not a goddamn peep." I stared up at him, not afraid. "Bang," he taunted, but I didn't flinch.

Now probably wasn't the best time to inform him he was under arrest, considering the fact my gun was still behind the counter in my purse.

After a moment, he stepped away and slipped the gun back on his hip as he continued to pry open and ransack the boxes. I had to give him credit. He had a talent for getting them open in record time.

I glanced around the room for a possible weapon. The only thing I spotted was the metal letter opener he was using to jimmy the boxes. He placed it on the table as he dumped the contents of the current box into the drawstring bag he brought with him. I snatched it from the table in one quick motion. Luckily, he didn't notice it was gone or that I moved from my spot.

The sound of gunfire erupted from the lobby, and he stopped. Straining to hear, I heard someone announce, "Federal agents." Then more shots were exchanged. Those words caused the bank robber to become frenzied. He dumped the rest of the box into the bag, pulled the string closed, and slipped it underneath his jacket.

"You're going to get me out of here," he said. "Is there a back door or another exit?"

"Nope." Like I was going to tell him about the second

entryway from the manager's office.

"Well, we're going to find one." He pulled his gun and grabbed my arm, hauling me to my feet. "After you."

The gunfire stopped, and my guess was his two partners had been subdued. We were in the hallway when Michael came down the steps directly in front of us. His gun was out and aimed. The gunman grabbed my hair and pulled me against him. Using my body as a shield, he pressed his gun into my clavicle.

"Federal agent. Drop your weapon and let the lady go," Carver ordered. I met Michael's eyes, hoping he'd just take the shot anyway. "Drop it," he repeated.

The gunman pulled me closer, and I reached into my pocket, grasping the handle of the letter opener. It was better than nothing.

"I'm going out that door." The guy dragged me backward toward the locked vault. The problem was he had nowhere to go in this narrow hallway. "Once I'm free, I'll let her go. Just get me out of this fucking bank."

"I can't let you do that. Look around. You're out of options. We can all walk away breathing, but you need to listen to what I say. Now. Get. On. The. Ground," Carver said, using his calm authoritarian voice. He was waiting for a clear shot, and in these tight quarters, I had to do something to give him one.

"Michael," I interrupted, "you don't have a choice." I wanted him to take the shot, but he shook his head ever so slightly. "Michael, please."

The man pressed the barrel into my neck, threatening to fire.

"All right," Carver took his finger off the trigger and eased his gun down, "be cool."

The reprieve from having the firearm in his face caused the man to relax his grip just enough for me to elbow him hard in the solar plexus. I stabbed the letter opener into his abdomen, and spinning around, I knocked the gun from his hand. It clattered loudly on the tile floor while he howled in pain, and I attempted to get away. Before I could, he ripped the sharp, metal object from his body and slashed forward. Michael pushed me out of the way and aimed his gun.

"Don't you fucking move or I will shoot you."

Picking up the fallen gun, I pointed it at our suspect while we waited for backup to come down the steps.

TWENTY-SEVEN

"Guys, we've got two more in the lobby with fucking Uzis. They winged Sharpe," Boyle said as additional agents came to check on us.

Two agents I recognized led the bank tellers to safety while Carver and I kept tabs on the only remaining bank robber. Because of his stab wound, we weren't able to move him, so we were camped out in the narrow hallway, separated from the lobby. Our bank robber was doing a great job making a nice pool of blood on the floor. Apparently, he didn't know he wasn't supposed to remove an impaled object. The rest of the team was assessing the situation and waiting for the EMTs to arrive. Boyle was running point and giving out instructions.

As soon as he got the chance, he came to check on us. "You kids okay?" he asked, knowing he just missed something major.

"Peachy." I handed him the robber's gun and ran up the stairs to get my own before someone tried to catalog it as evidence. On my return trip, I noticed the cut on my arm. "Dammit."

Carver and Boyle glanced at me, and Boyle radioed for the tactical team to cover our captive and make sure he didn't bleed to death while we waited for the EMTs to arrive.

"Alex, are you okay?" Carver asked as we went into the wide open space of the lobby. Boyle's expression read worry, and Carver picked up on it instantly.

"It's just a scratch. Nothing much," I said.

"Blood exposure," Boyle added quietly. "With the way he's bleeding, it's a possibility. You need to get checked out."

The bastard better not have anything communicable, or I'd kill him. That is, if I hadn't already set that in motion.

Jablonsky arrived, along with a couple of ambulances and the local police department. The FBI would be sending their own agents to evaluate things, but by the time they bothered to show up, I would be long gone. Mark found an EMT examining my arm and came over to see what happened. After Carver and I explained the situation in the hallway, Mark ordered me to the hospital and put Carver in charge of babysitting me. Some reward for a job well done.

*   *   *

As I sat on a bed in the ER, staring up at the ceiling and wishing to be anywhere but here, I tried to relax. This was all precautionary and a waste of my time. The man who attempted to use me as a human shield was in surgery now. He refused to answer our questions or allow us access to his medical records. Basically, he was being a spoiled brat and trying to ruin my day the way I ruined his. Clearly, his mother never taught him not to play with sharp objects. Since we didn't know what diseases he might have, I was being made into a pincushion.

The nurse came in with half a dozen needles filled with high powered anti-virals, antibiotics, and whatever other preventatives they used in the event of exposure to diseases like HIV, AIDS, hepatitis, et cetera. Grimacing, I looked away as she stuck me multiple times, checked the site of my cut for obvious infection, and said I had to wait before being discharged.

"Are you decent?" Carver called from behind the

curtain.

"You know me. Am I ever decent?"

He pushed the curtain aside. "Are you okay?"

"I'm annoyed is what I am. This is pointless."

"It's just to be on the safe side," he insisted as I considered leaving without waiting for medical approval.

"It better be. I'm only twenty-six. Just imagine how much sex I'll miss out on if I end up contracting something from that lunatic."

"I'd be willing to take the chance and hook up with you," he joked. At least I hoped he was joking. "My guess is you're worth it." I slapped his arm. "Is that foreplay?"

"Thanks for not accidentally shooting me. That would have been worse. But if you had the shot..."

"I didn't. He kept moving behind you. Winging him wouldn't have helped matters, but we made a good team. Where'd you get the letter opener from anyway?"

"He brought it to jimmy open the safe deposit boxes. Apparently, he couldn't keep an eye on his tools. What do we know about him?" I asked.

"His name is Isaiah Thompkins. He has a few armed robberies in his past. A team is scoping out his apartment and workplace. The other two men from the lobby were his former cellmates from two different stints. He's a three striker now, and considering everything that's happened," Carver whistled, "the asshole might be better off dead than facing twenty-five to life."

I nodded, and we fell silent.

"Parker," Jablonsky stormed into the tiny cubicle allotted to me, "what did I tell you about having an emergency contact?"

"I don't need an emergency contact. This is Boyle's fault. That is one paranoid agent you have working for you. First off, we don't even know if I was exposed to anything, and second, we don't know if he has anything deadly or contagious."

Carver looked at me, knowing I was slashed with the same letter opener that had been shoved through Thompkins' gut, making my first point moot.

"Well, we're going to find out. *I* will find out." Mark

looked like he was in no mood to be reckoned with. The nurse came back, checked the injection sites, and took my temperature. "Is she okay?"

"You might experience some flu-like symptoms. It's a common side effect. Headache, dizziness, fever, joint pain, some nausea."

I sighed. Medicines and I rarely got along. With the exception of OTC pain relievers, I was a total lightweight.

"Do you have anyone to keep an eye on you just in case?" she asked, speaking directly to me and not Mark, even though he was the one who asked the question.

"Of course, she does," he said. Apparently being my emergency contact gave him some kind of authority over me. I'd have to remember to get that changed sooner instead of later. I signed the release forms and stood up. I was probably imagining the queasy feeling. It was the power of suggestion, so I tried using reverse psychology to counteract it. "Carver, take her home. I'll be there as soon as I get some answers."

"Guys," I protested, "I'm perfectly fine. Can't we just go back to work?" But my words fell on deaf ears as Carver led me out of the building.

*   *   *

Arriving home at almost nine p.m., I still wanted to accomplish a lot of things tonight. The first was to shower and change. It was one of the few rituals I had, a coping mechanism to deal with horrible days. Today counted.

"Can you call in an order for some sandwiches and soup from the deli around the corner?" I asked Michael as I grabbed a pair of jeans and a t-shirt from my drawer.

"No problem." He knew my habits. "Take your time."

When I emerged, my head was throbbing and the nausea had set in. I took a seat at my kitchen table and glanced at the wrapped sandwiches and vat of chicken soup he ordered, along with the stack of individually wrapped saltine crackers. Opening a pack, I nibbled on a cracker as Michael poured a glass of ginger ale and put it on the table in front of me.

"You were starting to look a little peaked in the car. Also puce, which isn't a good color on anybody," he teased. I finished my crackers and got up to get a pen and paper. "Now what are you doing?"

"Newsflash, we have reports to file and debriefs to go through." I tossed him a questioning look. "How long have you been doing this job?"

"Oh, so that's what you're doing with all those late night hours in front of the computer at the office." He slapped his palm against his forehead. "I thought you were surfing for internet porn like everyone else." He grabbed the pen from my hand. "Tonight, you're not writing a report." I glared at him, thinking this was his way of telling me to rest. I had no desire to rest. I had a desire to work. Getting a couple injections at the hospital didn't mean there was anything wrong with me. "I'm writing your report tonight and conducting your debrief."

"Michael," I sighed, "I can do it myself."

"No. Jablonsky gave me strict instructions. Frankly, our boss is scary as hell."

After picking up another pack of crackers and taking a sip of the soda, I told Michael what happened, and he scribbled furiously to keep up. Having a personal assistant was something I could get used to. Now if only he could cook and clean, then maybe he'd be a keeper.

TWENTY-EIGHT

By the time Jablonsky showed up at my apartment, I was curled up on the couch. Carver finished my paperwork and was putting the final touches on his. Even though he suggested I go to bed, I was exercising my dominion. Here, I was in charge. Queen of the castle.

"What's the verdict?" I asked, sitting up. The pounding in my head had increased.

"Douchebag's out of surgery. We had a lovely chat. He's undergoing some tests now. It'll be a few hours until we know if he's clean or not." Mark looked over Carver's shoulder before coming over to the couch and pressing the back of his hand against my forehead. "You can take down a guy twice your size in under a minute but fill a syringe with antibiotics and it knocks you on your ass. Crazy world we live in."

"Tell me about it."

"Mind if I watch the game?" Jablonsky asked, sitting on the other end of the couch and picking up the remote as I slumped back down.

"What game?"

"The sports channel is showing classic basketball games all week long." I hated basketball, and he knew it. "I thought since I was hanging around here while we wait for news on Thompkins, I could at least watch some television." He tossed a glance to Michael. "Carver, why don't you join me and grab the rest of those sandwiches?" I stared at Mark like he was insane. "Would you mind sitting up so there will be room for all three of us?"

"Fine." I got off the couch and went into my room. The entire point was for me to go to bed. Frankly, I was happy for the excuse to drop the tough act, but there was no reason Jablonsky needed to know that. There was also a good chance he already did.

Snuggling under the covers, I tried to get warm. Eventually, I dozed as the sound of sports commentary and hushed whispers carried through my apartment and into my bedroom, lulling me to sleep. A couple hours later, I climbed out of bed in search of something to drink. Jablonsky was asleep on my couch, snoring slightly. Michael was sitting at my kitchen counter, looking exhausted as he went over the reports. Mark brought a stack with him when he showed up, but I didn't bother to give them a second thought.

"Why don't you go home?" I whispered to Michael. "You look beat."

"I'm okay." He searched my face, assessing my condition. "You look better."

"Flattery will get you nowhere." I sat down next to him.

Mark brought dossiers on the three bank robbers, apparent links connecting Thompkins to Slidle, but as of yet, the fourth man, a getaway driver, hadn't been found. Neither had our tipster. There was a lot of work that still needed to be done to connect these random individuals together. We had several long hours ahead of us.

A few hours passed before the phone rang, jilting Mark awake. I grabbed the cordless phone from the cradle and answered. They put a rush on the test results. Even though Thompkins never tested positive for anything, his two prison sentences, questionable background, and horrible decision-making abilities made everyone a little uneasy.

"Thanks," I said into the receiver, hanging up the phone.

"Well?" Jablonsky rubbed his face. "What's the verdict?"

"He's clean," I said, returning to the paperwork and doing my best to hide the rush of relief. Sometimes, even I didn't know why I tried to act calm and collected all the damn time. "I'll probably get tested in six months just to make sure, but nothing to worry about, which means I got all those shots for nothing."

"Not for nothing." Jablonsky picked up his discarded gun and put his jacket on. "Take the morning off. I'll see you at the OIO building after lunch. We still have more work to do," he met my eyes, "especially since you're healthy as a horse."

"Sir?" Carver asked, making me giggle. Somehow, he missed the memo on Jablonsky's irritation with the word *sir*.

"Fine, you can have the morning off too. Just don't spread it around. I'd hate for everyone to think I'm turning into a sentimental softie." Mark shifted his gaze from Michael to me. "It's getting late. You should head out and let Parker get some sleep. The reports can wait until tomorrow."

"Aww, c'mon, just five more minutes," I said in a whiny voice, attempting to be jocular. Clearly, I was in a good mood. Jablonsky smiled and went to the door. "Thanks, Mark," I added sincerely.

"No problem." He nodded once and shut the door.

"Wow, you're a total teacher's pet. First, he shows up at your house, and then you get to call him Mark. No wonder you're the favorite," Michael teased.

"You're just jealous because he got to crash on the couch while you had to sit at the counter and work." I put my pen down and leaned back in my chair. There would be no more working tonight. I wanted to celebrate, although, quietly because I still had a lingering headache and chills.

He looked at me, and the grin grew on his face. "Your 'I'm too cool to give a shit' façade has some cracks in it. Quick, get the plaster." He nudged my arm. "I've never seen you this happy before."

"Just thinking about all that sex," I snorted.

"Is that an invitation?" He tried seductive but missed the mark after all the kidding around.

"Absolutely not." I laughed.

"Alex," he sounded slightly more serious, "are you a clip's half empty or clip's half full kind of girl?"

"As in the bullets in my gun?"

"Uh-huh."

I thought about it for a moment. "Neither. With half a clip I could take down two suspects, possibly three."

He rolled his eyes.

"What?" I asked.

"Nothing. I was just trying to determine if you believed you have the worst luck or the best luck. Things tend to work out oddly when we're together on an assignment. But it's you, so you probably don't believe in luck."

"I believe in something. No clue what. But definitely something. And right now, I'm willing to say I have some fantastic luck. If you asked earlier when I was getting stuck with needles, I would have told you I had awful luck. It's all about outcomes and perspective, isn't it?"

"It is." He squinted, trying to hide the smirk. "You're either the most put together person I know or the most insane." He shook his head. "Things are a lot more interesting here than they were in Los Angeles." He got up and stacked the folders on top of my table.

"Are you glad you transferred?"

"Yeah. And after a day like today, I'm going to ask to stay at the OIO. That is, if you're not going to add my lack of firing on Thompkins as another tally against me, even though I didn't have a clear shot."

"It only counts against you if I get shot or have to shoot someone for you." That happened once before, and there was no need for a repeat performance. "Before you go, would you mind telling me what happened in the bank? My viewpoint on the matter is limited, and it'd be nice to be prepared for tomorrow." I glanced at the time. "Later today," I corrected.

TWENTY-NINE

Michael Carver was one hell of a storyteller. I never knew this until he began explaining in vivid detail what happened outside the bank, during the breach, and in subduing the two other robbers. His words had me enthralled as my mind created the situation he was explaining. Either that or the nurse forgot to mention hallucinations and delusions as possible side effects.

"Boyle and I were staked out across the street, drinking our coffee and waiting for everyone to clear out of the bank. The security guard locked the front entrance, and a few people were straggling out the exit. Frankly, we figured it was time to call it a day, and Boyle was just about to send the tactical units home, but I spotted you through the window, going upstairs with some guy in tow."

"And you didn't assume it was a customer or booty call?" I quipped.

"No. You take your job too seriously for shenanigans, and something just didn't fit the bill. So we waited. A few minutes later, my phone rings. Keep in mind, by this point, another three people have left the bank, and with the way the damn windows are, we aren't certain how many people are still inside."

"I'm glad you answered."

He laughed. "I put the call on speaker, and at first, all we hear is static and fabric rustling around. Boyle's thinking you pocket dialed me accidentally, but then your voice comes through, explaining the situation." He shook his head, almost in disbelief. "You gave us the description, the number of suspects, their location, everything. It was fucking genius. I leave the line open while Boyle calls in our tactical support. Things sound a bit heated, and I decide to go in."

"You decide to go in?"

"Boyle and I decide to go in." He raised an eyebrow as if to ask if I was happy with the correction, but I remained silent. "The tac team is on the way, so we go in the exit, trying not to make a scene. As we walk in, the security guard tells us the bank is closed, and the two thieves make us. They were carrying fucking Uzis. Who carries an Uzi? We're not in some noir gangster flick."

"Did they say *your money or your life*?" I asked, but Carver wasn't amused by my question.

"Mr. Big Shot security darts out the door, so I'm guessing he's probably not cut out for security work."

"You're great at reading people." I winked.

"The three tellers are still behind the counter, and one of them starts screaming like a banshee and hits the silent alarm which notified the manager. What's his name?"

"Sharpe."

"As in he isn't very." Michael sighed, probably to add to the theatrics and drama. "He comes out of his office. One of the two gunmen decides to spray the place in bullets. Boyle and I duck behind the furniture, and Sharpe gets winged. It's nothing serious. A flesh wound to the upper arm, but he's howling like a werewolf during a full moon. We made the announcement and told the bastards to drop their guns."

"Did they comply?" I knew they wouldn't. No one that well-armed ever does.

"Fuck no. Boyle gets to Sharpe, and I'm considering taking one of them out when our tactical team bursts through the doors. The sons of bitches flip out because of the dozen agents in full assault gear. The one who shot Sharpe tried to make a run for it, but he got hit by a beanbag round. The other one was on the ground without any of us even having to ask."

"Accommodating."

"Hardly." Carver rolled his eyes. "They secured the main room, and that's when I went up the stairs so I could go down the stairs to get to you. Has anyone else considered how moronic it is to have only one way to get to the vault and safe deposit boxes? Asinine to go up and then down."

"There's a back doorway from the manager's office," I added. It opened up into the safe deposit box room, and it was how actual clients got access to their property. The bank robber who attempted to take me hostage didn't know this. No one did. And I didn't offer to divulge this piece of information. It was need to know, and the dirtbag definitely didn't need to know. "It's a security measure to deter thieves, robbers, and gunmen from knocking over the bank."

"Obviously, it works like a charm," he muttered sarcastically. He met my eyes, wondering if he should continue the story since I knew the rest. "Then I come down the steps, and I'm confronted by you and the idiot with the gun."

"Fun times."

"Yep."

"Just for the record, was I supposed to swoon and say something like *my hero*? Because there was a class taught at Quantico on how not to swoon in the face of danger."

He chuckled. "It's okay. I knew you were thinking it the entire time." He stood up, getting ready to leave my apartment. "Honestly." His tone was serious, but whatever he was going to say, he decided against. Instead, he pressed his lips together and went to my door. "Good night, Alexis."

*　　*　　*

That weekend, we went through all the information we had on our five currently incarcerated thieves. Most of them had records, but only Slidle and Henderson worked at the auto body shop. The local police department moved them to central booking and kept them segregated.

Jablonsky and Boyle dragged each of them to the OIO building, one by one, for questioning. The two Uzi-toting robbers, Robert Dunne and John Black, were hired for the job by Isaiah Thompkins. They were last minute replacements for Slidle and Henderson and had no previous knowledge of the ATM heists. They were only involved because of their connection to Thompkins, whose record indicated he met both Dunne and Black while in prison. They each had a laundry list of misdemeanors and felonies on their rap sheets which didn't seem surprising given their artillery of choice. Other than being promised a percentage of the bank cut, they knew very little of what was going on. A job was a job. No questions asked.

The more interesting connection was figuring out who comprised the original four man team, or three man and one woman team. Roxie Henderson was romantically involved with David Slidle. They met at work, and at some point, the clothes had come off. The strange thing was instead of having a natural progression to their relationship, they went from romance to robbery. It made no sense to me. Maybe it's why dating anyone you work with was so strongly cautioned against. One minute, you're in love, and the next, you're taking a bank teller hostage or driving a getaway car. Still, it would be nice to believe normal people existed and didn't one day wake up with the unshakeable desire to become felons.

For whatever the reason, Roxie went along with David's plan or his friend's, since we were still uncertain who the ringleader in all of this was. She wasn't going to narc on her boyfriend, and even now, she remained adamantly opposed to giving us any more information. David Slidle claimed I used unnecessary force and there was no legal basis for the warrant issued to search his apartment. Due to the lack of evidence we found inside, he maintained he was innocent and this was a frame-up. None of those things were true, but his lack of cooperation was frustrating. Jablonsky and Boyle questioned him numerous times, but they might as well slam their heads into the wall.

Maybe David's instead, but that would be deemed brutality and a violation of his civil rights.

There was only one source left for us to exploit, and right now, he was still recovering from surgery. Whatever Mark did to ensure our access to Thompkins medical records made Mr. Thompkins particularly cooperative, but due to his unstable condition, the doctors limited our contact with him. Aside from the twenty-four hour police detail posted outside his room, we were stuck waiting until he was no longer in the ICU before we could question him further. I just hoped he'd be able to give us answers and not more questions.

THIRTY

"No," Jablonsky said. Thankfully, we were in his office, away from the prying eyes of my fellow agents. "You're not going to question Thompkins. In fact, that's an order, Parker."

"What do you think I'm going to do? I'm not going to stab him again."

"No." Mark stood up and leaned across his desk. "Now get back to work."

"Yes, sir," I said through gritted teeth. It was Monday afternoon, and he was sending Boyle to talk to Thompkins. While I understood the need not to further agitate our one remaining chance at closing this case, from a creative standpoint, any threat I made would carry much more weight.

Just the thought of Thompkins had my skin crawling. It had been three days since the situation at the bank, but instead of being relieved, I was angry. If anyone should get to throw accusations at the bastard, it should be me. *Cool it, Parker*, I reminded myself.

Taking a few deep breaths and making sure logical thinking had returned, ushering out all my emotional turmoil, I pulled out the dossiers we compiled on Dunne, Black, Thompkins, Slidle, and Henderson. We had their phone records, and although they were primarily used to determine the interconnectedness of our five detainees, we didn't get the chance to thoroughly examine all the numbers listed. Someone had to do it, so it might as well be me.

After cross-referencing common numbers among the five different phone logs, accessing the billing information for the unknown numbers, and making a list of commonalities, I had a few possible leads on our getaway driver and tipster. There was a slim chance they were one and the same. Honestly, it didn't matter either way. The tipster hadn't done anything illegal. All he did was report the crimes. It was just the fact he knew such intimate details that led us to believe he was involved or closely related to someone who was. Putting things into perspective, I began narrowing our possibilities.

Hours later, we assembled in the conference room to go over our findings. I made some progress on identifying the fourth man, and our technical savvy brethren were comparing driver's license photos to the grainy security cam footage from outside the bank and convenience store in the hopes of finding a match. Boyle returned from his outing with some additional information, so the four of us took turns catching the rest of the team up to speed.

After reading the dozen possible names off my sheet of paper, Boyle perked up. One name, in particular, Garrett Neville, brought a smile to his face. Glancing at Carver, who had been sent to interview Roxie again, he let out a snicker. Jablonsky and I seemed to be the only two in the dark.

"Garrett Neville," Carver flipped through his notes, "is a nice guy. Quiet. Was always hanging out at David Slidle's place, playing video games, and drinking beer. Always kept to himself. He was the outcast of their group. But he never caused any problems, so they let him hang around with them."

"Unless he was playing *GTA*, I don't think he's our getaway driver," Boyle surmised. "He's twenty-two. Enrolled in junior college. Probably the younger brother type. He wants to fit in but doesn't. He used to work part-time at the auto body shop until he quit. That's when they hired Roxie Henderson to replace him."

"If anyone knows what's going on with Slidle, he would." Jablonsky tossed a glance my way. "Parker, why don't you have a friendly chat with Neville? I'm sure he's not used to beautiful women talking to him. Maybe you can turn on the charm and get him to open up."

"On it," I replied.

Carver gave me an encouraging look, and I copied Neville's address before exiting the conference room.

*　　*　　*

I knocked on Neville's door. The apartment building he lived in was populated by co-eds, and the hallways were filled with loud, boisterous, and drunk young adults. Sometimes, I was nostalgic for my college years, but this was a great reminder to be thankful that was in the past.

"Hang on," a voice called from the other side of the door, "I just need to find my wallet."

"Mr. Neville," I said, about to announce I was a federal agent, but instead, he opened the door wide, holding out a stack of dollars and clearly surprised to find me standing in front of him. "I'm not a prostitute. I'm a federal agent." I flashed my badge as he turned crimson.

"So-sorry," he stuttered. "I thought you were pizza." He stepped back. "Not pizza but bringing pizza. Co-come inside, please." He gestured that I should enter. Stepping into his apartment, I made sure no one else was present. There were no obvious signs of drugs, stolen cash, or weapons with the exception of the light sabers hanging on the wall. Since I wasn't a Sith lord, I wasn't too worried about their implications. "What can I do for you, um, Agent?"

"Alex." I gave him a coy smile. "Your name has surfaced in conjunction with an ongoing investigation." It was apparent from watching him that he knew exactly what was going on. "This will go much better if you elaborate before I have to start asking questions."

"How'd you know it was me?" His Adam's apple bobbed uncontrollably as he swallowed repeatedly.

"We're the federal government. Big brother is always watching." From the science fiction memorabilia around the room, I was positive he bought into conspiracy theories too. I snickered and cracked a smile. "Relax. Why don't you sit down and tell me what you know?"

"Are they watching me right now? Is that what the drones are for?"

It would be too easy to toy with him, so I shook my head. "I was only kidding. There were a lot of long hours, phone records, and basic investigation tactics that led us to you. Now," my tone grew stern, "we can do this here, or I can bring you in. Which would you prefer?" I flipped my hair behind my ear and tried the smile again. Apparently, he was mesmerized by my charm or afraid of the drones lurking outside his window because he quickly became an open book.

"I didn't go with them. They never asked me to. But they talked about it all the time. Finding better ways to make money. Easier ways. A few months ago, I was tinkering with a computer, and Dave asked if I could show him how it worked. Then we got talking about how everything is computerized now and wouldn't it be great if you could hack an ATM." He looked up, flustered. "Not that I ever would."

"Of course not."

"But yeah, that's when it started. He tried to make sure I didn't know what was going on, but I overheard a lot."

After listening to everything Neville said, I phoned Jablonsky for advice on what to do now. Neville was a material witness. He knew the connections among the players and the identity of the getaway driver. We couldn't leave him here, especially if someone else realized what he knew. At the same time, it would be a tough sell to get the kid to willingly go into protective custody, at least for the short-term.

"I'll send Carver to meet you. He has some visual aids that might help your dilemma."

THIRTY-ONE

Michael and I convinced Neville to come with us and to provide invaluable testimony on the ATM thefts. The failed bank robbery was being prosecuted separately since it relied too heavily on a separate team, despite the fact it had been David Slidle's plan. Slidle would be brought up on conspiracy to commit charges in conjunction with the bank robbery, but the heavier penalties for him lay with the ATM thefts.

The bank robbery case practically made itself since three of the four team members had been caught red-handed and in possession of firearms. They were all going away for a long time. That allowed our focus to shift back to the initial case, the ATM heists. The only common denominators present at both the bank hold-up and the heists were the getaway driver, John Seymour, and Isaiah Thompkins. Both men would be charged to the fullest extent on the ATM case and the bank robbery.

Neville told us everything he could. He was our tipster. He didn't think robbing anyone, even banks, was a reputable way to make money. At least someone had ethical standards and a conscience. His tips might have put him in danger had Seymour been concerned with being sought after, but he wasn't. Being the getaway driver during the bank robbery, he just wanted a cut without as much risk. Fortunately for him, we were willing to deal if he cooperated.

David Slidle masterminded the plan with the help of his girlfriend, Roxie. The two of them found maps, blueprints, and schematics for the ATMs. From the information we found in Roxie's apartment, I was willing to wager she was the brains and David was the brawns. Despite the fact she had accused him of all of it, upon a second search of her apartment, this time for drugs, we found a false wall in her closet where she kept her stash. There were dozens of empty prescription pill bottles, and we believed she spent her money on pharmaceutical grade narcotics and needed more cash to refill her supply. David had the connections and the muscle to pull this off. He had questionable friends, namely Isaiah Thompkins.

Slidle used his friends as additional support during the ATM snatch and grab and the convenience store hit. His team consisted of his friends, Isaiah Thompkins, John Seymour, and Roxie Henderson. Thompkins and Seymour met Slidle while getting their cars repaired years ago, and they had been close ever since. Seymour had no prior record but was willing to go along with everyone else. He was a follower, and Slidle had been the leader, or at least believed he was. Roxie encouraged him, even though she denied this fact vehemently. The skeletons in her closet said otherwise. And while Thompkins might have boasted about being reformed, the statistics said differently. Repeat offenders continue to offend repeatedly.

After Roxie and Slidle got pinched, Thompkins wasn't willing to let the perfect plan go to waste, so he called in his two former acquaintances, Dunne and Black. The two had some B&Es and larceny charges, but neither was a criminal genius. They were simply continuing to do the only thing they knew how to do, steal things. This time they got caught. The Uzis they brought into the bank were provided to them by Thompkins, who by all accounts was the only actual hardened criminal in the bunch. The rest seemed to be wayward misfits, pursuing their own personal agendas.

"A drug addict, an auto mechanic, a dumb schlub, one hardened criminal, and two lackeys walk into a bank," Carver said. "Want to hear the punch line?"

"The punch line is we got them."

"Precisely." He pulled up a chair and sat across from me, putting his feet on the edge of my desk. "May I take you out to celebrate, Agent Parker?"

I shook my head. "I'm not in the mood."

"That's why we are going to drink. To put you in the mood."

Logging off my computer and putting my report in the top drawer for tomorrow, I leaned back in my chair and assessed Michael. "It's getting easier, isn't it?"

"What?"

"This job. The work is still daunting, but," I frowned, "it's not like I'm surprised to find out Henderson lied to us or Thompkins was so desperate to get away that he'd rip a letter opener out of his stomach to use as a weapon." I maneuvered through my muddled thoughts. "Easier isn't the right word, but I'm not sure what is. Maybe it's just me being cynical and jaded."

"You've always been cynical and jaded. You've got that agent prerogative. You always did." He stood up. "And now we're going to do what everyone else does to cope."

"Fine," I gave in, "but you're buying the first round.""

Part III:

The Final Chapter

THIRTY-TWO

A few weeks before the event...

The pain radiated up my side. I couldn't move, and I couldn't breathe. If the man above me applied any more pressure to my ribs, I was sure they would break. As it was, I wasn't positive they wouldn't be bruised and sore for the next few days. Resisting the physical urge to panic and flail, I carefully considered my options before making a decision. I slapped my palm against the dingy red mat. Agent Michael Carver immediately released his grip and leaned back on his haunches. I took a deep breath and flattened out on the floor, no longer forced into an uncomfortable contortion. I shut my eyes and put my hands over my face as I attempted to shut out the world.

"You're distracted. Where's your head?" Michael asked, laying on the mat next to me and staring up at the ceiling. We spent the early morning sparring in the FBI's gym. "First of all, I've never managed to pin you in that hold before, and second, since when do you tap out?"

I sighed and moved my hands to my torso, gingerly

assessing the area for tenderness. "I'm having an off day. Plus, it's too early in the morning for hand-to-hand combat." He hadn't done any damage. Well, maybe just to my pride.

"Alexis," he bumped his shoulder against mine, "what's going on?"

"Nothing." I considered sitting up, but that required too much energy. "I'm just tired. I haven't been sleeping well lately."

"When was the last time you got laid?" he asked, and I kicked him in the shin. "That long, huh?" He rubbed his leg. "I only ask because you might be in need of some extracurricular stress relief."

Carver tended to flirt. He also tended to be a jackass, and sometimes, he came off a little too pigheaded and misogynistic for his own good, despite my best efforts to knock some sense into him. But we were partnered together often enough that I considered him a friend and sometimes valued his opinion. However, this wasn't one of those times.

"Let me guess, you're offering."

"Maybe I would have, but you kicked me. So no. This well-formed male specimen is not available to be your plaything." He smirked. "Unless you ask nicely." I rolled my eyes. "In all seriousness, Alex," he offered a hand and helped me up, "is everything okay?"

"Everything's fine. Maybe I'm coming down with something. Change of seasons makes most people sick, right?"

He didn't buy it, but when it came to interrogation techniques, he knew I wouldn't budge. We parted ways, heading off to the separate locker rooms to shower and dress for another fun-filled Monday at the Office of International Operations.

I practically collided with him on my way out the door. My chest pressed against his, and he grabbed my shoulders, steadying me. From the look on his face, I knew he wouldn't leave well enough alone.

"Your head's still in the clouds, huh? Maybe I should have joined you in the shower."

"Maybe I'll report you to Jablonsky for sexual harassment, and you can spend the next few days watching the sensitivity training videos and brushing up on proper social etiquette with the legal department," I retorted. First, he tried to break my ribs, and now, he was busting my chops. Hell of a way to start the day.

Looking appropriately repentant, he held the door for me and dropped the sexist remarks. Once inside the elevator, I let out a sigh. Today began on the wrong foot, and it didn't need to get any worse. A bit of explanation for my snappish attitude might be in order.

"Michael," I stared at the bottom of the door, "this case is getting to me. I don't know why, but it is."

"It's getting to all of us," he admitted. "Bombers are a scary, disturbing lot. Particularly this one since we have yet to determine what he wants. Anonymous explosions scream terrorism whether it's one homegrown lunatic or an entire international sleeper cell. There's the possibility for mass casualties, hysteria, panic," he maneuvered around to stand in front of me, "that's why it's our job to keep it together. Can you keep it together, Agent Parker? Because someone's gotta think calmly and rationally about things if we have any hope of stopping these sick, twisted bastards."

I stared into his brown eyes. This was the first time I ever felt so overwhelmed and helpless since becoming a federal agent almost five years ago. Carver and I graduated from Quantico together, and eventually, we were both assigned to the OIO, a division of the FBI. After completing our two years of training, we had worked numerous cases from forgeries to bank robberies to arms dealing. Currently, we were investigating a local car bombing. There had been only one incident, but based on the crime scene, the bomb had been planted intentionally in a public place, just outside the courthouse. However, it had been inadvertently thwarted by a highly astute meter maid who reported the illegally parked vehicle and had it towed to impound where it had done nothing more than blow the nearby vehicles sky high. It was dumb luck that had prevented dozens of casualties and fatalities.

The motivation behind the car bombing would have been questionable if a threat hadn't been delivered to FBI headquarters after the explosion, warning of another impending attack. The ominous words declared this one would not be as easily avoided. We were on a collision course for destruction and death unless we pooled our resources and identified the bomber and the target. At the moment, we had no solid leads. Assuming this wasn't a bluff, we were running out of time. The uncertainty of our success seeped into my subconscious, affecting my sleep and everything else. Self-doubt and fear were my enemies.

"I'm afraid of the price of failure." I bit my bottom lip, hoping Carver would say something reassuring.

"We won't fail." He tried to play it off as a joke, but he was scared too. "You and I both scored off the charts. We've closed countless cases and impressed everyone around here with our superior deductive skills. The only reason we haven't cracked this one yet is to give someone else a chance to play hero, right?"

"In that case, I'll sit this one out, and you can play hero. Maybe afterward I'll even let you demonstrate some of those extracurricular stress relief techniques of yours." It was a joke, but it's what we did to avoid the seriousness of the situation. It was our coping mechanism and one that many in the law enforcement community exercised on a regular basis. To work a job like this, you had to find a balance from the harsh realities that existed in the dark underbelly of society.

"Empty promises, but on the off chance you're serious, I'll consider it added incentive for finding a lead." He winked.

The elevator doors opened, and SSA Mark Jablonsky spotted us as we exited the elevator. Our boss didn't look happy.

"Parker. Carver. Conference room. Now," Jablonsky barked, pausing after each word as if it were its own sentence. That was never good.

We followed him into the room and took a seat at the table. A dozen agents were already inside discussing the forensics team's findings concerning the makeup of the bomb and the materials used for the detonator.

"The residue found does not match the chemical composition of any military-grade incendiary device or any that are manufactured or used by any governments or private corporations that we are aware of," said Agent Sam Boyle. "The bomb was homemade and by someone who knew exactly what they were doing." He called our attention to an image of what was left of the detonator. "Although it was almost completely decimated in the explosion, our technical team has reconstructed what they believe was the detonator switch." The image on the screen changed to a computer rendition. "There was a built-in failsafe and a timer. On the bright side, it doesn't appear the bomb had a remote trigger. So assuming he sticks to the same signature, if this happens again, we should be able to disarm it without the bomber being able to cause a premature detonation."

"The problem is," Jablonsky took over the briefing, "it also means the bomber doesn't have to be anywhere in the vicinity. The unsub values his own life. He's smart and calculating. We can't expect him to make any stupid mistakes, so we have to be on top of this."

Closing my eyes for a second, I didn't feel on top of anything. Carver was right. I needed to get my shit together. All I needed was a decent night's sleep to give my mind and body time to regroup. Was that too much to ask?

Boyle began handing out assignments as he divvied up the list of materials used in the bomb. If we could figure out where the items were bought, then we might be able to identify the bomber. Half the agents left the conference room to begin locating suppliers. Another group of agents was assigned to scrub the surveillance footage from where the car had been prior to its impoundment. There was a chance the bomber might be identified from when he planted the bomb. The last few agents, including Carver, were sent to locate the owner of the vehicle and determine why someone would want to blow up his car.

"Parker," Jablonsky said as everyone filed out of the room, "you've barely left the building in the last three days, ever since we received notification of the explosion. So what have you got?"

"Not a damn thing."

Mark sat on the edge of the conference table and propped a leg up on one of the chairs. He wasn't about to accept that as a valid answer.

"None of it makes any sense. And if it does, I can't see it," I said.

"Okay, let's just talk it out. What do we know?"

"The car belongs to Douglas Haze, an assistant district attorney. It was parked in one of the reserved spots in front of the courthouse, and from the copy of the ticket, it remained in that spot for almost four days. After the permitted seventy-two hours, the city was notified of the violation, and the car was towed to the police impound lot. Six hours later, at approximately noon on Thursday, the bomb went off. Based on the blast, it is estimated there was enough explosive inside the car to take out a thirty foot radius."

"If the vehicle wasn't moved, it would have taken out nearby pedestrians, possible motorists, and other parked cars. What else?"

"As far as I can see, it would have been a random act of violence." I shook my head, hoping to knock something important loose. "I checked the court's docket. There weren't any high-profile cases on the schedule. Noon is in the middle of the day, and since judges tend to stay in chambers to enjoy their lunch hour, the likelihood the explosion was meant to target one of them doesn't seem very likely. And given that Mr. Haze hadn't moved his car in days, how could anyone assume with certainty he'd return on that day and time to his vehicle?" I got up to pace. "Could the target be the courthouse and not any particular person?"

"It was too far from the building to cause any structural damage."

"Maybe it's a political statement."

"All right, let's get back to the facts and stop with the conjecture for a minute."

"That's all I've got." I stopped pacing and slumped back in the chair. "Mr. Haze hasn't been to court in weeks. He's on vacation, according to his assistant, and he hasn't been assigned any new casework by the district attorney. None of this makes any sense."

"If Haze hasn't been to court in weeks, why was his car parked outside the courthouse for the last four days? How did it get there?"

"I don't know." There wasn't any way to determine how the car got there or who drove it when the only thing left was a charred, metal heap. It wasn't like it could be dusted for fingerprints.

Jablonsky looked like he had an idea as he stepped away from the table. "Let's go, Parker."

THIRTY-THREE

Jablonsky and I stood in the small office of Mr. Haze's assistant, Martha Reid. She was on the phone with someone and would periodically hold up her pointer finger in a *wait just a moment* gesture and then continue to scribble notes on the legal pad in front of her. If she held up her finger one more time, I might have to make a similar gesture of my own.

As we waited, Mark caught my attention and cast his eyes toward the door. Catching his drift, I whispered some excuse and left the office. Haze's office was across the hall, so I leaned nonchalantly against the door and turned the handle, but it didn't budge. Didn't the prosecutor trust anyone?

Wandering the hallways, I hoped to find someone more helpful than Mrs. Reid. The problem with these legal types was they were always busy, bogged down with paperwork, clients, or booze. Occasionally, a combination of all three. Eventually, I ended up in the copy room. An intern or paralegal worked the machine as she collated stacks of paper and cursed under her breath.

"Excuse me," I said, causing her to jump.

"You must be the new temp," she responded

automatically. "This place has been insane since one of the ADAs took a leave of absence. I don't see why they aren't looking for a temporary replacement for him instead of hiring more of us to handle the research for his current caseload and expecting us to keep the other prosecutors up-to-date on everything." She let out an annoyed sigh. "Had I known this was the amount of work I'd be doing, I would have become an attorney myself."

"Miss," I pulled my credentials and flipped them open for her to see, "I was hoping you wouldn't mind telling me about Mr. Haze."

"Great, now they expect me to deal with the cops too." Correcting her would only lead to further irritation, so I let it slide. "What do you want to know?" She continued collating and stapling.

"What's your name?"

"Courtney Dupree, paralegal to the ungrateful and self-righteous." And I thought I was having a bad day. "Sorry," she flicked her gaze to me, "I'm a temp. The agency sent me here two weeks ago. I only met Mr. Haze once." She laughed. "He was going out the door as I was coming in, and he spilled coffee on my blouse." Laughter seemed like a strange response to have in accordance with that type of recollection. "To make up for it, he hands me a twenty dollar bill to cover the dry cleaning cost, apologizes, and walks away. The joke was on him since I only own wash-and-wear."

"He sounds like a nice guy."

"Sure, I guess. I've never seen him again." She grabbed the final sheet of paper from the copy tray and finished stapling. "You were probably hoping I would be more helpful."

I shrugged. "Do you remember anything else about that day? What he was wearing or driving? If he seemed panicked or in a rush?"

"It's been two weeks, and it wasn't like I was paying that much attention. He had a great smile." She looked a little sheepish. "I guess he was probably wearing a suit or sports coat. And he seemed fine. Normal, just like everyone else. Maybe a little preoccupied since he did bump right into me, and less of a jackass than most, seeing as how he gave me cash for the coffee stain."

"He's a lawyer. Maybe it was consideration, so you wouldn't sue him."

She picked up the stack of papers and headed out the door. Perhaps she was too busy to laugh at my attempt at levity.

"Can you point me to someone who might know Mr. Haze a bit better?" I asked.

She came to a complete halt in the middle of the hallway. "Martha would be your best bet. She's his assistant. Why are you asking about him? Did he do something wrong?"

"His name has surfaced in regards to a current investigation," I repeated automatically. This was one of those lines I could utter in my sleep from overuse. "Thank you for your time, Ms. Dupree."

She continued down the hallway, and giving up on my pathetic attempt at snooping, I went back to Mrs. Reid's office to see if the woman had concluded her phone call or if Jablonsky ripped the jack from the wall.

"Frankly, sir, if you want information on any of Doug's current cases, you'll need a court order or permission from the district attorney," Reid's voice traveled through the closed door and could be heard in the hallway.

Going back inside, I shut the door and stood near the back wall so as not to interrupt. Apparently, Jablonsky was questioning her on upcoming trials and hearings.

"Fine." He pulled out his phone and made a call. He had a lot of professional acquaintances in a lot of different places, and it wasn't surprising that he had the DA's number saved in his phone. He gave a brief explanation and hung up. A second later, Reid's phone rang, and she answered, provided a couple perfunctory answers, and put the phone in its cradle. "Happy?" Mark asked.

"Here's the list of pending trials and corresponding court dates for the days and times you requested," she said. Since the information was already prepared for us, it made no sense why she tried to give us the runaround. I didn't like it.

Turning his back to her, he scanned the sheet and looked at me, hoping I would take over.

"Mrs. Reid, do you have any idea where Mr. Haze went or how long ago he made these arrangements?"

"I'm not his keeper. I have enough to do here."

"Does Mr. Haze have a family or a significant other? It'd be incredibly helpful to have some insight into his private life," I said.

"This is my job. This is a place of business, not some sorority house." She fixed me with a hard stare. "You should realize how important it is to exercise professionalism. If he didn't tell me, then I didn't ask." Her attitude seemed cold and detached, but when she spoke of him, she referenced his first name. There had to be a familiarity, despite her comments. My gut said she knew more than she was letting on.

"Of course, ma'am. Thank you for your time." I gave her a smile and headed for the door. Turning back to her, I asked, "When's Doug supposed to return from his absence?"

"He didn't say." Betrayal flickered across her face. "He didn't bother to tell me he wasn't coming back. It's not like I've been his assistant for years, always on top of things, making sure not to cut any corners, and that all the rules are followed to the letter." She sounded bitter. "Two weeks ago, he says goodnight, as he did every evening, and that was it. The next day, I was scrambling to get another ADA to cover for him. He didn't even have the courtesy to tell me to make preparations for his absence."

"Did he ever do that before?" I asked.

"No, but I got an e-mail the next morning saying he was taking a sabbatical and to pass along his caseload. No one questioned it, so I figured he must have spoken to the boss about it. I haven't heard from him since. Who knows what's going to happen to me or my job if he doesn't come back?"

Nodding, I continued out the door.

"Get anything useful?" Jablonsky asked as we left the building.

"Not really." I stopped, reconsidering. "I spoke to a

temporary assistant, Courtney Dupree. She said she was called in the same day Haze left. She also said they've been requesting quite a few temps to help with research to make up for the shortage of attorneys."

"It looks like Haze planned to leave all along, even if he didn't bother to inform his assistant," Jablonsky said.

Sighing audibly, I leaned my forehead against the glass window as we drove back to the OIO. "Our leads are so farfetched right now. Haze might not have anything to do with the explosion. I mean, seriously, who blows up their own car?"

"Parker, we work this case just like any other. You're trying to jump ahead because of the ticking clock, but keep in mind, just because some asshole calls in a threat, it doesn't mean it's real. It also doesn't mean we should be sloppy. We go where the evidence leads. Sometimes, it takes us to a dead end, and sometimes, it goes straight to the person responsible. Right now, we don't have enough to do anything else. This is square one."

"There has to be more," I argued. "Something has to be there."

He gazed at me for a long moment, probably too long for someone driving a car. "This might be it. We work with what we have and hope it's enough. Either it will lead somewhere, or it won't. We can't always stop things from happening."

That was something I wasn't willing to accept. If a train was speeding toward you, there had to be some way to stop it. We knew it was coming. Now all we had to do was locate the emergency brakes.

"I don't like it either," he said after a time. "I'm not saying we should throw in the towel, but you've been at this since we got the call. Tonight, you're going home early. Fresh eyes and a clear mind work wonders."

"Okay." For once, we were in complete agreement on the insane work hours I tended to keep.

THIRTY-FOUR

Arriving home, I phoned in an order for Thai food, showered, and changed into something comfortable. The wheels in my head were turning around the explosion, ADA Haze's sudden disappearance, and the comments Courtney Dupree and Martha Reid made. "Where is the freaking off switch?" I grumbled, turning on the television and channel surfing for a pointless distraction. Stopping on a movie that touted shirtless men with supernatural abilities, I reached for a notepad and started constructing a timeline surrounding Haze's sudden leave of absence. I just added the run-in with Dupree when there was a knock at my door.

"You're not Thai food," I said, sounding slightly disappointed.

"Glad to see your observational skills aren't suffering any." Carver entered my apartment without invitation. "By the time I got back, Jablonsky said you went home for the night." He gave me a look. "What gives?"

"I needed a break and some distance. Mark agreed or suggested it. At this point, I'm not sure which is more accurate."

Carver took his jacket off and wandered into my living

room. He picked up the notepad and read my scribbles before dropping it on the couch cushion. "This is what you call taking a break?" He sat down and stared at the TV. "I've seen this movie. Is it the second or third? Either way, they all turn into werewolves at the end."

"Michael, why don't you come in and make yourself comfortable?" I remarked.

"Sure, thanks." He unhooked his gun from the holster on his hip and put it on my end table. "I figured you'd be burning the midnight oil and thought you'd like an update on what we uncovered today."

"You could have called."

"True, but we both work better with visual aids," he picked up my notepad as if to demonstrate his point, "so this made more sense." He made an obvious pretense of looking around my apartment. "Unless I'm interrupting something. Maybe a date or a meeting with a male prostitute." I glared at him. "Female prostitute?" I made a disgusted sound, and fearing for his own safety, he cracked a smile. "Take it easy. I was only teasing. I thought you might like some company. If you don't want to talk about the case, we don't have to. Or I can go. No hard feelings either way."

Before I could answer, there was another knock at the door. This time, dinner arrived. I paid the man and brought the cartons into the living room, dropping them on the coffee table.

"I might have been overzealous in my ordering. I'd like you to stay for dinner, and we can go over whatever you and the other guys found today. Just stop with the quips, I'm not in the mood."

He smiled, appearing as if he just won some kind of prize. "Okay, Alex. Thanks."

He picked up the plastic utensils as I selected a carton of noodles, leaving him two other options to choose from. One of these days, I would learn to order one thing at a time, but on the plus side, leftovers often lasted through the week.

"We couldn't locate Douglas Haze," he said around a mouthful of shrimp. "Sam and I checked his house, spoke to a couple of his neighbors, pulled his phone records, and talked to his friends and family. The guy disappeared."

"What'd we get on the bomb materials and the vehicle?"

"When I left, they were still trying to identify the suppliers, but nothing was out of the ordinary. My guess would be the bomb could have been constructed from the products they sell at any hardware store. We have a few experts from the PD's bomb squad checking for a signature on the detonator. The real kicker is the footage we have of the car prior to its impoundment."

"The suspense is killing me." Leaning back against the sofa cushion, I curled my legs underneath me, too worn out to pace.

"From what we can tell, the guy who dropped off the car in front of the courthouse resembles Haze. It might even be him. We're working on angles and facial recognition right now, but suffice it to say, it doesn't appear anyone else approached the vehicle except the meter maid and the tow truck driver." Carver put the carton on the table. "The problem is," he chewed on the inside of his lip for a moment, thinking, "we ran Haze's credit cards to try to locate him. He bought a bus ticket two weeks ago for Indianapolis, and there hasn't been a bit of financial activity since then."

Either Haze was our bomber, or someone with a slight resemblance was. "Any possible ideas what his motivation would be, assuming Douglas Haze is behind the explosion and threats?"

"Disgruntled employee or a worker drone disenchanted with the entire legal system."

"Aren't we all?" I blew out a breath. "And if it isn't Haze, we need to determine who had access to his car. Were there any signs of tampering?" Michael looked at me as if I were insane. "Right, it blew up." I rubbed my eyes. "I guess that means I really do need a break." I tossed the notepad on the coffee table and settled into the cushions. Closing my eyes, I added, "Talk me through your thought process. Have you reached any conclusions?"

"Besides the fact you're suffering from sleep deprivation and have horrible taste in movies, I think Haze might be our guy. No one drops off the face of the earth. Maybe he needed to take the leave of absence so he could build the bomb. It's not like he's an engineer."

"But if you're planning an attack and you don't want to get caught, you don't plant the bomb in your own car. You don't dramatically change your routine, and you don't leave it parked someplace you know it's going to get towed away." I opened my eyes and studied Carver. "That's it." I smiled as the light bulb came on.

"The target wasn't the courthouse. It was the impound lot. But how'd he know the vehicle would get towed there?"

"A good guess," I shrugged, "but why target an impound lot? It seems contradictory to the follow-up threat we received."

"Unless," he grabbed his phone, "what if the explosion was to throw us off the scent of something else?" He finished dialing as I tried to process what he said.

"Like what?" It made no sense, but he ignored me as he waited for whoever was on the other end to answer.

Eventually, he hung up. "Dammit. I wanted Boyle to get a manifest of the other impounded vehicles. Maybe one of them was used in the commission of another crime, and the police haven't made the connection yet. An explosion would detract from any other pending investigations."

"Apparently, I'm not the only one who needs sleep. Your speculation sounds like a conspiracy theory."

"Do you have any better ideas?" he asked, and I shut my mouth.

We were getting closer in our assumptions, but we needed facts to support the beginnings of this new theory. It was almost eight. In twelve hours, I'd be back at work.

He turned around to see what I was looking at. "Okay. Tonight, we'll leave the investigating in the hands of our capable co-workers, and tomorrow, we'll see if anything they uncovered supports my theory."

"Okay."

"Now, do you want to finish watching the movie? I think there's another forty minutes until they all turn into werewolves."

"Sure, mindless drivel is precisely what I need right

now."

He found the remote and put the TV back on as I grabbed the throw from the back of the couch and got more comfortable. As the movie played, it became apparent the only saving grace it possessed was the shirtless men. The forced dialogue and overacting droned in the background as my mind tried to wrap itself around Carver's newfound theory.

At some point, I fell asleep because when I opened my eyes again, my head was resting against his shoulder and the sun was peeking through my blinds. Sitting up, Michael opened his eyes and stretched.

"What time is it?" he asked.

"I don't know. Seven, maybe?" I blinked a few times to clear the blurriness from my vision. "Seven-fifteen," I confirmed. "Shit. We're supposed to be at work in forty-five minutes. Why didn't you wake me last night?"

"Oh sure, blame me. I'm not the one who fell asleep on your shoulder." He went into the bathroom and shut the door while I set the coffeemaker to brew and got changed in my bedroom. "Do you think anyone will notice I'm wearing the same clothes from yesterday?" he asked as he went past my room.

"Lose the tie and keep your jacket on to hide some of the wrinkles." I finished dressing and opened the door. "I'm sorry. You should have woken me." I went into the bathroom and shut the door.

By the time I came out, Michael was halfway through a cup of coffee. He holstered his gun and folded the blanket on my couch. He looked like he had been putting in some long hours with his one day's worth of stubble and dark circles underneath his eyes, but that wasn't anything out of the ordinary for a federal agent.

"You said you haven't been sleeping lately, so I wasn't about to sabotage your only opportunity to get some rest." Sometimes, the jackass could be a sweet guy. "Thanks for the coffee." He took a final sip. "I'll see you at work."

THIRTY-FIVE

I arrived twenty minutes late. Jablonsky didn't say a word as I snuck into the back of the conference room and caught the tail-end of the briefing. The bomb-making materials had been tracked to two local hardware stores. If the bomber paid with a credit card or check, we'd have solid ground to stand on. The DA's office sent over Haze's employment records because he was currently our only person of interest. Agents were evaluating his caseload to determine if the ADA's sudden disappearance had anything to do with an upcoming case. Right now, we assumed Haze was the bomber or someone he pissed off was.

Right before everyone was dismissed, Carver spoke up. "Parker and I reevaluated the circumstances surrounding the explosion, and we think the intended target was actually the impound lot."

"It wouldn't hurt to check into that," Agent Boyle said. Prior to their reassignment at the OIO, Boyle had been Carver's supervisor at the LA field office.

Jablonsky nodded. "Since it's your idea, why don't the two of you go make friends with the local LEOs and see what they have to say?"

No one else wanted to go to the precinct and step on the police department's toes. The PD didn't like us, and this would probably make things worse. Pissing contest here we come.

"This seemed like a much better idea last night," I mumbled, signing a sedan out of the motor pool. "Do you have any cop friends you can ask for a favor?"

"I don't spend my time with cops," Carver said, illustrating exactly why two branches of law enforcement couldn't get along. "But I'm sure they won't have a problem. Bombings fall under federal jurisdiction."

"Wow, someone's an optimist." I turned the key in the ignition.

"Hey, maybe it's because I got to sleep with you last night." He chuckled, but I remained silent, driving out of the parking garage faster than necessary. "Y'know," as he continued his diatribe, he began to sound more sincere, "we're trained to be on alert all the time. Every minute of the day we might be expected to report in because of some crime or catastrophic event. The training and muscle memory become our default settings. Back at Quantico, they knocked out our casual, relaxed attitudes, so it's no surprise when everyone ends up wound tighter than a ball of yarn, especially when we're led to believe another attack might be imminent." I felt his eyes on me but kept mine trained on the road. "It's that constant unease that was keeping you awake. Last night, you had the opportunity to let your guard down because someone was there, watching your back." His words caught me by surprise, and I turned to look at him. "Confession time," he admitted, "since we've been investigating this case, I haven't slept more than four hours straight through. I bust your balls, Parker, but I get it."

"Don't you dare start saying crap like that. I'd hate to have to like you. You've been the bane of my existence for so long." I pretended to shudder. "My god, are you trying to make hell freeze over?"

He laughed, and for the first time in days, the job didn't seem quite as burdensome and isolating.

I pulled to a stop at the crime scene tape surrounding

what was left of the impound lot and got out of the car. Finesse. The plan was finesse.

We approached the uniformed officer standing guard to keep the looky-loos away. Displaying my credentials, I paired the federal agent badge with a warm smile.

"That was quick," Officer Molitao said as his gaze shifted from my photo identification to my face. "We only called your office ten minutes ago."

"Excuse me, sir," maybe I was overdoing the politeness, but it couldn't hurt, "but what are you talking about?"

"The body. Homicide's been here all night. But they just got the results back on the dental records."

"Officer," Carver stepped forward, reading the man's nametag but not attempting a pronunciation, "can you direct us to the detective in charge?" Molitao pointed his finger to a man standing in the midst of the rubble, and Carver lifted the crime scene tape. "After you," he said to me.

"Thanks," I said to the cop as I ducked under the tape. Grabbing Carver's arm, I whispered in his ear, "Did you hear anything about a body at this morning's briefing?"

"No, but if they just called, it's probably running around the circuit board at the office. I'll bet you twenty we end up getting a call before we finish talking to the detective."

"You're on."

Detective Jacobs was in charge of the scene. The impound lot looked like a junkyard after a massive fire. There were dozens of scorched vehicles. The initial blast had set off a few additional explosions as shrapnel and flames pierced the gas tanks of nearby cars and trucks. Honestly, the remnants looked like a scene out of an action movie. I stared at the destruction, amazed the damage had been reasonably contained.

Carver and Jacobs discussed the scene, but I couldn't concentrate on what they were saying. When I returned to reality, Jacobs was gesturing to a nearby van. "I guess you can understand why it took us so long to locate the body." He attempted a smile, but it didn't make it any further than his lips. "One of the clean-up crew found him yesterday afternoon when they attempted to move that derelict. The

ME had to run dental records because he was too well-done for anything else."

Resisting the urge to cringe at the crude comparison, I remained silent so he could finish the summation.

"We've scoured the rest of the area and tore everything else apart. There was just one body. Preliminary suggests he was dead long before the explosion since he had a bullet lodged in his chest."

"Who is he?" Carver asked.

Jacobs flipped open his notepad and skimmed the sheets before answering. "ADA Douglas Haze. Goddammit if someone on our side didn't get killed for fighting the good fight."

"This is an elaborate way to conceal a murder," I said. "We need records on the van, when it was brought in, who it's registered to, everything you have."

"My guys are already running down leads. I'd be happy to pass along our results," Jacobs said.

"Look, the explosion is federal jurisdiction, and your DB is in the center of our crime scene. Don't you think it might be in everyone's best interest to share? We can work conjointly."

"You want to catch a murderer," Carver chimed in since we were taking turns playing nice. "We want to stop a bomber. Our goals might not lead to the same person, but it'd be foolish to think they're unrelated." He spun in a circle to ensure a panoramic view of the lot. "The most important thing is to make sure this doesn't happen again."

"I'll get copies of everything we've found. Photographs, preliminary reports," Jacobs narrowed his eyes at me, "we'll share. But make sure you extend us the same courtesy if you make any headway on identifying the murderer."

"Thanks, pal." Carver extended his hand. "You got it."

"Detective." I nodded once, acknowledging his request and handing him my card. "I hope you'll be in touch."

On the way back to the car, Carver dialed our technical team and informed them of the incoming information. They could decide if they wanted to evaluate the scene themselves or if the PD did a decent job of cataloging everything.

After he hung up, I glanced at him. "You owe me twenty."

"Dammit. I shouldn't have believed a word that officer said." Despite our banter, the reality of the situation set in. "At least we found Haze."

"He's dead. We have no suspects. No leads. And all the work we've done on finding Haze in the hopes he was our bomber was a total waste of time and resources. Fuck." I slammed my palm against the steering wheel. "Now what are we supposed to do?"

"It's a start," Carver insisted. "Relax. If the intent of the bomber was to disguise the murder, then maybe there won't be any more bombings. This might be a single isolated incident."

"From your lips to god's ears."

THIRTY-SIX

Our priorities concerning the investigation shifted. There was no reason to focus on locating Haze. He was cooling his heels in the morgue. We were still trying to determine if Haze drove his car to the courthouse or if he planted the bomb. Although, that seemed completely convoluted given that he was dead and the threat was issued postmortem. Then again, we had to explore all avenues.

The purchase histories from the hardware stores resulted in a dead end. The items were bought almost three weeks ago with cash from one of the two stores. When we requested security footage from the store's CCTV, we learned they only maintained a digital copy for fourteen days before the files were deleted. One of our windows of opportunity just slammed shut.

"Carver and I are going back to the DA's office," Boyle announced, entering the conference room where we were camped out. "We'll question Haze's co-workers and see if they have alibis for when his car was left in front of the courthouse. With any luck, maybe someone will have something useful to say, particularly now that he's dead."

Jablonsky looked up and nodded. We should have been more thorough, but we didn't know that at the time.

"All right," I went to the whiteboard we were using to

diagram the progress we were making on the investigation, "where are we on identifying the car's driver?"

"We've input what we have into the facial rec software, but it's not much. There weren't enough points of reference. We've requested the data from the DOT cams. Backtracking, we might be able to determine where the car came from. It might be the only way to identify the driver," one of my fellow agents said.

Selecting a marker, I scribbled several questions on the board. We needed to identify Haze's killer, the car's driver, the bomb maker, and a possible next target. As I leaned against the table, I absently chewed on the marker cap while I studied the post-explosion photos.

"Here, Parker." Mark shoved a file box in my direction. "That's what the police department sent over. I know you've been itching to dissect it, so have at it."

"Thanks."

The rest of the world blurred into nothingness as I separated the information into relevant categories such as crime scene, bomb materials, Haze's remains, and miscellaneous items. By the time I finished sorting and updating the board, I was the only person left in the room.

Enjoying the solitude, I sat on top of the table and examined my handiwork. Haze's time of death was estimated to be between Sunday morning and Tuesday afternoon. The explosion occurred Thursday at noon, and the car was left in front of the courthouse on Monday. We needed to narrow the TOD window if we wanted to clear Haze as the bomber.

The rest of the scene was a mess of twisted metal and charred materials. Upon a secondary analysis, the bomb might not have been as powerful as we originally thought. The gasoline in the car combined with the gas tanks from surrounding impounded vehicles made the blast grow exponentially. It was a wonder the entire lot didn't go up in smoke.

Focusing on the courthouse parking lot, I noticed the vehicles were spaced farther apart and the parallel spots limited the chances of setting other cars asunder. If the car had not been moved, the explosion would have been smaller, but innocent bystanders might have been killed or maimed. Either way, it seemed like a lose-lose, and since this line of thought was neither here nor there, I returned my focus to our current theory. The explosion may have been designed to conceal Haze's murder, but why?

The ballistics report insisted the bullet came from a .38 caliber handgun. Based on the trajectory of the shot, it was fired from above. Perhaps the shooter was standing at the top of some steps or on a balcony when he shot Haze, or Haze was lying on the ground when he was killed. The striations were being run through the databases for a match to other crimes, but as of yet, the weapon hadn't been identified.

"You're still here?" Carver asked, coming into the conference room.

"Where else would I be? Any leads on identifying Haze's killer?"

"One of his most recent cases, a murder charge against Forrester Cline, got thrown out for improper procedure." Carver took a seat on top of the table next to me and studied the whiteboard. "Haze had the files and evidence locked in one of his desk drawers. He also hired a private investigator to tail the guy."

"That seems like stalker behavior instead of due diligence."

"Sam's checking into it now, but I'd say Cline seems like a good bet. Speaking of which," he reached into his pocket and fished out a twenty, "here."

I took the offered money and shoved it in my pocket. "Thanks."

"Why would an ADA still be investigating a closed case? Do you think they were gathering additional evidence to bring the guy up on other charges or in conjunction with another case?" Carver thought through the potential ramifications each answer held. He squinted into the distance and got off the table, flipping through the box of Haze's pending casework. Finding whatever he was searching for, he smiled brightly. "I gotta talk to Boyle." He dashed out of the conference room.

"I'll just wait here and continue to feel useless," I

announced to the empty room. Normally, I was on the ball, but this case left me flummoxed. Being stumped wasn't something I enjoyed. Shaking it off, I climbed down from the table, scribbled a few final notations on the board, and went to my desk to wait for Carver or Boyle to come back with something definitive.

"Okay, everyone, listen up," Boyle said, "it seems our man, Haze, was working on something off the books. Right now, we don't have any proof this is what led to his demise, but dimes to dollars, I'd say it's a reasonable assumption. Until it's proven otherwise or something else occurs, we're keeping tabs on Forrester Cline. I've forwarded copies of his arrest record and Haze's investigation to your inboxes. Get familiar with Cline, and tomorrow morning, we'll work out an assignment schedule to maintain round the clock surveillance on our newest person of interest. Until then," he glanced into the empty conference room, "continue what you're doing. We need to identify and locate the bomber before anything else goes up in flames."

Forrester Cline had been arrested on a first degree murder charge but was released because the search warrant wasn't properly filled out and signed. Everything the police recovered, including the murder weapon, was fruit from the poisonous tree and thereby inadmissible in court. Shit like this happened more often than it should, but it was the only way to attempt to create a fair judicial system. The theory was men like Cline would commit another offense, and as long as protocol and procedure were followed, the system would eventually win out. As the old adage goes, you don't bet against the house. After the charges against Cline were thrown out of court, ADA Haze began investigating Cline in conjunction with some conspiracy charges.

As I read the scanned pdfs of Haze's files, I realized the district attorney's office was in the process of compiling an extensive case against a homegrown militia group thought to have a stockpile of illegal weapons. The militia group was comprised of only three brothers, Tim, John, and Frank Farlow. Each was an outspoken anarchist, opposed to the government and everything it represented. The gun

Cline allegedly used in the commission of his crime traced back to the militia group.

The rest of the file detailed the selling and trading of weapons and munitions by the Farlow brothers. The DA hoped to add conspiracy and accessory charges before bringing a case against the Farlows. The state didn't want to have to dismiss another case without solid, irrefutable evidence. That read as motive to me.

Either the Farlows or Cline got wind of Haze's investigation and decided to pull the plug. Going so far as to blow up the man's car might be construed as a warning. However, if the explosion was a warning and not intended to conceal a crime, then why the cover-up? Why put Haze's body in the back of some van that might have only accidentally been blown sky high?

"Anyone have any information on the van they found Haze's remains in?" I asked.

A couple agents shrugged, but one of the more astute members of our team responded, "It's registered to a delivery service, Bates Movers." She clicked a few buttons on her keyboard. "They're a small independent service, but at least one of our suspects works there." I leaned over her shoulder as she pointed to a picture with a caption listing their employees. Frank Farlow.

"I'll be damned." I smiled. "How long was the van in impound?"

"According to police records," she clicked to a different window, "since Sunday."

A thought gnawed at the edge of my mind. I accessed Haze's phone records. A few calls came in over the course of the week, but based on duration alone, none of them had been answered since Saturday night. Had Douglas Haze been receiving threats? Running reverse lookups, I found seventeen calls, all lasting less than five minutes, from Bates Movers. Since they were placed after the close of business, I didn't think they were related to any moving needs. Aside from the frequency of calls to Bates Movers, there was only one other number that called numerous times over the last month. The number originated from a prepaid, unregistered cell phone. It was also the last number that phoned Haze on Saturday night.

"Does anyone have any friends at the NSA who can tell us what was said for three minutes on Saturday night between Haze and the mystery caller?" I asked. Most of my co-workers ignored me, a couple shot me dirty looks, and Carver chuckled. "C'mon, you know they're illegally wiretapping the entire nation."

Carver laughed, but Jablonsky and Boyle scowled at me. Apparently, I didn't need to take my political commentary comedy tour on the road.

"Parker, give me the number, and I'll see what turns up," one of the IT guys offered.

I highlighted the number and brought the copy of the phone log to him. With any luck, we'd eventually identify the caller, determine the reason for the constant calls back and forth with Bates Movers, and figure out who murdered Haze.

Over the course of the next few hours, the IT department determined the location where most of the calls were made. We couldn't narrow it down to a precise address, but it was in the vicinity of Forrester Cline's apartment building. There was a good chance Cline threatened Haze or lured him into a trap.

I let out an exhale as some of the weight lifted off my chest. There was still much more to do, but we had four suspects who could be killers, bombers, or both. Going back inside the conference room, I wrote each of their names on our board and everything we knew about them. I stared at the words, hoping for answers and coming up with nothing more than plenty of additional questions. Finally, I created a web overlay detailing the connections which reinforced my conclusion that we were on the right track, and then I called it a night.

THIRTY-SEVEN

The next morning, I was ready to dive into the investigation, but as I exited the elevator, I found Jablonsky standing at my desk. "Don't get comfortable," he warned. "Fill your thermos and let's go." Knowing better than to ask what was going on, I grabbed my travel cup from my bottom drawer, filled it with coffee, and met Jablonsky at the elevator. "There's an empty storefront across from Forrester Cline's apartment. You and I are staking the place out. With any luck, this chucklehead will do something incriminating, and we can nab him."

"What about the Farlows?" I asked as I followed Mark to the car.

"Boyle and Carver are set up in a surveillance van outside Bates Movers. We have another mobile unit on standby prepared to follow if any of them leave. We're going to divide and conquer."

"Have there been any additional threats from the bomber? Chatter? Anything?" Perhaps I was raining on our parade with my pessimistic attitude.

"Not a word." We fell silent as he maneuvered through the city. "We're trading off on eight hour shifts. Three teams." He glanced at me. "Cheer up. I brought cookies."

He grinned, and I laughed. "Plus, we're lucky. There's indoor plumbing."

"Awesome." Stakeouts typically meant calculated bathroom breaks and limiting the coffee and liquid intake. That wasn't going to be a problem this time.

*　　*　　*

Three days in the drafty, dilapidated storefront and the indoor plumbing no longer seemed like such a great perk. Patience. Stakeouts were about patience. The radio chirped, and Jablonsky grabbed it from the card table we set up, along with a couple of folding chairs.

"Sir, we've received verification of a second bombing. Agents are en route now." The location was a restaurant across the street from the municipal building. "First responders on scene found the explosion completely contained in the storage room. No injuries or fatalities to report."

"What the hell?" I muttered. Why plant a bomb where it couldn't hurt anyone? Was this about making a statement or was the body not found yet, just like with Haze at the first scene?

"I'm on my way. Have the police cordon off the area, and don't let anyone leave." Mark ended the radio transmission. "Parker, you're keeping eyes on this son of a bitch. He knows something. And I want to know exactly what that is." He picked up the radio again. "Boyle, have there been any changes in the Farlows' behavior?"

"Negative."

"Have someone from the standby unit rendezvous with Parker at this location. I'm going to the explosion site, and I don't want any of our agents to lack backup when it comes to surveilling murderers."

"Copy that. Someone's on the way," Boyle promised.

"If something happens before your backup arrives, radio for police assistance. Do you understand?" Mark spoke as if I were a child.

I nodded, and he threw one last look across the way to Cline's apartment before exiting the back door.

Twenty minutes later, the door opened, and being overly jumpy, my hand went to my gun as I heard a familiar voice announce, "Pizza delivery."

"You didn't want to spend another six hours inside the surveillance van?" I asked Michael as he dropped a box on the table. At least he wasn't kidding. Tossing a questioning look his way, I wondered where he found pizza at ten o'clock in the morning. Opening the box, I grabbed a slice, took a tentative bite, and made a face.

"Not good?" He picked up a piece. "It came from a convenience store. Ready-to-eat, just microwave."

"It tastes like soggy cardboard."

He bit into it and put the rest of the slice back in the box. "Guess we can toss this."

After spending another hour staring across the street into the curtainless windows of Forrester Cline's apartment, Carver and I unknowingly managed to consume almost half of the pizza. Boredom always resulted in horrible decision-making. Michael rubbed his face and shifted in his seat.

"Do you want to get some shuteye? Because we can trade off on watching Cline. And if something occurs, I'll wake you or trip over you on my way out." I smirked.

"Nah," he shook his head and picked up the Styrofoam cup of coffee, "I'm fine." He inhaled and sighed heavily, putting the cup down without drinking. "Can you believe there was another bombing? We got the threat. We assessed the situation. We've been investigating leads and motives and," he gestured to the window, "conducting surveillance, and there is still another explosion. This is fucking ridiculous."

"Tell me about it. Don't forget to address the elephant in the room. Since we've been keeping tabs on Cline and the Farlows, that means we have no leads on the bomber. None of them could have done it, unless we didn't notice. And I'm sure we would have noticed." I paced the space from the table to the window, my eyes never leaving Cline's apartment. The guy was a damn homebody.

"No, there's no way they aren't connected. It's the only thing that makes any sense."

"It could be a random lunatic. It happens." Defeat didn't look good on me, but I was tired, cranky, and ready to do something besides stare across the street at the flickering television lights.

"Or," he leaned back and bit his thumbnail absently, "what about a delivery? Postal service or a package maybe? Couldn't the bomb have been sent instead of being planted?"

"I guess." The only thing I knew was the explosion occurred in the storeroom. If the device had a timer and was delivered to the restaurant, could it have been mistaken for another parcel and fortunately placed in the back? "But it's just theory until we hear something concrete from Jablonsky."

The silence was filled with frustration as we continued to hope something more substantial would occur at Cline's apartment. Twenty minutes later, the bedroom light flipped on. Narrowing my eyes, I checked the time. Something seemed off.

"This guy is like a fucking ghost," Carver said. "I haven't caught a glimpse of him once. No wonder you're so bitchy. You must be bored out of your freaking mind being stuck here for days."

"I don't think he's home." I stepped closer to the window. "We haven't seen him at all." I picked up the log sheet from the other two shifts. They had both seen the guy in person coming home or going out since there were requests for a mobile team to maintain visual contact with the subject.

"We have the only exit in our sights." Carver checked the building's blueprints. "He can't honestly be a ghost. From what I know, ghosts can't kill, and Forrester Cline is definitely a killer." He got up and stood next to me at the window, touching my arm gently. "Getting him off the streets is a priority, so we have to play this by the book. I know how you can get."

I chuckled. "You're one to talk." Together, we bent the rules a couple of times, sometimes because of sheer ignorance and other times because something needed to be done. "But if he never does anything incriminating, what are we going to do? How can we just sit around drinking coffee and eating crappy food while we wait for more bombs to explode?"

As if on cue, the radio chirped to life. "Parker, respond," Boyle's voice came through staticky. I picked up the radio and affirmed my presence. "Frank Farlow should be arriving at your location momentarily. The mobile unit followed him. He just parked a block away from Cline's apartment. Monitor the situation from your location. The mobile unit will continue to tail Farlow. If Cline exits the apartment, you and Carver will need to maintain a visual in the event the two subjects split up. Do you copy?"

"Aye, sir." I tucked the radio inside my jacket pocket and checked the clip in my gun. "Looks like our stakeout might turn into something a bit more exciting."

"It's about damn time," Carver said.

Farlow entered the building, and less than two minutes later, he and Cline exited the front door. Apparently, Cline had been home the entire time. Carver spotted one of our agents casually walking up the block in pursuit of the two men.

"Looks like it's show time," he said as we exited the back door and hovered nearby, waiting for the two men to pass.

Michael put his arm around my shoulders, and I turned into him so we wouldn't seem as conspicuous. That was one of the few perks of partnering with a male agent close to my own age. We had tons of practice selling ourselves as a couple, and as predicted, the men went past without any hesitation. After they were half a block ahead of us, we strolled after them, allowing the other team to leapfrog with us to prevent alerting our suspects.

Farlow and Cline entered a laundromat three blocks away, so Michael and I entered a boutique nearby and browsed the racks closest to the window to maintain a visual. One of the other agents went around to the back of the laundromat to make sure our suspects weren't going to elude us by slipping out a back door and exiting into the alley.

"Can I help you?" the clerk asked.

"Federal agents, ma'am." Carver covertly flashed his

credentials. "Please step away."

She obliged, slightly frightened.

"I'm so going to use that the next time I go shopping," I whispered, cracking a smile.

Five minutes later, Farlow and Cline exited with a medium-sized package. The radio in my pocket chirped, reminding me I forgot to silence it. Thankfully, it didn't go off when we were outside. The other agent radioed in the circumstances, and Boyle gave the go-ahead for a takedown. Maybe a decent defense attorney would argue this was circumstantial and we didn't have enough proof to make an arrest, but considering that only hours earlier a bomb detonated in the back of a restaurant, we weren't going to wait around for another explosion.

The two agents keeping tabs on Farlow approached and announced themselves before Carver and I even exited the boutique. Both men ran. Farlow kept a tight grip on the package. With any luck, the other team would stop him and secure whatever might be inside the brown cardboard box. My thoughts went to the possibility of a bomb, and I shuddered to think what would happen if it went off out in the open.

Carver, as usual, ran ahead of me as we chased after Cline. From our suspect's trajectory, I felt confident he was going home. We continued after him, but he made it inside the building and up the stairs before we could apprehend him.

"Second floor, third from the right," I shouted to Carver as we began our ascent.

We drew our guns and slowed our pace, not sure what to expect. When we reached Cline's apartment, the door was wide open, but there was no sign of Cline.

"Mr. Cline, we're federal agents. Come out slowly with your hands up." Carver braced himself against one side of the doorjamb, and I took up the other. "Mr. Cline, we know you're in here."

Still nothing.

I cautioned a glance around the door. "Bedroom?" I mouthed to Carver. He shrugged and tried again. When we still got no response, I took a steadying breath. "Cover me,"

I whispered and slowly entered the apartment. The bedroom door was open, and I approached silently. I leaned around the frame. No one was inside. I shook my head but went in to make sure he wasn't hiding in a closet or under the bed. "Clear."

Michael stood outside the closed bathroom door. The rest of the apartment had been checked, and it was the only place left for Cline to hide. "Mr. Cline, come out. Now."

I strained to hear, but there was no sound or movement. Leaning against the jamb, Michael held up his fingers for a countdown. When he got to one, I turned the doorknob as he raised his gun and stepped forward into the room. The only sound I heard was a loud click.

THIRTY-EIGHT

Against the bathroom wall was a motion sensor attached to an incendiary device. Right now, the sensor was green, but as Michael fidgeted, it let out clicking sounds and briefly flashed red.

"Alexis, get out of here." He swallowed, holstering his gun.

"I'm not leaving you. Let's both just take a breath, and you need to stop moving." I crouched down to examine the sensor Michael inadvertently tripped. "Listen to me." I stood up and stared into his eyes through the mirror's reflection. Since his back was to me, it was the only way we could see one another. "I'm going to radio for assistance and get someone from the bomb squad down here to deactivate that thing. Until then, you aren't going to move a muscle. I'll be right back."

Having a barely workable knowledge of detonators, I knew stray radio signals could cause a premature detonation, but leaving Carver standing on top of a bomb wasn't something I wanted to do either.

"Okay. Call it in and then stay out there. No reason why we both need to be blown to bits."

"My god, you'll do anything to be a hero, won't you?" I attempted to joke, but my heart hammered mercilessly in my chest and my hands shook uncontrollably. "Don't go anywhere."

"Hey," his tone stopped me in my tracks, "be careful. We don't know where Cline went."

"You're one to talk."

I went into the hallway and radioed Boyle, requesting immediate assistance. He would make sure the bomb squad rushed to our location. In the meantime, I was going radio silent. After turning off the radio and steeling my nerves, I went back inside.

"I was just thinking," Carver said as I stood behind him, "wouldn't it suck if that piece of soggy cardboard, as you so eloquently put it, was my last meal. It really makes a guy reconsider the things he puts in his body."

"Michael, as soon as we get out of here, I'll treat you to anything you want."

"Promises, promises." He smirked, but then his jaw clenched. "Don't stand so close." He pressed his lips together in a tight line. "And make sure you watch where you step. Just because I found one booby-trap that doesn't mean there aren't more."

"It's going to be fine," I insisted, hoping at least one of us would believe it. Serious wasn't helping. All it did was make the situation seem more dire. "And just think, I was relieved not to have to apprehend the perp with the cardboard box for fear that could be a bomb. It's ironic how things work out. How much do you want to bet the cardboard box held nothing but the guy's laundry?"

"If you put twenty on that, you're on," Michael said. He fell silent, and I tried to come up with something positive to say. When I attempted to meet his eyes, I noticed his were screwed shut, and his shoulder blade was twitching. "There are some things I'd like to discuss," he began, opening his eyes and sounding resigned to whatever his fate may be.

"Tell me later."

"No," the fear in his brown eyes shocked me, "just in case. I want to do it now. First of all, this has been one hell of a ride."

"Don't you fucking dare. If this is the kind of shit you're going to be sputtering, then I'll wait downstairs for the bomb squad."

"Alex, in the event," he attempted to clear his throat, "have them tell my mom first. She's a strong lady." He let out a long exhale. "And inside the locked safe in my bedroom closet are copies of my personal files. The Bureau will want those."

I nodded.

"Next to the bed is–" he began, but seeing a perfect opportunity to lighten the mood, I interrupted.

"I'm sure Sam or Mark will clear out your porn collection," I teased, and I caught a smile. "But just for my own clarification, they aren't going to find any crazy ass shit like S&M gear or some fluffy suit. Damn, what are those people called?" My mind went blank, but hopefully, the banter would keep him focused on more positive things. "Y'know, the ones who dress up like giant stuffed animals to screw. Stuffies or fluffies?"

"Plushies," he chortled. "Is this your way of confessing to it being your kink?"

"I don't have any kinks. You're the one with a closet full of porn, S&M gear, and a plushie suit."

"You do realize you're absolutely insane, right?" he asked. I shrugged, and his reflection smirked at me. "Only a lunatic would stand inside an apartment with a ticking time bomb."

"You're not so bad. Sure, you get moody sometimes, but I've learned to ignore it," I teased.

"Alex," his tone was back to serious, and I rubbed a hand over my face, "make sure you get these bastards."

"I promise." Before either of us could say another word, I heard the sound of sirens getting louder. "Stay put. Help has arrived."

By the time I made it to the ground floor, officers were clearing the building. The bomb squad arrived, and Boyle pulled up. "Agent Parker," Boyle called as he got out of the vehicle, "fill us in."

I told the group of bomb technicians everything I knew. One guy nodded, donned the heavyweight protective gear, and went into the building to evaluate the situation.

"We lost Cline," I said. "He was too far ahead of us, and when we reached his apartment, we found the door open. We assumed he was inside, but he wasn't. I guess he opened his door and continued running. The fucker completely threw us off the scent." I shook my head. "And now Carver is standing on top of a bomb."

"This isn't your fault." Boyle looked nauseous. "Frank Farlow was arrested with a box full of plastic explosive. It's stable since it wasn't attached to a detonator. But this is the smoking gun we needed." He stepped closer and lowered his voice. "At this moment, I couldn't care less if that psycho makes it out of interrogation alive. We'll find out how to deactivate the bomb upstairs and what other targets these fucking yahoos are planning to hit. For once, I'm actually in favor of the Patriot Act and deeming someone an enemy combatant."

"Can I call dibs on the waterboarding?"

"We'll take turns," he said. Clearly, we were both worried about Carver.

Most of the time the risks associated with this job seemed minimal or reasonable. For example, the risk of being shot could be minimized by wearing Kevlar, or I could decrease my chances of being caught by surprise by going over advanced hand-to-hand combat maneuvers. But how were we supposed to prepare for situations like this? There was no way to control the situation or the outcome, and that was one thing I would never accept.

Ten minutes later, the bomb tech came outside. The building had been cleared, and a few of his team members followed him inside with various tools and equipment. As Sam and I waited, praying to whatever entity might be willing to listen, Jablonsky's SUV screeched to a stop a few feet from us.

"Where's Carver? What's the status of the bomb? Do we have an update on Cline's location?"

"Michael's still upstairs. The bomb squad is," I faltered

slightly, "they're upstairs, working on deactivating it. Cline's in the wind. He got away from me. He tricked us. That's why Michael is where he is." I was starting to lose it. "Dammit," I swore and kicked the tire on Mark's SUV.

"Agent Parker, go back to the office. Review the information on Frank Farlow and get whatever information you can out of him. There is work that needs to be done, and you standing here isn't helping anyone." Jablonsky pointed to the open driver's side door on his SUV.

"I don't want to leave Carver."

"I wasn't making a request. Get to work. You don't need to be here."

Obeying his orders, I climbed into the SUV, shut the door, and drove back to the OIO, unwilling to consider the possibility of what might be happening inside the apartment building.

THIRTY-NINE

"Listen up, you son of a bitch," I circled the table like a shark, "your actions scream terrorism, and you are one phone call away from being sent to Guantanamo. Unless you want to avoid becoming some camel jockey's bitch, I suggest you answer my questions to the best of your ability."

Frank Farlow glowered at me with disdain. "I'm the only true patriot in this building. I'm taking a stand and protecting what our forefathers worked so hard to create, and you can't do a thing about it."

"You wanna bet? Where's Forrester Cline?"

"Who?"

I slammed his face into the tabletop.

He screamed in pain and sat back, blood running down his face. "You broke my fucking nose."

"That's just for starters." Exhaling and loosening up my shoulders, I stood in front of him. "Where's Forrester Cline?"

"I don't know." He leaned down, trying to stop the bleeding with his handcuffed hands. "And even if I did, I wouldn't tell you."

"Did you sell him explosive devices or any other

weapons?"

The cameras were off, and no one was watching from the observation room. Boyle had given me the go-ahead to treat our captive as an enemy combatant, which greatly limited his civil rights. Although, bashing the guy's skull in might still be questionable. Violence only sought further violence, but god help him if Carver didn't make it out of that apartment in one piece. Right now, I needed Farlow to fear me.

"The second amendment gives us the right to bear arms."

"Did you provide him with any explosive devices?" I asked again, my patience thinning. The brief look of glee that passed over his bloodied features was enough of an answer. "What did you give him?"

"Oh, you'll see." The asshole smirked.

Putting on a pair of gloves, I went behind his chair, grabbed his short, greasy, brown hair and yanked his head backward and gave his nose a hard squeeze, refusing to let go.

"Shit," he cursed and attempted to wriggle out of my grasp. He was handcuffed to the bar in the table, and his chair was bolted to the floor. He wasn't going anywhere. "Help. Someone. Help. Get this crazy bitch off of me." But my fellow agents, Michael's friends and colleagues, wouldn't take pity on this excuse for a human being.

"Answer my question," I growled in his ear.

"Plastic explosive and instructions on making pipe bombs and letter bombs," he frantically exclaimed. "Now, let me go."

"What about the sensor in Cline's apartment? How can it be disarmed?"

"What?" he genuinely sounded confused. "I didn't give him any sensors. I just gave him the basics."

"Why? For what purpose?" My jaw clenched. I believed he didn't know anything about the motion sensor detonator which meant Cline was acting on his own.

"Forrester wanted to take care of some problems."

I released the pressure on Farlow's nose, and he winced. Walking around to the other side of the table, I stared at him, waiting for some elaboration.

"He was wrongly accused, and the state was harassing him. They were following him, tapping his phones without just cause. He was being set up. Framed for a murder he didn't commit. And the sickest part is this nation claims to be protecting its citizens, but it's completely subverted from what it was intended to be. Only the true patriots can understand what is constitutional. You stand there with your badge and gun claiming to have some authority over me, but you have none."

This guy was a nutbag. He had a lot to say, particularly when it came to ratting out Cline's motives and maybe explaining the circumstances surrounding Haze's murder, but I didn't want to go near any of that. That needed to be on the up and up, and I already tainted my interview with violence.

"How much explosive did you give Cline?"

"Enough for three small bombs. He wanted more, but," Farlow shut his mouth, and I knew the rest of the explosive he wanted was in the package we confiscated.

Slamming my chair against the table and jarring my captive, I stormed out of interrogation, stopped the first person I found, and told him to send someone to get our suspect cleaned up after he accidentally hit his nose on the table while trying to strong-arm his way out of the cuffs. I had gotten everything I could out of him, and there was no reason why the man needed to make a bloody mess in our interrogation room. It wasn't very sanitary for any future persons of interest who might be forced to sit in the same chair at the same table.

Back at my desk, I made a few calls to get arrest warrants signed for the other two Farlow brothers. If their family militia group was buying and selling explosives, we had reason to bring them in for questioning. After issuing a BOLO on Forrester Cline, I went to talk to the mobile unit that brought Farlow in. They said the package was left in an out-of-service washing machine which must have been used as a drop. They already pulled the laundromat's video surveillance and were hoping to identify whoever left the plastic explosive for Farlow. Just as I picked up my phone to call for an update on Carver's situation, the elevator doors opened and out came Jablonsky, Boyle, and Carver.

"Are you sure, kid?" Jablonsky asked.

"Yes. I want to nail these bastards," Carver said.

Jablonsky nodded once, clapped him on the back, and went into his office. Boyle threw an arm around his shoulders and whispered something to him. Carver grinned, and Boyle went into the conference room, calling the two agents from the mobile unit to join him.

"Hey," I launched myself into Michael's arms, "you're okay. I'm sorry for leaving you there and everything."

"It's okay." He hugged me back. "Careful, Alex, people might think we slept together," he whispered teasingly in my ear.

"Jerk." I filled him in on everything that transpired while he spent the afternoon standing around in Cline's apartment. "We have some strong leads. Someone else will have to do the follow-up interview, but we're making progress. Are you sure you don't want to take the rest of the day off?"

"Nah, but I have a few things I need to take care of while we wait on the other two Farlows to be brought in." He glanced at the rest of our team. "Thanks for having my back. Can you do me a favor and stay on top of whatever breaking news is going on with the earlier bombing from today?"

"Yeah, no problem." I gave him a strange look, wondering what he had to do instead.

"Great. You can read me in over dinner. I'm thinking surf and turf. After all, you did offer to buy whatever I want."

"Apparently, I should have been more concerned with my pocketbook than your well-being."

He snickered, and I grabbed a notepad and headed for the conference room. Charts and dozens of pictorial representations of the explosion from this morning covered a corkboard someone had pushed into the conference room. Jablonsky came in and asked that we all take a seat. For once, our fearless leader also sat instead of standing as he gave us the update. Today had taken a toll on him too.

The cause of the explosion was the result of a package bomb. The restaurant was expecting a shipment of jarred pickles, and the box thought to contain them had been unopened and left in the storage room. The photos of the scene indicated scorch marks, broken glass, and charred wiring. To the untrained eye, it looked similar to the detonator remnants used in Haze's car.

"Our team is going over the scene and checking for leads on who sent and delivered the package." Jablonsky locked eyes with each of us. "I'm sure everyone's aware of this morning's situation. Agent Carver is fine, but it is imperative we locate and apprehend Forrester Cline. However, if any of you end up in pursuit, feel free to exercise extreme prejudice in taking him down. I'm not willing to risk any of our lives for his apprehension."

No one was opposed to these more stringent measures. If you fuck with one of us, you fuck with all of us.

A junior agent opened the conference room door. "Sir, John and Tim Farlow have been brought in for questioning."

"Thanks, Cooper," Mark said. After Cooper left, Mark surveyed the room. "Okay, we'll let them stew for a few minutes. In the meantime, I need everything you can get on the three Farlow brothers, Forrester Cline, and anyone who might be able to give us some answers. The more ammunition we have against them, the better off we are." He stood up. "Parker, I need a minute."

I followed him to his office. He waited for me to take a seat, and then he shut the door and sat on the edge of his desk in front of me.

"Boyle said I could exercise some creativity," I began, but Mark held up a hand to silence me.

"I don't care what happened with Farlow or how it happened. It doesn't matter." He swallowed and blew out a breath. "But you're not going anywhere near him or his brothers. Whatever we get out of him might be the key to putting Cline behind bars for the rest of his life, and nothing any of us do should jeopardize that. I was told he broke his own nose while fighting against his restraints. No one can contradict that, so we're keeping this as the official story, understood?"

"Yes."

"Good."

I got up to leave.

"And Parker, we protect our own, even if the methods we employ aren't always particularly sound," Mark said.

"It wouldn't have mattered. He didn't know anything about the motion sensor or how to disarm the bomb. If," I looked away and began again, "I regret my actions."

"Then don't do it again." He jerked his chin toward the door.

Under different circumstances, I would have been suspended, pending an investigation, and possibly charged with assault. However, Carver's life had been hanging in the balance, so desperate times and all that. It didn't make it right, but it did make it understandable.

FORTY

In the last six hours, much of our case had fallen into place. We still hadn't located Cline, but if Farlow was correct in the amount of plastic explosive Cline possessed, there were no other targets. Bomb number one went off inside Haze's car. Bomb number two went off early this morning at the diner across from the municipal building, and the third bomb was rigged to a motion sensor in Cline's bathroom. Perhaps Cline was the innovative type and researched how to rig an explosive to a motion sensor without asking his supplier for assistance. Too bad he didn't accidentally blow himself up. That was just wishful thinking on my part.

"Hey," one of the techs said, and I opened my eyes to find him standing over me, "I just got into Haze's voicemail box. You need to listen to this."

I took the offered thumb drive and plugged it into my computer. There were countless threats from Cline to Haze dating back almost a month. Each message became more heated than the last until Cline finally threatened to kill Haze. More specifically, he threatened to shoot him in the heart.

"Did you pass this along?" I asked.

"Yes. SSA Jablonsky and SAC Boyle both have copies."

He retreated from my desk, and I checked the call logs and cross-referenced the number.

The prepaid burner cell's timestamps on the phone log matched the voicemail messages left by Cline. We had him for first degree murder. We also had him for an attempted bombing, and I was certain by the end of the night we'd have him for the detonations at the impound lot and the diner.

Picking up the phone, I dialed Det. Jacobs and shared the newest development on his homicide case. It was only fair. The police department tossed Haze's apartment and found the original crime scene. Haze had been shot on the landing of his fire escape. From the looks of his apartment, there had been a struggle, and Jacobs determined the ADA tried to escape his attacker by going out the back. Unfortunately, Cline had come prepared and shot him from the level above.

"Agent Parker, we've been reviewing the security tapes from Haze's building. The shooter is Forrester Cline." Jacobs muttered barely audible expletives. "I guess it's a tossup to see if the state or federal government indicts first."

"The state's got the death penalty, so just make sure you have a damn solid case."

An eye for an eye would make the whole world blind, but it was hard to act enlightened or evolved when shit like this kept happening. Every day, there was another serious threat, whether it was a mass shooting, explosion, or some other multi-casualty event.

"Parker," Boyle called, and I went into his office, "Tim and John Farlow are hoping for immunity if they cooperate. How much insight do you think they possess? You're probably the best judge after your chat with their brother, Frank, this afternoon."

"Sam," I wanted to rip my hair out as the day continued to weigh on me, "I have no idea. Farlow, Frank Farlow," I specified, "seems to be the ringleader. From the things he said, he's all about his doctrine and proving himself to be a real patriot. I'd say from what we witnessed today and the things he might have mentioned, he's running the show.

He sold the explosive. He explained to Cline how to use it, plant it, and detonate it. From their records, the three Farlow brothers reside together. They work at Bates Movers together. They probably masturbate together for all I know."

He waited for my rambling to ebb. "Okay. I'll see if we can cut them a deal. The problem is they're all accessories to an ADA's murder. That tends to grate on the nerves of both the DA's office and the US Attorney's office. It might be a hard sell."

"Obviously, our jobs aren't supposed to be easy." I rubbed my eyes. "Do we have any idea who's supplying Farlow with weapons and explosives?"

"Tim and John are offering names if we deal." Boyle studied me. "Alexis, you look like hell. Grab a hold of Carver and get out of here. He should have taken the rest of the day as a personal day instead of sitting at his desk being profoundly morbid." I cocked an eyebrow up. "He's spent all afternoon writing out specific instructions in the event of his demise."

"Dammit. I'll see what I can do."

I was ready to go home. My partner had almost been blown sky high, I had assaulted a handcuffed prisoner, and I wanted the party responsible to be executed by the state. At the moment, I was so far beyond cynical and jaded that I was bordering on apathetic with homicidal tendencies. Granted, I heard of agents burning out but never within a matter of sixteen hours. No, today we had to celebrate life. And tomorrow, whatever was left to be handled could be handled.

"Alex?" Michael glanced up from whatever he was doing. "Is something wrong?"

"Yes, and I need you to come with me."

"Just give me ten minutes." He looked confused, but I wasn't about to waver. Yes, I was a workaholic who could easily spend the entire night working this case, but it wouldn't be good for my mental stability or Carver's. Occasionally, I needed to prioritize.

"Fine." I went to my desk, turned off my computer, tacked every new lead and theory to the board in the conference room, and collected my belongings. Michael grabbed his coat and met me at the elevator. "Boyle's sending us home for the night. Don't argue. I'm starving, and I promised you dinner." I reached into my pocket and found a twenty, probably the same twenty he gave me. "Oh, and you were right. The box didn't have Farlow's laundry in it."

"You really shouldn't bet against a surefire thing," he said. On the way down to the parking garage, his cell phone rang. He turned away and answered. "Hi, Mom. I'm glad you called back." He paused, and I wished we weren't stuck in a tiny metal box so he could have some privacy. "No, everything's fine. I just wanted to see how you're doing. How's Dad?" I fumbled through my purse, looking for my car keys. "I should go. A friend is taking me out to dinner." He paused. "Yes, a lady friend. I love you too. Bye." He disconnected and caught me looking at him. "Alexis, don't look at me like that."

"Like what?"

"You know like what. I'm fine."

"I'm glad." I led him to my car and unlocked the doors. After both our doors were shut, I turned the key in the ignition. "I broke a guy's nose today."

"Thank you."

"It wouldn't have helped. He didn't know how to," I stopped at the traffic light, waiting for it to change to green and pausing as I did in the hopes of figuring out what I wanted to say or what needed to be said, "deactivate it. He didn't know anything about it."

"Alex..."

"I'm sorry, Michael." I turned to him. "I was supposed to have your back, and I couldn't do anything to help you." My jaw clenched tightly, and I faced forward again, hitting the accelerator the moment the light changed.

Carver remained silent. Maybe he blamed me, or maybe I was just adding my own fears to his.

After the silence became unbearable, I cleared my throat. "So, where do you want to eat?"

FORTY-ONE

Carver and I had lobster tails and steaks for dinner. It was the surf and turf he wanted, and I didn't begrudge him the price. After we finished eating, we ended up at a dive bar a few blocks from his apartment. It was where he'd go occasionally to have a drink and seek out some non-OIO company. Allowing me to join him was probably sacrilege, but I was buying.

Michael was a bourbon guy, and it seemed easier to order the rounds in twos, even if I didn't particularly care for the stuff. Although we spent the last two hours alone together, I couldn't remember who spoke last or what was said. Talking wasn't one of my strong suits, and he shut himself off from the world. He finished his third drink and flipped the glass upside down. Mine had barely been touched.

"You have to know it wasn't your fault," he said out of the blue. "You and I have been through a lot." He snorted. "Damn, if that's not an understatement. Right now," he shook his head, "I don't even know what I'm doing. Can we get out of here?"

"Yeah." I tossed some cash on the bar. "Whatever you want."

"I just want to go home."

We left the bar. My car was parked almost halfway between the bar and his apartment building, so as we got closer to my vehicle, I slowed my pace.

"I guess I'll see you tomorrow."

"Come with me. I could use a friend," he insisted.

"Michael, I don't want to see your plushie suit." I smiled and gave him a friendly nudge.

The silence returned for the next two blocks as we made our way to his apartment. He unlocked the door and ushered me inside. He had a small two bedroom apartment. There was a good chance my one bedroom apartment had more square feet than his, but I couldn't be sure.

"Like I mentioned earlier, my personal case files are in my bedroom closet, but this computer has copies of all the reports I've compiled for the OIO. Inside the locked drawer is a list of passwords. The key to that drawer is on my key ring." He reached into his pocket and brought out his keys. "It's this one." He had five keys on the ring. "This goes to my car. These two are for the apartment. I just showed you the one for the desk. And this is for the lockbox in my closet."

"Michael, stop," I begged. "We are not doing this. You're okay. Today was just a bad day."

"And what if one day it's more than a bad day?" He looked away. "Someone needs to know what to do just in case."

"I don't want to be that someone." He ignored me and continued listing where things were and what to do. "Please, stop."

"I've written out specific instructions in case anyone has questions. They're in my bottom drawer at work." He was scared, and this was the only way he could take back control. "It's just in case. Don't worry about it, but just know it's there."

"All I want is for you to be there." I couldn't stand it any longer, and I hugged him, holding him tightly.

At first, he stood completely rigid, but eventually, he caved in my arms. One of his hands got tangled in my hair, and the other forced me closer. There was no telling how long we stayed in that embrace. Neither of us was willing to let go or pull away. At some point, our grips loosened, and we both withdrew. Leaning forward, I kissed him. It was gentle and meaningful, and then I stepped back.

"It was one bad day. Do not let it get inside your head. We deal with shit all the time. This is nothing new." Even I didn't believe it.

Everything Carver was doing felt like tying up loose ends and putting his affairs in order. His foundation had shifted, and it frightened me to think what that could mean.

*   *   *

The next day at the office was business as usual. Maybe a good night's sleep gave Carver some perspective. He returned to his normal workload and routine habits instead of spending his day writing out worst case scenario instruction manuals. I compartmentalized and stuck everything from yesterday into a neat little box at the periphery of my psyche. It didn't matter that I assaulted Frank Farlow or didn't make as much progress on the case yesterday as I should have. I was chalking it up to a bad day. It was over now. It was tomorrow, and my energy needed to be focused on locating Cline and following up on our new leads.

"Sir," I knocked on Boyle's open office door, "what happened with Tim and John Farlow?"

"They got immunity," he said, nonplussed. "I just sent two agents to bring in their supplier. The police department is canvassing the area and checking for eyewitness accounts on Haze's murder." He cautioned a glance at Carver, who had just gone into the conference room where most of the team was working. "He seems to have pulled himself together. How is he?"

"Honestly, I have no idea."

Boyle assessed me. "And how are you?"

"I'm ready to close this case."

He jerked his chin toward the conference room, and I

went back to work. Inside, everything had been updated, and our theory board was in practical working order. Most of what we knew was no longer unsubstantiated conjecture. It was simply what happened.

Frank Farlow posted his anti-government rhetoric all over the internet. He designed websites, blogs, and social media pages that shouted what he interpreted true patriotism to be. He chastised the government for taking control of our lives, illegally monitoring us, and requiring licensure for what he dubbed every aspect of our civil rights. Like I determined upon my first encounter with the man, he was a nutbag. Even if any of the arguments he made were solid, there was a right way and a wrong way to go about doing things, and clearly, his way was the wrong way.

His outlandish claims filled every part of his life. His brothers did his bidding, but as far as we could determine, they weren't the instigators. They seemed passive and possibly even in denial about the lengths Frank would go for his cause. Even his co-workers at Bates Movers didn't realize how unhinged and destructive he was. They simply thought he just took every opportunity to spout nonsense from atop his soapbox. It reminded me of the Edmund Burke quote, "The only thing necessary for the triumph of evil is for good men to do nothing," and briefly, I wondered if Farlow was a fan. It was easy to find justification by spinning words to fit any set of goals.

Forrester Cline somehow came across Farlow's ramblings, and given his current plight, the two men quickly hit it off. Forrester Cline might have been acquitted of the initial murder on a technicality, but his insistence on seeking revenge and threatening ADA Douglas Haze made the attorney dig in his heels. After receiving some less than pleasant voicemail messages, Haze was dead set on finding something that would stick to Cline. My mind scowled at the inappropriate pun.

The more Haze tried to make a case, the faster Cline developed his plan for revenge. Although some details concerning the exact times and dates Frank Farlow met with Forrester Cline were still cloudy, Tim and John insisted there had been half a dozen different meets in which Cline and Farlow discussed ways of getting payback. Farlow's main concern was making a political statement. He encouraged Cline to plant the explosive devices outside the courthouse and at the restaurant near the municipal building. Both places were frequented by government officials, judges, law enforcement officers, legislatures, and Haze himself. Farlow believed he found the perfect delivery system for his message, and Cline would make the ideal patsy. At least now, we had proof the threat we received concerning future bombings had been made by Frank Farlow.

However, Forrester Cline didn't care about making a statement. The only thing he cared about was silencing Haze. The dozens of menacing voicemail messages began almost a month ago. After Haze received the death threat, he decided to take a leave of absence from work and lay low until the state had an undeniable case. It was what prompted him to buy the bus ticket and disseminate some misinformation about leaving town, except he didn't leave. He continued to work with the private investigator on finding additional evidence against Farlow and Cline.

But since Farlow was willing to take the heat on the bombings, Cline decided there was no reason to wait before silencing the nosy ADA. From what was revealed during the follow-up interview with Farlow, Cline had gotten impatient, went to Haze's apartment, and killed him. It was a game of cat and mouse, but I couldn't help but wonder if Haze had just let Cline's acquittal go, if any of this ever would have happened.

"Parker," Michael said my name, and I looked up at him, "since it seems we have a handle on Haze's murder, Jablonsky wants us to go through the files once more and then drop them off at the precinct. I could use some help."

"All right."

I pulled up a chair, and we began going through the information and making final notations. Neither of us mentioned yesterday or last night, and as I watched Michael work, I was relieved things seemed to be back to normal.

FORTY-TWO

Carver carried the boxes into the precinct, and I asked for directions to Det. Jacobs' desk. Arriving at his cubicle in the major crimes unit, we watched as most of the squad rushed around in a hurry over the latest call.

"And I thought things at the OIO were hectic," Carver whispered in my ear.

"Detective Jacobs," I called, making the man swivel in his chair, "we've brought the information back to you."

"Amazing," he shifted his gaze from me to Michael, "there must be a first time for everything." He stood and took the boxes from Carver. "Agents, walk with me."

We followed Jacobs down the hallway to evidence storage. He handed the boxes across the counter to an officer on duty, signed the chain of custody form Carver produced, and handed the officer the same form to sign. Handing the duplicate copy back to Carver, he took to leaning against the counter.

"Since you've been forthcoming in your investigation, it's only fair for me to tell you we've got eyes on Forrester Cline. Uniforms in the area are keeping tabs on him, and we've sent a couple of black and whites to bring him in."

"How'd you find him?" I asked.

"We've been canvassing the neighborhood where his mother lives. A neighbor spotted him entering her house. When he left this morning, we tailed him." Jacobs looked smug. "You mean to tell me the federal government can't locate a suspect?" He couldn't resist the dig, but I let it go.

"Do you mind if we hang around until he's brought in?" Carver asked. There was a score that needed to be settled, but this was not the time or place for it.

"Suit yourself. But it's our collar." Jacobs faced me. "After all, the state's got the death penalty." He winked, and I couldn't help the tiny smile that crept onto my face. It was sick and twisted and made me feel disgusted with myself, and yet, there it was. Apparently, I needed a vacation. We went into the hallway, and Jacobs left us alone.

"Once we know he's in custody, we should get out of here," I insisted. Carver was wound tight, like a coiled spring, and he didn't need to stick around. "I know why you want to be here, and it's not worth it."

He met my eyes, blinking back whatever he was feeling. "You're right, Alex. He's not worth it, but I am. I deserve to know this is over and that fucking asshole is behind bars."

Silently, we waited in a few empty chairs near booking for Cline and his escorts. I phoned Jablonsky and gave him the update. All he said was be careful. There wasn't much else to say.

Almost two hours later, Cline was dragged into the precinct in handcuffs. I couldn't imagine what Michael must be feeling. But as Cline was shoved past us, Michael remained motionless, watching with a level of disinterest usually reserved for particularly tedious infomercials. That sight worried me more than anything else ever did.

"Let's go," he said, standing up. "It's done."

"Why aren't you celebrating? Why aren't you fighting to go bash his skull in? What the hell is going on, Michael?" I asked as soon as we exited the double doors.

"Nothing's going on. It just feels different. Maybe I feel different." He opened the car door and got inside. "C'mon, we're wasting daylight."

There was no point in arguing. We had a job to do. Since

the police had Cline and we had the Farlow brothers, the only one left was the supplier. Boyle said he was being brought in, so with any luck, this case would conclude by the end of the day. Hopefully, all we needed was a fresh start and a new beginning on a different case.

*   *   *

It had been a week since Forrester Cline's arrest. The OIO had conducted numerous interrogations with Cline, the three Farlows, and the bomb supplier. The police department had a solid case against Cline for the murder of ADA Douglas Haze. They had eyewitness accounts of Cline entering Haze's apartment building and sounds of an argument. The building's security cam footage and Haze's phone records were the icing on the cake.

After the murder, Cline called Frank Farlow for help. He had a dead body on his hands and needed someone to assist with the clean-up. Farlow left work with the van, met Cline outside Haze's building, and dumped the body inside. Afterward, the two men went back inside Haze's apartment, located the keys to Haze's car, and planted the bomb. While this was happening, the two geniuses left the van parked in a tow away zone. When they returned the next morning to retrieve it and the body, the police already impounded the car.

This was the impetus that encouraged the relocation of the car bombing. Originally intended to be a political statement, it was now going to be used as a cover-up for a murder. Additionally, based on what Tim and John said, Frank hoped the police would mistakenly believe the ADA set the explosive himself to illustrate his distrust for a corrupt legal system. But as Frank and Forrester continued to plot and plan, they realized how unrealistic that sounded, and instead, Farlow decided to keep on track with his other target, the restaurant.

Cline wasn't going to disagree, especially since Farlow could turn him in for killing an ADA. The plan continued, but once again, fate interfered with Farlow's scheme. The package sent to the restaurant exploded in the closed storage room, not doing any real damage or causing any injury. Frank Farlow failed twice. Thankfully, the only person hurt in this venture was Douglas Haze, and that had more to do with Cline than anyone else.

I rubbed my eyes, staring at my completed report. Right now, search warrants were being signed for Frank Farlow's storage unit. His brothers tattled on him for amassing numerous weapons and other illegal devices. It could only further solidify our case by adding additional charges and more years to the laundry list of felonies and decades' worth of prison time Farlow was already facing.

Looking across the room, I spotted Carver at his desk, searching for something. He had been off his game since the near-miss in Cline's apartment, and I wondered what he was planning to do.

"Want to grab a drink?" I asked.

"Not tonight."

"Are you planning to engage in some extracurricular stress relief techniques?" I asked.

He chuckled, looking up and smiling. "That depends on if you're offering." He was joking, but I couldn't help but think there was a sadness to his eyes.

"Well, I think we might need to go have a few drinks first. My inhibitions need to be greatly lowered."

"Alex, you're such a tease. But in case you aren't kidding, can I have a rain check?"

"Sure," I replied, wishing he'd speak his mind. "Just in case you reconsider, I'll be at my usual watering hole." He nodded. "Good night."

"Yeah, you too."

I stopped by the bar near my apartment, took a seat, and ordered a soda. Carver didn't show up, and I didn't expect him to. I had no intention of sleeping with someone I worked with, but I thought he might want some company. There were only so many times you could walk away from a life or death situation unscathed.

FORTY-THREE

The next morning, the warrant was signed for Frank Farlow's storage unit. It was a converted warehouse typically leased to businesses to house their stock. It was located a mile from the OIO offices, and we had teams checking the area for anyone suspicious. Since Farlow was a fan of guns and artillery, there was the possibility his stockpile might draw the attention of some undesirable individuals.

I had barely read over the morning reports when one of the techs summoned me. I followed him into the elaborate room of monitors, surveillance feeds, and communication devices, and he explained the logistics for the current operation. I listened as he went through the placement of surveillance equipment, the location of the warehouse, and the basic layout.

"Okay," I said, uncertain why I was getting this briefing, "why are you telling me this?"

"Jablonsky said you're coordinating the operation from the office."

"Me?" This had never happened before. I was always sent out in the field, either to investigate or to surveil, so this made no sense. "Um, just wait a minute." I went down the hall and knocked on Mark's door.

"Parker, you're running things from inside today."

"Why am I being punished?" I asked as Boyle and Carver entered Mark's office in tactical gear.

"You're not, but if you think it's beyond your capabilities, then I have some paperwork that needs filing," Jablonsky retorted, checking his service piece and putting it into his holster. "It's IT's game anyway. You're just relaying the go-ahead over comms."

"Fine," I said.

Boyle gave me a pat on the back. "See, this is what happens when you actually get your reports filed on time, unlike the rest of us." He tossed a pointed look at Carver, who chuckled.

"We leave in ten," Jablonsky announced as he left the three of us in his office while he went to speak to the director.

"Seriously, what gives?" I asked.

"Nothing," Boyle hesitated, glancing into the hallway, "and you didn't hear this from me, but they might be grooming you for a promotion. Try not to screw it up." He winked and left the office.

I eyed Michael suspiciously. "Is that why you've been giving me the cold shoulder lately?"

"That wasn't my intention. I've been contemplating making some changes. I'll fill you in when I get back, and I'll try not to have too much fun without you."

"Hey," I stopped him as he tried to leave the office, "be careful. I'm only your telephone operator, so it makes it difficult to watch your back from here."

He smirked and went to join the other two men.

Blowing out a breath, I went back to the operations room to learn how to run point from off-site. As I settled into the chair, the techs hooked me up with an earpiece and radio, turning the dial to the proper channel so I'd be in contact with Jablonsky and his team. While technically this was deemed a raid, it was for evidence gathering. The surveillance teams monitored the area all night but didn't spot anyone in the vicinity, so this was just a simple enter, search, and retrieve mission.

"Jablonsky thought this would be good practice. Something easy for you to cut your teeth on," the tech said. "How long have you been with us, Parker?"

"Almost five years." I shook my head, wondering where the time went. It seemed like only yesterday I was being made a full-fledged agent, and somehow, it was three years later. Maybe I'd just been too busy to notice. No wonder I was more pissed off than usual, I hadn't taken more than two consecutive days off since I started working. "Just wondering why I'm the last one to hear about this advancement opportunity?"

"No one's offered you the job yet," the tech pointed out. "This is just a practice to see if you'd be able to handle more responsibility one day."

"Frankly, I'd rather be outside the warehouse."

The radio made some staticky noises in my ear before the tech adjusted the dial, and I heard Jablonsky's voice over the speaker. They just arrived on scene. Boyle and Carver were going around to the back exit while Mark took the front door. The tech nodded, and I leaned into the microphone.

"No sign of any activity outside the warehouse. It's been converted into four separate units. Farlow's is on the eastern end of the building. From the blueprints, that unit has two exits, a single door in the front and a large cargo door in the back. The interior is approximately twenty-five hundred square feet." I reread the warrant to make sure it was filled out for the right subunit within the warehouse.

"Are we cleared to breach?" Boyle asked. He chuckled at the absurdity of how seriously I was taking my new duties.

"What do you think, Jablonsky?" I asked. Mark was still senior, so things like this should be his call.

"It's your show, Parker."

Taking a breath, I looked at the tech, trying to determine my thoughts on this new position of power. The monitors in front of us were local traffic cams near the area. They didn't provide a great view, but by squinting and turning to the side, a portion of the warehouse could be seen between another building and a tree. He gave a curt nod.

"Affirmative. Move in." Within a second of my command, the radio let out a shrill noise, and static filled the airspace. A dark cloud of smoke billowed on to the edge of the screen. "What the hell happened?" I squawked into the radio and to the tech.

Frantically, I tried to get someone to respond, but there was nothing but static. The tech took over, spinning dials and flipping switches, but I was out of my chair and halfway down the hall. I dialed as I ran down the stairs.

"911, how may I assist you?" the dispatch operator asked.

"This is Agent Parker." I rambled off my credentials as I raced down the flights of stairs, concluding with the warehouse address and a request for immediate support from all emergency services. Reaching the bottom with keys in hand, I sprinted to the car, putting it in gear and speeding from the garage.

The warehouse was only a mile from my location, but driving through city traffic was hell. I was on autopilot, and as I screeched around a corner, I briefly wondered how long I had been driving on the sidewalk. The flashing lights and sirens were on, and thankfully, pedestrians leapt out of my way as I flew to the location. I made it to the warehouse within five minutes to find fire trucks and ambulances already on scene.

The fire department had a stationhouse only two blocks from here and responded immediately to my call. Throwing the car into park and bolting from the door, I spotted Jablonsky sitting on the concrete as an EMT ran a flashlight in front of his eyes.

"What the hell happened?" I asked, relieved to see him alert and functioning. Only then did I notice the dark plumes billowing from what was left of the building.

"Those sons of bitches rigged the building to explode." He tried to push the EMT away. "Where's Boyle and Carver?" he asked. "Oh for fuck's sake, I'm fine." He tried to stand, but his balance was off. And the EMT pushed him back into a seated position.

"I'll find out," I replied, already circling toward the back of the building as fear overtook my senses with every step.

"Ma'am." A fireman tried to block my path, so I flashed my credentials at him, not slowing my pace. "Ma'am," he tried again as I sprinted toward the back. His job was to put the fire out; mine was to find my friends.

As the rear of the building came into range, I saw a fire truck and two ambulances. There was a bloody sheet on the ground, and I found myself racing to it. No, this can't be happening. My mind kept screaming in protest as if that would change the outcome.

"Michael," I exclaimed. He was on a gurney. Two EMTs were on either side of him. He was bleeding from his temple, but he seemed alert. "Oh my god, Michael," I ran to him, "are you okay? What happened?"

He looked distraught. "Sam opened the door. He had just gotten inside before the blast," he swallowed.

One of the EMTs pushed me out of the way. "Ma'am, we have to get him to the hospital, now."

I climbed into the back of the ambulance after Michael, not thinking about anything except making sure he was okay. One of the two EMTs shut the doors and went around to the front while the other strapped Michael in and connected him to a few monitors and started checking his vitals.

"Sam's dead," Michael said.

His skin looked so pale against the ash marks from the blast. He coughed, and I saw blood. The EMT was stripping the tactical gear off of him, and I clutched his hand.

"This is all my fault. I'm so sorry."

His eyes started to flutter, and his voice was barely above a whisper. He was saying something, but I couldn't hear him. I leaned closer and felt his lips brush against my cheek.

"It's okay, Alex," he insisted.

As I leaned away, his body jerked, the warning bells sounded on the medical equipment, and the EMT shoved me out of the way. With the Kevlar off and his shirt cut open, I saw that his torso was covered in deep purple and black.

"Hurry it up," the EMT yelled to the driver. "He's bleeding into his abdomen. Have trauma prepared to get him into surgery as soon as we arrive."

Michael flatlined, and the EMT charged the defibrillator and shocked him. After two jolts, the monitor beeped an unsteady rhythm. A moment later, the ambulance slowed, the doors were yanked open, and they carried the gurney out of the ambulance. I didn't move. Boyle was dead, and Carver was dying.

"Ma'am? Ma'am?" That horrible word kept repeating as if on a loop, and I jumped when someone touched my shoulder. "Ma'am," the EMT said again, "they'll do everything they can. Were you at the warehouse when the blast went off?"

"No, but I should have been." I stepped out of the ambulance on shaky legs and studied the hospital doors. I couldn't go inside, fearing what the outcome would be.

As I stood motionless and staring, the second EMT from the rig returned. "He's in surgery, but," his expression looked grim; he already knew what the outcome would be, "they'll keep you updated on his condition."

I shook my head, fighting back tears. "The other agent, Jablonsky, any word on him?"

The two exchanged a brief look. "We'll give you a ride back to the scene," one of them finally said, acknowledging that I wasn't going to wait inside the hospital for the doctors to tell me Michael didn't make it.

FORTY-FOUR

The ambulance dropped me off next to Mark's location. By now, the place was crawling with police, fire, and OIO agents. Jablonsky was sitting in the back of an ambulance as someone removed debris from his cheek. He looked at me and shoved the man away, stepping down. At least his balance returned.

"Sam Boyle's dead," I choked out, biting the inside of my lip. "And Michael," I stopped and forced my chin to stop quivering, "it doesn't look good. He's in surgery."

"Parker," he said my name softly, but I stepped away. Any human contact would cause the tears to spill, and now wasn't the time or place for that. "Do what you need to."

Brushing past all the acronym-emblazoned jackets, I found my car still parked haphazardly with the driver's side door open and the keys in the ignition. It really must be a crime scene if no one bothered to steal a perfectly good car. On autopilot, I climbed inside and somehow made it back to the OIO.

No one said a word to me, which I was thankful for. Everyone heard what happened, and the place was silent. Glancing at my computer monitor, I had no idea how I managed to write my incident report, but there it was. My eyes looked across the room, first at Boyle's empty office and then at Carver's desk.

"Alex." Jablonsky had just arrived. There was a bandage along the side of his face and blood on his collar, but other than that, he seemed fine. "Come into my office." His tone made my heart break, and my breath hitched in my throat.

"No," I shook my head, "please, Mark. Don't." His eyes shone wet, and I went into his office as the first tears that I would shed began to fall. "Don't say it."

"Alex," he swallowed and pulled the door closed behind me, "I'm sorry." He hugged me, and I sobbed, feeling his own tears moisten my shoulder. Eventually, I forced my emotions into check and pulled away from his embrace.

"This is on me," I declared, opening the door and going back to my desk. I printed my report and went to the director's office. Knocking but not waiting for permission to enter, I went inside. "Sir, after the events of today, I'd like to take full responsibility for what happened to our agents." My chin quivered, and I gritted my teeth, forcing my body to obey simple, rational commands. "I hope you'll open an investigation into their deaths." The word caught, but I forced it out. "I will be at your disposal for any questioning." Without waiting for a response, I went back to my desk and started a new word document.

When I was finished typing, I saved it on the computer, printed a single copy, placed it in an envelope, and tucked it neatly into my purse. Giving Carver's desk a final look, I got up. It was almost eight p.m. Jablonsky watched as I left the building. He didn't say anything because there was nothing to say. I screwed up, and two agents paid the ultimate price.

Somehow, I ended up at the hospital where they had taken Michael. After flashing my credentials, I was directed downstairs to the morgue. After answering a few more questions, I was given access to Michael's body. The assistant pulled the drawer open and left me alone as I looked at his lifeless form.

"I'm so sorry, Michael." I kept repeating the words over and over, hoping he'd open his eyes and tell me it was okay. How ironic that the last thing he ever said to me was that it was okay. It was almost as if he'd known. Thinking back, I wondered if he knew all along that something like this was going to happen. Remembering the instructions he forced me to listen to, I wept.

The door behind me opened, but I didn't bother to turn around. "I knew you'd be here," Jablonsky said, wrapping his arm around me. "Did you say your goodbyes?"

I nodded, unable to answer, and he gave Michael's shoulder a squeeze and led me from the room.

"His parents are on their way. They should be here in the morning. It's so fresh, but I'm going to move the files out of his apartment tonight so they can have some privacy without us interfering."

Finding my voice, I rambled all of Carver's instructions. We left my car at the hospital, and Mark drove me home. Before I could get out, he grasped my wrist.

"Alexis, right now this won't mean much, but later on, it might bring you some comfort." He swallowed, keeping his own sorrow in check. "You're the reason Carver didn't die in an alley four years ago. You bought him more time, and he used that time to make countless differences in this world."

"It's not fair, Mark. It wasn't enough time."

"It never is." A tear escaped his eye, and he rubbed it away immediately with the back of his hand.

* * *

That night, I didn't sleep. The next night, I didn't sleep. Eventually, my pattern turned into crying myself to sleep, oftentimes on the couch. Sam and Michael were dead. There was nothing I could do to fix it, and I would have given anything or done anything to change what was unchangeable.

By the end of the week, I had attended two funerals. Both unbelievably difficult, but each time, I stood completely still, no longer crying or showing any emotion. I managed to turn it off in public, to appear numb. On the inside, the pain and guilt were unbearable.

Every day, I went to work and found myself staring at

Carver's desk or Boyle's office, waiting for one of them to return to ask me to do something. They never did. While the warehouse explosion was under investigation and my actions on that day were being called into question, largely due to my insistence that this was my fault, I was chained to my desk. It only made the agony and longing for my fallen friends that much worse.

"Parker," Jablonsky called, "in my office." Following him, I noticed the dark circles under his eyes, the weight of the world on his hunched shoulders, and I knew he was hurting too. "Everyone in the office is being sent for a mandatory psych consult. I think we're calling it grief counseling. Just a word of advice, try not to be so surly." I shrugged noncommittally. "By the way, the internal investigation has concluded. You weren't at fault. You didn't do anything wrong." He exhaled. "No one could have known. I thought it would be an easy op, which is why I gave it to you. I did this to you."

"No, you didn't," I insisted. The rage suddenly boiled to the surface again. "What's happening to those bastards who sent us into the building without warning?" I snarled, finding it increasingly difficult not to visit the Farlows in lockup and put a bullet through each of their brains.

"They'll get what's coming to them." He handed me a card with my assigned time to speak with the FBI psychologist, Dr. Weiler.

"I wish Carver was here, so I could bitch to him about how you think I'm insane."

Mark nodded, and I went back to my desk.

*   *   *

For the next two weeks, I worked from my desk. Dr. Weiler hadn't cleared me for field work and insisted I continue to meet with him a few times a week. It was pointless since I never felt the need to be forthcoming in any of our sessions. Also, I didn't particularly care for the forced therapy. It was one of the things I despised about this job.

"Agent Parker," Dr. Weiler said, and I looked up from the spot on the carpet where I'd been staring, "you have to open up. Mourning is a process. Don't you want to heal? Don't you want the pain to go away?"

"No."

He looked baffled by my response. "Parker, if you want my approval to go back to work in a full capacity, you have to say something."

I was tired of this. Tired of the nagging, the bullying, the picking. I was tired of sitting at my desk, waiting for people who were never coming back. I had grown to hate this job, this man, and the person I had become. The price was too high to pay, especially after Boyle and Carver already paid the ultimate price.

"Y'know what, Doc?" I stood up, angry for being forced to this point. Without it ever being explicitly said, I was given an ultimatum. "I don't want to heal. I don't want the pain to go away because it's the only thing I have left of Michael and Sam. I don't need this. And I sure as hell don't need you." I stormed out of his office, hearing him protesting in the background that this wasn't any way for a stable person to act. Who the hell ever said I was stable?

I went to my desk drawer, pulled out my purse, and removed the envelope I placed inside the day my friends died. Continuing on my path, setting fire to the bridges as I went past, I knocked on the director's door and waited for permission to enter. Once inside, I handed him the envelope and removed my service piece and credentials.

"I quit," I blurted out before he opened the seal.

"Agent Parker," he sounded stern, "you can't quit." He launched into a long-winded tirade on how this was a position granted to me by the US government and not some insignificant part-time job. Then he explained how I was a valuable asset and could not be replaced. Finally, when I failed to waver, he buzzed his assistant to get Jablonsky.

"It doesn't matter," I insisted, "because I quit. There's my resignation, my gun, and my badge. I'm done."

"Jablonsky, did you know about this?" Director Kendall asked as Mark came into the office, completely unaware of what he was walking into.

"Alex, let's talk about this," Mark said, but I shook my

head.

"Two agents aren't coming back because of me, so there's no reason in this world why I should still be here. Good day, gentlemen."

There was no point in arguing. It was what it was, and it was over. I quickly cleared out my desk. Having minimal personal effects made it that much easier, and I threw a final glance at Carver's desk, wishing with all my heart this was a nightmare I would wake up from.

FORTY-FIVE

My days and nights held no differentiation since I spent all of my time curled up on the couch, flipping through television programs that I didn't have the focus to watch. Occasionally, I would shower, change my clothes, or seek out sustenance, but for the most part, I remained on the couch. It didn't take a fancy Ph.D. to determine I was depressed, and it took even less to determine I couldn't give a rat's ass. Now whether or not the depression was what made me not give a shit or vice versa, well some fancy credentials and extensive research might have been required to figure that one out, just like the chicken and the egg. Luckily, I didn't care enough to worry about it.

It had been a month since I left my job. Mark would visit or call every few days to check on me and suggest I come back to work. I was stubborn, and I wanted nothing to do with the only career I had ever known. Not only was I mourning the two obvious losses, but I was also mourning the loss of the life I had. The one I wanted and tried so hard to achieve. In a single moment, everything changed. Until it happened, I never believed it could.

There was a knock on the door, and I sighed, not wanting to be bothered to answer. "Parker, I know you're in there," Mark yelled from the other side. "I've brought you dinner, and I won't leave until you let me in."

Relenting, I answered the door and retreated to the couch. "I'm not hungry. You should save yourself some time and effort and stop coming by. I'm not suicidal. I'm just sad."

"You're telling me." He snorted. "Look at you. You're just skin and bones, not like there was much more to work with before either. But I swear," he shook his head, annoyed, "I'm surprised that TV remote hasn't been permanently implanted in your palm."

"They can do that now?" I asked sarcastically.

"No." He brought over a carton of orange chicken and shoved it into my free hand. "When are you coming back to work?"

"I'm not." I dug into the carton and ate automatically. No thought went into the process. "I resigned."

"Like I've said, the paperwork has not been filed. You're on a leave of absence. Hell, you had so many sick days and vacation days accumulated that you can take a few months off without a problem. And since this is a temporary leave of absence, there's no reason not to tack on some extra non-paid days if you need more time."

"Mark," I protested, but he put up a hand.

"You're acting like a spoiled brat. You're being selfish. Everyone else is getting their ass off the couch and going to work and making a real difference in this world. What the hell are you doing except making a dent in the sofa cushion?"

"Get out," I snarled. But he wasn't backing down. It turned into a screaming match, and I found myself standing inches from him as we fought bitterly. "Go."

"Do you think hiding here is going to bring either of them back? Is this what Michael would have expected you to do?" he bellowed, and I slapped him across the face. He took a step back and rubbed his cheek. "There's the Alexis Parker I know." He grinned proudly. "She would stand and fight, not cower in the corner."

"I don't know what to fight for," I admitted. His words jolted me from my self-induced pity party. "Not anymore. I can't go back to work. Seeing what was there and isn't anymore, it's too much. It hurts too much."

He nodded, comprehending the emotional toll being at the office took. "I have something for you. Carver left it for you actually, but you weren't ready before. I think you might be now." As I stood in a daze, he left my apartment and returned ten minutes later with a small box. "Did you know he was planning on leaving the OIO as soon as we finished the Farlow case?" I shook my head, finally understanding what Carver was planning to tell me all those weeks ago. "This was left with all the doomsday instructions he had written. He made it very clear he wanted you to have this, but you better not have been kidding about not being suicidal."

"If I was, I'd have done it already," I said, wearily studying the container. By the time I looked up, Jablonsky had left, giving me privacy and solitude.

Inside the box was a nine millimeter, almost identical to my personal handgun. It had been Michael's. Next to it was documentation, transferring ownership to me, and there was a note. Unfolding the piece of paper, I took a deep breath and read.

Alex, in the event I am no longer your partner, I wanted to make sure you were never left without adequate backup. On our first assignment together, you saved my life, and I hope at some point you feel the favor has been returned. This job has been one hell of a ride.
~Michael

I spent the rest of the evening cleaning and polishing Michael's handgun and mine. Maybe resigning was for the best. Carver intended to do it, and instead, I was the only one left who could. Something changed, and I felt the shift. Whether it was Mark forcing me to fight or receiving one final message from Michael, I couldn't be sure of the impetus. That night, I slept in my bed, once again reliving the nightmare of the warehouse explosion and hearing Michael's words in my ear, as if he were in the room with me. "It's okay, Alex." It was the beginning of getting back to some semblance of okay.

*   *   *

Little by little, I started to forge a new normal. Although, oftentimes I still preferred the comfort of sleeping on the couch, remembering falling asleep on Michael's shoulder. Only now, I was starting to take back control of my life. Every day, I spent hours training, running, lifting weights, shadowboxing, whatever. Then I'd spend countless hours searching for jobs in private security. Being a rent-a-cop wasn't a top priority, but I hoped to find some work as a security analyst, consultant, or investigator. I submitted dozens of applications, but the only time I'd get a response was to say I was either overqualified or underqualified for the position.

Money was still coming in on account of my accumulated personal days, but that would end soon enough. Maybe I should do something else entirely. On a whim, I perused the classified section, disgusted with the lack of options and even more disheartened by the number of things I wasn't qualified to do. I had no idea how to be a plumber, a nurse, or how to construct a building.

Mark stopped by, as he did weekly. We ate dinner while he spoke about his current investigation and I complained about my lack of employment options. His eyes held a strange glint, and I waited for an elaboration that never came. He simply shook his head, helped me clear the table, and called it a night.

A few days later, he asked if any of my pending prospects panned out. I laughed at the ridiculousness of the question since I didn't seem qualified to do anything now that I was no longer a government employee.

"I know someone who needs some help. He's been receiving threatening phone calls, and there's been some corporate espionage involved," Mark said. "I'm not sure it's anything you'd want to handle, but he's getting desperate. Can I pass your name along?"

"That's what I'm left with?" I asked. "Maybe I can get a job if you know a guy who knows a guy who's desperate." I shook my head. "Sure, he can reject me like everyone else."

"It's not a friend of a friend. It's *my* friend," he insisted. "Submit your résumé to Martin Technologies, and I'll make sure they schedule an interview for you within the week."

"Are you sure about this?" Now that an actual job opportunity presented itself, I wasn't sure I wanted it. The couch started to look appealing once more, but maybe I was just scared of screwing up again.

"Parker, you didn't fuck up here. You're still one of the best agents I've ever seen, and there will always be a place for you at the OIO. But give this a chance. I can't guarantee you a job, but it wouldn't hurt for you to try to get back out there. With any luck, you can resolve this issue for Marty within a couple of weeks. His name will be a great résumé booster, and then you can find something permanent to your liking."

"Marty?"

"James Martin, CEO of Martin Technologies." Mark paused, trying to come up with a better way of explaining who this guy was. "The fifty-year-old scotch I got with my last divorce, that was from him."

"What the hell," I replied, resigned to taking this unintended avenue, "at least he has good taste in scotch."

Here's a preview of *Likely Suspects*, the first full-length Alexis Parker novel. Now available in paperback and as an e-book

ONE

"Yes, I'm Alexis Parker. Pleased to meet you." I extended my hand and watched my reflection in the mirror. To say I was nervous for my interview was an understatement. After turning in my letter of resignation to the Office of International Operations, I hadn't been able to get so much as a call back from anywhere else, despite the dozens of applications I submitted. I wasn't ready to admit my leaving the OIO was a bad idea; the job required too much bureaucracy and red-tape for my liking.

I had spent four years of my life working investigations, chasing art thieves and smugglers, and I had nothing to show for it except a fairly sparse résumé and a meritorious service award. I sighed and continued to get ready, straightening my long brown hair and putting on the proper amount of makeup to look professional and serious without being over the top. I didn't want the guys at the Martin Technologies security office to confuse me with either a clown or a call girl.

I'm twenty-nine, single, and unemployed. *Who wouldn't want to hire me*, I thought bitterly, *especially when I'm such a great catch?* The truth of the matter is I always had what one would have considered a bright future. I'm fairly intelligent, well-educated, and decent enough looking. The problem is I lost my focus and drive to stick with one thing, which would probably explain my current lack of employment.

Before I could continue farther down the path of figuring out how my life had gotten so derailed and my internal thought processes could reach the combustible point, my cell phone vibrated across the vanity. I flipped off the flat iron and looked at the caller ID. Taking a deep breath, I hit answer, fearing my scheduled interview had been a clerical error.

"Hello?" I said, fumbling with the now unplugged flat iron I was trying to wrestle into the bathroom cabinet.

"Ms. Parker, please," the woman on the other end sounded annoyed.

"This is Alexis Parker." Two could play at this game.

"Ms. Parker, I am calling on behalf of the Board of Supervisors at Martin Technologies regarding your nine a.m. interview. Mr. Martin would like to be privy to the interviewing process, and he requests we move your interview to," the voice paused, as if rereading a memo to make sure the details were accurate, "10:15 today."

"That's fine." I was relieved my interview had only been rescheduled and not canceled.

"Okay. I will update the security office in the lobby to be prepared for your arrival at 10:15 instead of nine. Do be prompt. Mr. Martin does not like to be kept waiting." And with that, she hung up.

"Nice talking to you, too." I hit end call, wishing this was a landline so I could have slammed the receiver down. I took another breath and looked in the mirror. I was an experienced and capable investigator. I should be able to handle some security consulting work for a corporation, I tried to reassure myself.

At 9:30, I walked out my front door with my résumé and copies of my degrees in hand. What else would Mr. Martin of Martin Technologies need in order to properly assess my qualifications for the job? A certified copy of my birth certificate, a blood sample, and maybe my last will and testament? Perhaps these were just details the woman who called this morning had failed to mention during our brief conversation.

During the drive, I thought about how I had come to apply for the job at Martin Technologies in the first place. Mark Jablonsky had put in a good word with Mr. Martin, the company's founder and CEO. Mark had been my training officer at the OIO and insisted this potential opportunity would fit my personality and interests like a glove.

Mark and Mr. Martin were friends or colleagues of some sort. The actual connection was still a mystery, but Mark assured me I would at least get a chance to interview based on his recommendation alone. Initially, I resisted, thinking this was just another sign of quasi-nepotism, or at the least favoritism, running rampant in the workplace. However, after several weeks and no other job offers, I figured what the hell. It was at least worth looking into.

I pulled into the parking garage and checked my reflection once more in the rearview mirror. My nerves were getting the best of me. It was amusing to think I had been less anxious chasing armed thugs through the streets than I was going into an interview. There was something a little off inside my brain, and I suspected I was never properly socialized.

"Here goes nothing." I tried to bolster my confidence as I hurried to the MT building and pulled on the monogrammed brass door handle.

Entering the lobby, I was amazed at how open and airy the room felt. Light was filtering in from all sides. The security office was a circular desk, set about twenty feet away from the front doors. There were a few couches throughout and a row of elevators at the back of the building. It looked like a classy hotel, but as I approached the security station, I noticed numerous surveillance cameras, keypads, and other protocols in place.

"Can I assist you, ma'am?" one of the security guards asked from behind the desk.

"Miss Parker," I corrected automatically. I hated being called ma'am. That one word triggered too many bad memories. "I'm here to interview for the consulting position with Mr. Martin."

The security guard smiled and asked to see my driver's license, so I pulled out my wallet and handed it to him.

"Right this way, please."

He went to a filing cabinet, pulled out a visitor's pass, handed it to me, and led the way to the elevator banks. He swiped his security badge through a card reader and pressed the elevator call button. The elevator dinged, and the doors whooshed open. We stepped inside. He pushed seventeen, and up we went.

We exited into a hallway lined with lavish offices and conference rooms. The guard escorted me to conference room three and gestured inside. "Please wait here." Before I could say a word, he was gone.

"Friendly group of people," I muttered, taking a seat in one of the rolling office chairs surrounding the large rectangular table. I opened my bag, pulled out my documents, and placed them neatly on the table. I was fidgeting with the corner of the stack of papers when I heard footsteps.

"Hello," a woman's voice greeted. I spun around in my chair. "I'm Mrs. Griffin. I believe we spoke earlier on the telephone. You're here for the consulting position, correct?" I nodded and bit my tongue, ignoring the urge to mention her rude hang up from earlier. "I see you arrived with no issues. That's a good sign." She appeared to be speaking to herself, so I continued to nod, unsure how to respond to her odd comments. "Mr. Martin shall be in momentarily. Can I get you anything while you wait? Tea? Coffee? Water?"

"No, thank you. I'm fine." I couldn't get an accurate read on the woman, and before I could, she walked swiftly out of the room and closed the door behind her. I took a deep breath. The Martin Tech employees must be trying to perfect their disappearing acts.

Before I could muse much further, the door opened again. This time, a man in a three-piece Armani suit and Rolex walked through the door. If given the opportunity, I would have bet his shoes were Italian leather. His dark brown hair was cut short and expertly styled. He had the lean athletic build of a runner, probably in his mid-thirties, and his green eyes sparkled, indicating the wheels were already turning inside his head.

"James Martin." He extended his hand.

"Alexis Parker," I responded. "Pleased to meet you."

He frowned slightly. "To be perfectly honest, Miss Parker, I expected you to be male." I looked at him, unclear if this was an insult or flattery, but instead, it just seemed to be a comment. "My assistant wrote this appointment down as Alex Parker."

"Well, I don't plan to have any gender reassignment surgeries in the near future, but feel free to call me Alex. Most people do."

He smirked slightly but remained professional. I was quickly beginning to feel like a child sitting in the principal's office. "Miss Parker, you come highly recommended by Agent Jablonsky. He was your supervisor at the OIO, correct?"

"That's right." I sat up a little straighter. Despite the fact I had only stayed at the Office of International Operations for four years, I had spent the first two being trained by Mark and the second two running operations for him.

"Jablonsky claims you were one of the best and brightest agents he's ever seen, but you only stayed at that job a few years. Why is that?"

"Well," I honestly didn't know how to verbalize the answer succinctly, "I wanted to make more of a difference, and with an endless string of crime, things started to feel hopeless. The work became monotonous." I struggled to find the proper terminology to explain my feelings.

"So, you don't like structure or rules?" He stood and began to pace, clasping his hands behind his back.

"I'm okay with rules and following orders. To be perfectly honest, I'm not too fond of the red-tape, especially when I continued to see the same injustices day in and day out and knew my hands were tied. It made it difficult to accept the small wins in regards to the bigger picture."

"So you want to be a superhero out to save the world? A vigilante?"

"No." Was this a trial instead of an interview? "I want to step back and do something more impactful." The voice in my head screamed kiss this job good-bye, working for a company isn't what really counts, and Mr. Armani Suit should realize it by now.

However, to my surprise, Martin clapped his hands together. "Exactly." He was actually excited by my response, and I wondered if he had multiple personalities or suffered from an extreme mood swing disorder. He gave the briefest smile, or at least I thought he did because it appeared and disappeared so quickly I couldn't be sure. He looked down at his watch. "It's almost eleven. I have some business to attend to, but if you can have the assistant copy your documents," he glanced at my pile of papers, "I'll be in touch." He left the room and disappeared down the hall.

I sat there absolutely stunned. What just happened? I had the urge to pinch myself to see if I was dreaming, but before I could implement such actions, Mrs. Griffin appeared in the doorway.

"Follow me this way." She proceeded back into the corridor, and I hurried after her. Her office was situated next to the conference room, and inside, she copied my résumé and walked me to the elevator. "Someone from Martin Technologies will be in touch with you shortly."

"Thanks," I said, still somewhat dazed by the whirlwind interview.

The door to the elevator opened, and the security guard from earlier was waiting inside. We rode the elevator back to the lobby in silence, but as the doors whooshed open, he turned to me. "Badge, please," he said politely, and I handed him the visitor's pass. "I hope your interview went well."

"Thank you."

Once I got in my car, I pulled my cell phone from my purse and dialed Mark's home number. I knew he'd be at work right now, so I left a message on his answering machine. "What have you gotten me into this time?"

TWO

What a strange day, I thought as I rifled through the freezer looking for something to make for dinner. I had gotten home so incredibly baffled by the interview at Martin Technologies that I had put on my sweats and gone for a nice long run to clear my head, followed by a second shower for the day, and a nap. When in doubt, nap. This had become my philosophy as of late and continued to work fairly well. Perhaps I should write a book on the art of napping since I didn't see why anyone at Martin Technologies would actually want to hire me. Not to mention, I wasn't even sure if I wanted to work for someone who seemed to have a few screws loose.

"Ah ha!" I exclaimed, pulling out a microwavable dinner which had been buried under a pint of chocolate ice cream and a bag of peas. "Dinner is served."

I scanned the carton for an expiration date and cooking directions and checked the time. It was almost eight. Napping had a habit of making the day fly by; maybe that should be the title of my first chapter. Just as I popped holes in the plastic wrap, the phone rang.

"Hello?"

"Get dressed," a male voice I didn't recognize

responded.

"Excuse me?"

"Semi-formal for dinner. There is a car downstairs to pick you up."

I pulled the receiver away from my ear to check the caller ID, but it only listed 'private' as the source of the call.

"All part of the interviewing process, Alex."

"Mr. Martin?"

"Of course." He paused. "Why? Are you interviewing elsewhere?"

"Can you ask the driver to wait? I'll be ready in ten minutes, or I can drive myself if you tell me where to meet you." I ignored his other question since jobs were like dates. I didn't want to appear too eager or too available, but at the same time, I didn't want to seem overly aloof or uninterested.

"Nonsense, why waste a perfectly good, chauffeured town car? The driver will wait until you are ready. No rush."

I tossed the frozen dinner into the trashcan and headed for the bedroom. Who uses a surprise dinner as an interviewing technique? I pondered this while rummaging through my closet, trying to find something semi-formal to wear. Settling on a black skirt, lavender blouse, and a black blazer, I put my hair in a ponytail and slipped on some open-toed pumps. *This better suffice*, I thought as I quickly put on some eyeliner and lip gloss, grabbed my purse, and headed for the door.

As I exited my apartment building, I spotted a black town car parked in the fire zone. James Martin was leaning against the back door with his arms crossed, chatting with the driver.

"Stunning." Martin smiled, and I blushed, despite my better judgment. He glanced at his watch. "And accurate too. It's only been eleven minutes."

"I try to be punctual." The driver opened the rear door, and I got into the car. "I didn't realize you were waiting outside my apartment, Mr. Martin," I said, implying the creepy nature of his sudden appearance, but he didn't seem to catch on.

"Please, it's no longer office hours, so it's James."

"Okay, James. Pardon me for being so blunt, but why the surprise dinner? If you wanted to continue the interview, you could have said so this morning or had your assistant notify me." Before I could continue explaining how his actions could seem a little stalker-like, he interjected.

"I like to see how potential employees react under surprise conditions. Based on your previous employment with ol' Jabber, I know you can handle stressful, volatile situations, so I wanted to see how you handle yourself during overly civilized functions." He grimaced slightly at the overly civilized.

"I see," I said, even though I didn't. "How am I doing so far?"

"So far, so good, but the night is still young." He might have winked, or it was just a trick of the lights.

For the rest of the drive to the restaurant, he asked questions about my background and experiences with ol' Jabber, which was his nickname for Mark. I answered easily and wished my morning interview had been this simplistic, without the interrogation. The driver pulled to a stop at an expensive looking French restaurant I had never heard of. The valet opened my door, and I stepped out. Mr. Martin, or James as I was supposed to call him this evening, came around to my side of the car and offered his arm.

"Shall we?" he asked politely.

This high-class scenario was probably to see how well his potential new security consultant could blend in with the hoity-toity aspects of his life, so I tentatively looped my hand through his arm.

"I guess so." The familiar nervous pang resonated in the pit of my stomach, and arm in arm, we entered the building.

The interior was decorated extensively in crystal and glass fixtures. The dining room was comprised of less than two dozen tables situated in concentric half circles with a waterfall cascading behind the back of the bar. The bar stood against the far wall, completing the space the half circle of tables had left bare. To say the décor was exquisite would be an understatement. The maitre d' greeted us immediately.

"Mr. Martin, it's so nice to see you again. Would you care for your usual table?" she asked, her expression and body language indicating she'd seen him without his clothes on in the not too distant past.

"If it's not any trouble," he replied, oblivious to her smile. "But we will need another chair. There is a third party joining us this evening."

I looked at him quizzically as we were escorted to a table near the back of the restaurant where we could gaze directly at the waterfall fixture and watch the bartender mix drinks. Once seated and situated with our beverage orders and menus, I turned to Martin.

"Is another executive joining us for dinner?" I wanted to know what other obstacles I might be facing tonight.

"No. I just thought Jablonsky could meet us here and praise you in person instead of in these nicely written form letters I keep getting."

I studied my menu to avoid further conversation. I hated interviews; although, if I were being honest, I'd say I wasn't a fan of intimate dinners either. Looks like a lose-lose tonight, Parker.

"Well, if it isn't Marty trying to scoop up the best and brightest yet again," Mark Jablonsky teased as he approached our table and extended his hand to Martin. "How the hell are you, you old son-of-a-gun?"

I looked at my former boss and my potential new employer. Since when did we transport back to the 1950s when people used phrases like old son-of-a-gun? The terminology didn't faze Martin. He merely stood and shook Mark's hand. The same look of mutual respect reflected on both of their faces despite how incredibly different they seemed.

Mark was older, in his early fifties, with graying light brown hair and a mustache. He had put on a bit of a gut from too many late nights in the surveillance van eating Philly cheese steaks and potato chips, and his suit, regardless of price, always looked as if he slept in it.

The two men sat down, and Mark beamed at me. "You look like a million bucks."

Before I could respond, Martin chimed in. "That goes without saying, but the better question is does she look like she could protect a million bucks."

"Alexis Parker is one of the most capable people I know. I wouldn't have recommended her otherwise. I know what you need, and she can handle it." Mark picked up his menu to read. "I always tell you if you need proof, test your hypothesis, just like your workers do in the lab."

"Just so we're clear," I piped up; being silent was never my strong suit, "what exactly does this job even entail because security consultant is a vague term?"

Martin turned to me. "Martin Technologies is responsible for the development of many different things from cooking utensils to airplane parts. I personally try to provide more economical and eco-friendly alternatives worldwide, and therefore, I've made quite a few enemies." He paused briefly and picked up his glass. "Recently, there have been death threats, a kidnapping attempt, some manufacturing sabotage, and corporate espionage. I need a new face I can trust to keep an eye on things at work. Not to mention, the Board thinks it might be a good idea to update my personal security, seeing as how I have majority control of the company." He took a sip before continuing with what seemed to be a level of melodrama. "If something happens to me, there could be a coup, stocks could plummet, and the world could explode. You know, things of that sort." Although he attempted to joke, his eyes were as serious as I'd ever seen. Was the great James Martin actually afraid, or was that something else I saw flicker behind his eyes? Anger, perhaps?

Before anything else could be said, the waitress returned to take our orders. I requested a steak with Portobello mushrooms in a cream sauce, as did Mark, while Martin ordered the Chateaubriand. As she walked away, I glanced around the dining room. Most of the tables were empty, which seemed odd since this was an upscale restaurant, and it was early in the evening.

"If you need someone who can do all that, you've found your girl," Mark said, lauding my capabilities.

Martin considered it as he lifted his scotch and slowly swirled the golden brown liquid around the glass. "Perhaps you're right. You've been right so far."

I was about to ask for more job details and what the actual relationship between these two men was when I heard glass shatter. It was a much louder sound than if a waitress had dropped a tray of glasses. This sounded as though a wall of mirrors had simultaneously broken. Turning to the cause of the cacophony, I saw a group of masked gunmen enter the restaurant. The maitre d' was cowering on the floor next to her podium, and the entire glass façade in the foyer was shattered.

"Ladies and gentlemen, if we may have your attention, please," the masked leader bellowed. An older woman sitting on the other side of the restaurant gasped as the men invaded the dining room. "We shall make this as brief and painless as possible. Do not call the cops, and do not use your cell phones. Stay seated and place your valuables in the center of the table. This is a robbery."

Martin carefully set his glass on the table and whispered in my ear, "Congratulations, you're hired. Now do something."

ABOUT THE AUTHOR

G.K. Parks is the author of the Alexis Parker series. The first novel, *Likely Suspects,* tells the story of Alexis' first foray into the private sector.

G.K. Parks received a Bachelor of Arts in Political Science and History. After spending some time in law school, G.K. changed paths and earned a Master of Arts in Criminology/Criminal Justice. Now all that education is being put to use creating a fictional world based upon years of study and research.

You can find additional information on G.K. Parks and the Alexis Parker series by visiting our website at
www.alexisparkerseries.com

CPSIA information can be obtained
at www.ICGtesting.com
Printed in the USA
LVHW042244140822
725927LV00003B/235